INSIDIOUS THREATS

SASHA MCCANDLESS LEGAL THRILLER
BOOK 16

MELISSA F. MILLER

BROWN STREET BOOKS

1

January 2023

The early morning sunlight streamed in through the large window in Leo Connelly's home office. A beam bisected his face and fell across the card he held loosely in his big hands. He had the note memorized by this point, but stared down at the elegant cursive writing on the thick linen paper and read the words aloud in a soft voice as if, this time, their meaning would reveal itself to him:

> *Agent Connelly,*
> *I must apologize for my behavior earlier. I was reel-ing, having realized that I have made a grievous mistake.*
> *I have made other mistakes in my life. Lord knows I have. But I have always tried to do the right thing. I may not always have succeeded, but I did try.*

Everything I did, I did in Josh's memory, as an effort to honor him. Please bear that in mind when you judge me. But all my work is about to be used for ends that are dishonorable at best, dangerous for certain, and dystopian if they prevail.

I must find a way to make amends for my recent errors of judgment. If you're reading this, then I have failed, and I must ask you to pick up the task. I don't know where else to turn, and I feel seeing you out my window was a sign of some sort.

Enclosed is a program that you can use when the time comes to stop Mjölnir. It will not complete the task, but it will get you in the door.

Best regards,
Landon Lewis

He twitched his lips and dropped the card onto his desk. Nope. Still gibberish.

He flipped through the small notebook in which he scribbled down his thoughts every time he studied the blasted letter. The notes dated back to last summer. For half a year, he'd been trying to tease out the meaning of the dead man's words. Some bits made sense, but the overall picture remained murky, muddy, and mysterious.

What had Landon been thinking? Surely job one in giving someone instructions to be carried out posthumously was to be clear. Clear, unmistakable, explicit directions were vital. Was it really so much to ask?

He grabbed a pen and reviewed his scrawled notes

from the last time he'd engaged in this exercise in futility.

"All my work" had to be a reference to Cesare, Landon Lewis' ill-conceived artificial intelligence tool. The AI was designed to predict and prevent crime by identifying law-abiding citizens with a latent propensity for criminal behavior. To the surprise of absolutely nobody but its creator, Cesare had proved to be a disaster—and a racist one, to boot.

But the rest of Landon's sentence was a head-scratcher. There was no way Cesare could be used for *any* purpose, let alone a "dishonorable, dangerous, dystopian" one. Sasha had seen to it. His formidable, pocket-sized wife had gotten the Justice Department to shove a consent decree down Landon's throat. He couldn't do a blessed thing with Cesare.

Leo straightened in his chair. *No, that wasn't true.* At least, he didn't think it was. He was pretty sure the consent decree prohibited the use of Cesare for any predictive policing purpose. Maybe, if Sasha had been very pushy—which was almost a certainty—it might also prevent using the program's predictions for other purposes. He'd heard about an AI program used in the Netherlands to weed out welfare fraud. Like Cesare, it had created a mess.

But even Sasha had her limits. Leo bet that the consent decree wouldn't stop Landon if he'd tried to tweak Cesare to serve a purely financial purpose. Like what? Predict whether someone would file an insurance claim? Or default on a mortgage?

He bobbed his head back and forth. Maybe. But that didn't seem dramatic enough to warrant Landon's note.

As someone who believed in the concept of free will, Leo was willing to describe fiscal determinations made by an AI algorithm as dishonorable. But he couldn't imagine Landon describing those predictions—no matter how poorly made—as dangerous or dystopian. No. It had to be more than that.

And, he suspected, it was related to the one hundred million dollars wired into Landon's account the day he died. Landon Lewis had sold Cesare to the highest bidder and then gotten seller's remorse when he learned what the buyer intended to do with it. There was no way Landon would have reacted to someone using his creation to set insurance premiums by sending Leo … what, exactly?

He dropped the pen and picked up the flash drive that had been tucked into the package with the note. The drive had a physical keypad. To unlock the drive, a person would have to enter a PIN on the keypad. For further protection, the drive was coated with an epoxy, and the information on the drive was encrypted. Any effort to break into it without the PIN would destroy both the data and the drive itself.

Landon's note referred to the data on the drive as a program. One that could help stop "Mjölnir." Leo knew from his extensive understanding of Norse mythology —okay, fine, his love for Marvel movies—that Mjölnir was Thor's mighty hammer. But he had no clue what it meant in this context. Was Mjölnir Cesare? Was Mjölnir a copycat technology? Maybe Cesare was on the flash drive. Maybe Landon had, in fact, suffered a psychotic break the day he died and the note was the sheer unhinged raving of a mentally unwell man.

Leo had *almost* convinced himself that was the case. He'd been *this* close to deciding that he didn't need to do anything at all with the drive because Landon had been suicidal and most likely not lucid when he wrote the note. He'd keep it tucked away in his safe, untouched.

He huffed out a heavy sigh. But then, right before the new year, Maisy—Sasha's long-time friend—had roped Sasha and Leo's babysitter into starting a true crime podcast with her. And less than a week later, Maisy and Jordana had disproved Leo's theory by exposing Landon's alleged suicide as a murder, landing a police detective and a well-heeled commercial real estate broker in jail in the process. And he was back to trying to puzzle out what he was supposed to do with this freaking USB drive.

He glanced at the time. Sasha would be getting the twins up to get ready for their day any moment, which meant this sliver of quiet contemplation was about to end. He returned the card, the drive, and his notebook to the biometric safe in the closet, and headed downstairs for breakfast duty. As he dodged the cat lounging in a sunbeam on the top step and avoided the dog's apparent efforts to trip him by weaving between his feet, the word "Mjölnir" looped through his mind.

What the devil was Mjölnir?

Two thousand-odd miles away, in a nondescript office park in Sun Valley, Idaho, Garwood March stifled a yawn while waving his ID badge in front of a card reader. He stomped his boots against the snow-packed pavement while the reader blinked. Once, twice, *beep.*

He hurried inside as the wind blew a smattering of snow into the lobby behind him and yanked the door closed. As he sipped his hot chocolate and waited for the elevator, a persistent thought—the thought that had been dogging him for months and that dragged him out of his comfortable bed in his warm apartment at this indecent, predawn hour—looped through his mind.

What the devil was wrong with Mjölnir?

Gar was a talented software developer with a particular gift for debugging. This statement wasn't arrogance or pride; it was a fact. He knew it. Everyone knew it. After all, that was why Rosen, that weirdo from Pinpoint Partners with the cringy title—data tracking evangelist and application integration sherpa or guru or whatever—had specifically requested Gar for this project. Pinpoint was some kind of silent investor in the tech company that employed Gar. Gar neither knew nor cared about the details. But his supervisor, the acerbic and anxious Antonia, cared. She cared a lot. And she'd taken to hovering.

Gar couldn't work his magic with someone standing behind him, peering over his shoulder, second-guessing his decisions, and fretting. He needed solitude, loud French metal music, and assorted snacks. Also, hot chocolate. Unlike the stereotypical computer programmer or coder, Gar didn't survive on a steady stream of energy drinks or cold brews. His go-to drink was hot chocolate made with full-fat milk and topped with a healthy dollop of whipped cream. In the dead of summer, he swapped out the hot cocoa for a cold glass of chocolate milk. The son and grandson of dairy farmers, he came by his beverage of choice honestly.

The elevator dinged, the doors whooshed, and he stepped inside the car. He stared blearily at his distorted reflection in the highly polished metal doors as the compartment rose to the third floor. He wasn't a morning person—not by any stretch. He did his best work late at night. But so did Antonia. And if she wasn't lingering around his desk, asking how it was going, then she was pinging him at home, well after midnight with incessant requests for progress reports. Managing his manager had become a distraction. So Gar had started coming into the office before sunrise to get a few uninterrupted hours of work in before she started peppering him with questions. Not that the new schedule was making any difference. He was still utterly, hopelessly stuck. Flummoxed, even.

The elevator came to a stop and the doors parted. Gar sighed and stepped out into the quiet hallway. The motion-sensing lights clicked on, and he shuffled toward the bullpen where the coders, programmers, software engineers, and developers all worked together in a jumble. He suspected this arrangement had originated because the human resource team in charge of seat assignments didn't know enough to differentiate one computer geek from another. Unintentional or not, it had been a stroke of brilliance. The layout encouraged the worker bees to bounce ideas off one another and to get fresh perspectives and different spins on their projects.

But even access to the bullpen brain trust hadn't helped Gar tease out the problem with Pinpoint Partners' pet program. He flopped into his chair and powered up his computer.

Across the room, Petra Vuković glanced up from her code. She kept her earphones on but raised a hand in greeting. He lifted his hot chocolate in a return salute before turning his attention to the program that had become his nemesis. He wasn't sure how long he'd been wrestling with the blasted thing when Petra wandered over. Long enough to have drained his drink, leaving only a skin of dried milk clinging to the edge of the mug.

"What are you working on?" Petra raised herself onto the filing cabinet, where she perched like a bird.

At some point, while he'd been immersed in the code, she'd removed her hoodie and tied it around her waist. Her sleeveless tank top showed off her defined upper arm muscles, distracting him from her question. He realized he was staring, and his face heated as he pulled his eyes away from her toned biceps and triceps.

"Uh, sorry. Still trying to figure out what's wrong with Mjölnir."

"That thing. Why's it named Thor's hammer?"

He shrugged. "No clue."

She drew her eyebrows together. "What's it supposed to do?"

"It's an AI-powered algorithm that's supposed to predict a person's shopping habits with unmatched accuracy so companies can serve up the perfect ad."

"Lovely. Now even the robots work for our capitalist masters."

He couldn't tell from her dry tone if she was joking or about to launch into another one of her socialist rants, so he quickly went on, "And it does that—sort of. But in addition, for no apparent reason that I can see in the programming, it also volunteers a prediction of the user's propensity to commit one of any number of felonies."

Her pierced left eyebrow shot up. "Felonies, really?"

"Well, crimes. But, yeah, so far, they've all been felonies."

"Wouldn't most people's likelihood of committing a felony approach zero?"

"You'd think so. Or, at least, hope so. But according

to Thor's trusty hammer, pretty much everyone has a criminal hidden inside them."

She blinked at that. "And you can't find the string that's making it happen?"

"No. I'm ready to rip my hair out. The only possibility left is that the trigger is so deeply buried in the AI's 'brain' that it only activates when the algorithm is already running. You know?"

"Gar, bro, if that's the case, you know what it means."

He didn't, though. He shook his head, confused. "No. What?"

She held his gaze steadily. "It's a feature—"

"—not a bug," he joined in.

She hopped off the filing cabinet and brushed off the seat of her dark jeans. "Yup. I'm going to the kitchen. You want a coffee?" She eyed his mug. "I mean, another hot cocoa?"

"No, thanks."

Usually, he'd tag along, savoring the minutes with her in light of the not-so-secret crush they both knew he had but neither acknowledged. But her words had shaken something loose. "You go ahead."

She shrugged and strolled off. He stared down at his hands. It was the logical conclusion—obvious, even. Despite zero evidence that it had been coded to predict crime, Mjölnir predicted crime—consistently, and regardless of what Gar tweaked in an effort to make it stop.

If Petra was right, and Mjölnir was functioning as intended, that raised an even bigger question: Why would a commercial advertising algorithm be designed to predict crime?

He needed to talk to Pinpoint Partners and get some clarity. He checked the time. It wasn't even seven-thirty on the West Coast. Too early to call Silicon Valley. He doubted anyone was even awake yet.

3

Another nine hundred or so miles to the west, Amanda Teale-James exited the driverless car, smoothed the nonexistent wrinkles out of her custom-made suit, and strode purposefully into the sleepy private airport nestled on a cliff near the edge of the Pacific Ocean.

Silicon Valley Aviation Center exclusively served a roster of well-known tech titans. A dozen disrupters and innovators had pooled their pocket change to build the facility so they could jet off to Wall Street for finance meetings or to Capitol Hill to be raked over the coals for televised congressional hearings without having to negotiate the inefficiencies and inconveniences of mass air travel—not to mention the indignity of sharing space with the occasional belligerent drunk or racist soccer mom who got on the wrong side of a flight attendant and caused a stink that would inevitably result in the police being called and the interaction going viral.

Flying out of SVAC was a different experience altogether. The bad boys of the industry—a group known for moving fast and breaking things, asking forgiveness and not permission, and throwing money at their problems—had effectively built themselves a time machine. It was a portal back to an era when air travel was civilized, men wore suits and hats, and leggy would-be models prowled the aisles of jets plying booze and fancy meals. At least that's what Amanda assumed. Her knowledge of the 1960s and its aviation experience was formed entirely by old movies and reruns of "Mad Men." But it sure *felt* like a blast from the past.

The waiting area for Leith Delone's private jet was a far cry from the crowded, noisy terminal of a commercial airport. The area managed to be somehow both small and intimate, and airy and spacious. The wall-sized windows overlooked the gray-green ocean and the fog rolling over the water, and a small fire was lit in the freestanding glass fireplace in the middle of the room, taking the early-morning chill out of the air. She made a beeline for one of the white club chairs in front of the fireplace.

As if to prove Amanda's point, Stasia, the six-foot-tall platinum blonde who was Leith's favorite attendant, beamed at her from behind the small bar that was tucked away in one corner. A moment later, the hostess was standing in front of her with a Bloody Mary festooned with three olives, just the way Amanda liked it.

"Good morning, Ms. Teale-James," she practically purred.

Amanda eyed the cocktail with a mixture of tempta-
tion and disdain, then gave her head a mournful shake.
"Morning, Stasia. I'll have to pass on the drink. I'm on
my way to a mediation meeting."

"Of course. Double espresso, then?"

"Please."

"Perhaps you'll have a glass of champagne to celebrate a positive outcome on your way back from Pittsburgh?" Stasia suggested before heading off to make the
coffee.

"From your lips to Lady Justice's ears," Amanda
murmured more to herself than to the hostess as she
slipped her laptop out of its case and began to review
the electronic file.

Mediation was not her strong suit as a lawyer. It
involved too much negotiation and cooperation. She
was a trial shark, not a consensus builder. Her nose for
weakness and, more importantly, her willingness to
exploit it made her a sharp litigator. But she loathed
settlement talks.

She'd tried to dump the meeting off on one of her
junior attorneys or one of the innumerable associates
employed by the high-priced outside law firms that
Leith had on retainer. But he didn't want to hear it. He'd
shown a rare flash of impatience with her.

She could still hear the irritation in his tone as she
replayed his words. "Blast it, Amanda. You're my
general counsel. I want the other side to realize how
seriously I'm taking this. I want you there. Get them to
agree to my terms. End of discussion." And then he'd

chopped his hand through the air to let her know she was dismissed.

It was clear he meant it: Leith Delone, eccentric billionaire and one-time wunderkind, had a major bug up his butt over the employment dispute. Less clear was why. As far as Amanda could tell, the case was trivial. Some local news anchor had criticized Leith on the air after he bought the station where she worked. Word got back to Leith, and he had her fired.

Despite her age and gender, the anchor—a woman with the improbable name of Maisy Farley—hadn't bothered suing to allege age or sex discrimination. She was content to take the golden parachute offered by her contract—a meager million dollars—and walk away. But for reasons that Leith wouldn't explain and Amanda couldn't fathom, he was dragging his feet. The Farley woman had been fired at the end of July, and, here Amanda was, six months later, flying to freaking Pittsburgh in the middle of winter to make a series of bad-faith arguments to justify the delay and to try to extract a completely unenforceable concession out of the woman.

The only question was why?

"Why, Leith?" she said aloud in a low voice as she scrolled through the case notes her assistant had prepared.

Stasia returned with the espresso. Amanda thanked her, closed her laptop, and leaned back in her chair to savor her first sip of the hot, robust drink. She rolled the strong coffee around on her tongue like a wine sommelier, then sighed with contentment.

Her reverie was interrupted by her buzzing phone. She reluctantly set down the cup and dug the device out of her calfskin bag.

"ATJ," she answered briskly, saving precious seconds by forgoing a greeting and abbreviating her five-syllable name to three letters.

"Um, hi, Ms. Teale-James. It's Oliver. I hope I'm not calling too early? I have that background on the Pittsburgh lawyers you wanted."

She rolled her eyes at Oliver's wholly unnecessary sucking up. Of all her obsequious associates, he was the worst. And that was saying something.

"I told you I have a seven-thirty flight. I'm already at the airport. Did you email me a report?"

"Yes, ma'am. But I wanted to call, too," he stammered.

"Why? Do you think I don't know how to read?"

"Y-yes. I mean, no. No, of course not. I know you can read. I just … well … I've put these dossiers together before, and this one's weird."

"Weird, how?" She wondered whether the roughly seventy grand a year that Stanford Law charged in tuition included any instruction in the fact that *weird* wasn't a legal concept. Poor Oliver had certainly not taken the class if one existed.

"Well, um, the one lawyer, she's gotten a lot of press. Like, a lot."

Amanda closed her eyes briefly and suppressed a sigh. "That's not unusual. I'm sure Ms. Farley retained the best attorney she could afford. Well-regarded attorneys tend to garner news articles, Oliver."

"I know, but not like these."

"Like *what?*" While she waited for Oliver to spit it out, she drained her espresso, caught Stasia's eye, and raised the empty demitasse cup. The attendant nodded her understanding.

"So, there are two attorneys on all the paperwork. The firm is McCandless, Volmer & Andrews. Two of the named partners are handling Ms. Farley's case. Naya Andrews, who's a top-notch transactional partner, and Sasha McCandless-Connelly, who's a litigator. She founded the firm after leaving Prescott & Talbot. You know it?"

She did. It was an East Coast white-shoe firm. Big on tradition and full of old-money legacy types.

"Ms. McCandless-Connelly couldn't cut it, huh?" Those types of firms had a strict up or out policy.

"No, the opposite. They offered her partnership the first year she was eligible. She turned them down and struck out on her own."

Amanda's eyebrows crawled toward her hairline. That *was* surprising. Then she shrugged. "Maybe one of her supervising partners was handsy. It happens. It used to happen a lot. How long ago was this?"

She heard pages flipping. "Twelve years ago."

"It was a different world back then, Oliver." She felt positively ancient saying it, but it was true.

"I guess. But she's supposed to be a civil litigator. Volmer's the white-collar criminal guy."

"Okay?"

"Well, her resume doesn't say civil litigator to me. She solved the murders of a couple attorneys and, sepa-

rately, the murder of a state court judge. She's represented a serial killer, broke up an international human
trafficking ring, sued the police and the local prosecutor's office for misconduct, and a bunch of other wild
stuff. She was stabbed by some forensic pathologist who
was mixed up in a political scandal, and she nearly died.
The list just goes on and on. I didn't know if I should
put all these articles in the background file because they
don't really have anything to do with her practice, but
… I thought you'd want to know."

From his hesitant tone, if Oliver had been a puppy,
he'd have had his tail between his legs, waiting to be
reprimanded for piddling on the floor. She relented.

"Send me everything. You're right, most of it is likely
irrelevant. And you're also right, it's unusual enough
that I'd like to know about it. Good work."

"Yes, ma'am," he chirped. She could hear the smile in
his voice. "Oh, there's one more thing."

"What is it?"

"I was surprised to see Maisy Farley's name featured
prominently in one of the more recent articles. She's
apparently started a true crime podcast and solved a
murder that the local cops had misclassified as a suicide.
The dead guy was supposed to be the star witness in
McCandless-Connelly's case against the prosecutor's
office. That's a weird coincidence, right?"

There he went with the *weird* again. How had the
Supreme Court missed snagging this guy as a clerk?

"I suppose it is. Pittsburgh's not *that* small of a town,
is it?"

"No, ma'am. At the last census, the population—"

"It was a rhetorical question, Oliver. Just send all the articles and make a note of which one involves Maisy Farley."

"Will do. I'll put them all in a folder on the document site. The headline for the one about the suicide that was really a murder is 'Peach of a Podcaster Takes a Fresh Look at Landon Lewis Death.'"

Stasia returned with the fresh coffee and an apologetic smile. "It's time to board," she mouthed.

"I have to go." Amanda hung up on Oliver and stowed her phone in her bag before he could formulate a hesitant goodbye.

As she followed Stasia out to the tarmac where the glossy white private jet waited, she drew her eyebrows together and searched her memory. Landon Lewis. She knew that name. She just didn't know why.

"How long is the flight?" she asked as they crossed the carpet to the stairs.

"Five hours from wheels up to wheels down," Stasia told her.

Five hours. That gave her plenty of time to figure out who Landon Lewis was and what connection, if any, he had to this plain-vanilla case. Or to take a nap.

4

S asha stuck her head through the doorway and peered into Connelly's home office. "Aha, *here's* where you've been hiding. The kids were about to relent and let me make them breakfast."

He turned from the closet and feigned a horrified expression. "Anything but that!"

She smiled and handed him her necklace. "Do me a favor before you rescue them from their green smoothie fate. I can't get this clasp to close."

She lifted her hair from her nape and bowed her head. He stood behind her and draped the silver chain over her collarbone. She shivered at the touch of cold metal against her bare skin.

"Sorry." He eased the microscopic hook into the clamshell clasp. "There." He dropped a warm kiss on the back of her neck.

She pivoted to face him. "Thanks."

He studied her. "Turquoise and silver necklace from Aroostine. Your mom's matching hairpin that doubles as a weapon. You're dressed for battle. Court, I hope, and not back alley."

She grinned. "Neither. A mediation. Well, not even. It's a meeting with the mediator and WACB's lawyers to discuss the station's persistent failure to either pay Maisy or provide a reason why they haven't."

"Not even a mediation, and you're breaking out the *kanzashi*."

"Leith Delone's consigliere is flying in from California to attend the meeting along with the station's employment lawyer, so ... yeah."

He raised one eyebrow. "He has a consigliere? Really?"

She sighed. "Well, no, she doesn't *call* herself that. She's his general counsel. But she's his GC, not the GC for one of his businesses. And from all the opposition research Jordana pulled together for me, that's how she functions—like a trusted counselor to a mob boss."

"Wait, I thought Jordana quit. Isn't she working for Maisy as her podcast producer now?"

She tried not to pout. She wasn't sure she succeeded. "She did. But this is for Maisy and, ultimately, Jordana, too. After all, if her new boss runs out of money, she'll be forced to come back to work for me, heaven forbid."

"I'm glad to see you're over the betrayal."

She pretended not to catch the sarcasm in his tone. "Thanks."

Sasha didn't feel betrayed by Jordana's defection. Not really. Her feelings were more complex than that. She'd watched the girl grow into a teen and then a young woman and had seen her develop the insightful, sharp intellect of a lawyer. In her view, Jordana would be wasting her abilities by not pursuing the law. But she'd never stand in the way of Jordana's happiness and personal fulfillment. For some reason, though, everyone —including her own husband—thought she was taking the decision personally.

"Speaking of the podcast, what's going on with the murder investigation?"

"Which one?"

"Fair question. Either of them. Landon's? Zane's? The attempted murder charges?"

Maisy and Jordana had exposed Landon Lewis' death as a murder—or at least a killing—at the hands of an amateur boxer named Zane Novak, who'd been had been hired by a dirty police officer to intimidate Lewis. The details of the intimidation and how it had gone wrong had sadly died with Zane, who was stabbed to death while in police custody by none other than Detective Colchis. Colchis, the rogue cop, was somehow tied up with Bella Steptoe, the commercial real estate agent who'd leased Landon his office space. After Zane's death, the cop and the realtor had turned on each other, and Maisy had witnessed their dueling confessions, accusations, and attempts to shoot one another. After their arrests, both Bella and Tim Colchis had lawyered up. Nobody was talking. As far as Sasha knew, the authorities had no idea as to who had hired them.

She shrugged. "Unless Bella or that jag-off Colchis starts talking, Landon's death is a dead end. They can pin Zane's death on Colchis, and Maisy's testimony is enough to bring attempted murder charges against both of them. But until one of them strikes a deal, the details about who wanted to shake Lewis up and why aren't going to come to light."

His jaw tightened and his gray eyes narrowed.

She knew that look. Her husband was still beating himself up for being the last person (aside from Zane) to see Landon Lewis alive. She rested her hand lightly on his forearm. "You have to let it go, Connelly. It was a chance meeting. You weren't put in his path to save him."

He jerked his head back, and his eyes snapped to meet hers. "I never said I was."

"You didn't have to."

She held his gaze until he nodded. Then he said, "Are you still storing Landon's papers at the law firm for Maisy?"

"Yes. Naya told her she could use the space as long as she needs to. Why?"

He shrugged. "No real reason. Just don't you think it's odd that the police haven't asked to go through that stuff? There might be something in there that shows who was calling the shots."

"There might be, but I think the authorities are pursuing other avenues right now. They have a political nightmare on their hands with a cop who murdered a prisoner in custody."

"I guess so," he allowed. "What about Maisy and Jordana? Are they still trying to run it down for their podcast?"

"I think they're focusing on the financial angle right now."

Connelly nodded. "That makes sense. Presumably, whoever transferred a hundred million dollars to Landon's account the day he died knows something."

"Ya think?"

He laughed. "Yeah, probably." Then his expression grew thoughtful. "Do you think Maisy and Jordana would want some help going through the documents?"

She gave him a close, questioning look. "Are you volunteering?"

"Maybe. Hank and I are between assignments. If nothing else, it's an excuse to hang around your office."

"Mmm. You have a crush on one of the lawyers?"

He brushed a kiss over her lips. "I might."

She leaned in and pressed her mouth harder against his. He pulled her close, holding her hips against his thighs.

"I'll talk to Maisy," she breathed. Then she reluctantly took a step back and smoothed down her bunched-up dress. "I should get going before you distract me. I need to prepare for Ms. Teale-James, and Finn and Fiona are probably going to burst in here any second, demanding sustenance."

"Watch out for Ms. Teale-Jones. I hear those lawyers with the double-barreled names are crafty."

She smiled. "I've heard that, too. Don't forget, Naya and I are taking Maisy out to dinner after the meeting."

"To celebrate?"

"Or commiserate. Time will tell."

"To celebrate," he said firmly. "Don't walk home. Call a ride share."

"Connelly, it's four blocks. And I'm the deadliest five-foot-tall woman you know."

"Please?"

She rolled her eyes and gave him one more quick kiss. "Only because you said please." She glanced at the time and groaned. "I really do have to go."

"Go get her, Ms. McCandless-Connelly."

"Oh, I will. After all, I'm one of those crafty hyphenated lawyers."

His laughter trailed behind her as she left the office.

5

S tasia stood in front of the etched glass front door and waited for someone to answer the chimes that echoed through the Steptoes' massive marble entryway. She passed the time studying the visible portions of the mansion through the door and betting with herself whether a butler or a maid would answer.

As it turned out, it was neither. Bella Steptoe, dressed in a workout outfit—colorful leggings and a long, fitted tank top—opened the door herself. Her expression turned from one of welcome to one of confusion when her eyes landed on Stasia.

"Oh, you're not Laura."

The statement didn't seem to require an answer, so Stasia stood quietly and waited.

"Laura's my Pilates instructor," Bella prattled on as if Stasia might care. Then she dropped her voice and leaned forward. "Are you from ... pretrial services?"

Stasia allowed herself a small smile and flicked her

eyes down to the monitoring bracelet circling Bella's slim ankle. Bella watched her with parted lips, anxious and alert.

Finally, Stasia answered, "No. I'm not here to make sure you're following the terms of your house arrest while you await trial."

Bella's shoulders relaxed. "Home confinement," she corrected, as if she couldn't help herself.

"Whichever."

"So, then, how can I help you?"

"Our boss sent me."

Bella's shoulders shot back up to her ears, and she shook her head violently. "You can't be here," she whispered. "Please, go."

Stasia studied the woman without pity. "You know I can't do that."

"You can't come in."

"I don't need to come in. I have a message to deliver. Mr. Delone wants you to remember how important it is that you maintain the confidentially that you agreed to when he retained you."

"Retained me in my capacity as a real estate broker to manage his commercial properties in the area, you mean?"

Stasia gave her a blank look. "You know that's not what I mean."

Bella pursed her lips and shifted her weight from one bare foot to the other, antsy now. "Then I have no idea what you're talking about."

"That's a good answer. Just remember. Because Detective Colchis forgot."

"Wait. What?"

"Tim Colchis, your co-defendant? You know, the police officer who stabbed the boxer in a failed effort to clean up the Landon Lewis mess."

Bella dropped the innocent act like it was hot. "Look, Leith—our employer, rather—didn't involve me in any of that last summer. All I did was tell Colchis when Landon was alone in the building. That was the full extent of my participation in that botched operation. Since then, I've done everything I could do to limit the damage."

"Just be mindful that you don't decide to talk. The detective decided to roll the dice. He told the district attorney's office that he's ready to deal."

"He's going to sell me out?" Bella exploded.

"That would be exceedingly hard, considering he fell in his cell this morning and sustained extensive brain damage. He's comatose and unlikely ever to wake up."

Bella opened, then closed, her mouth. After a moment, she found her voice. "Did you …?"

Stasia gave her a long, cool look. "I don't think you want to ask me that question, Mrs. Steptoe. Your take-away here is not to get any ideas about cooperating with the prosecution. In many ways, your position has improved. With Novak and Colchis both dead, there's really nobody who can testify against you."

"You're forgetting Maisy Farley."

Stasia waved a hand. "She's an irritant. A fly. Nothing more. Now, one last question: the errand Leith asked you to handle last month—the trip to upstate New York—was it successful?"

"As far as I know. I did what Mr. Delone told me to do."

Stasia held her gaze for a long, intense moment. "Good. See that you continue to do so."

She heard a car rolling up the driveway behind her and turned up her hood so the Pilates instructor wouldn't glimpse her face. She left Bella standing open-mouthed at her front door and slipped away as if she'd never been there.

6

Amanda hurried off the elevator into McCandless, Volmer & Andrews' brick-walled lobby, still shivering from the bracing winter air.

An older White woman with impeccably coiffed silver-blonde hair looked up from behind the reception desk and greeted her warmly. "Ms. Teale-James?"

"Yes, that's me. I'm here for the Farley meeting."

The receptionist smiled. "Of course. Mr. Collins' office called; he's running late. Let me take your coat, and then I'll show you to the conference room."

Amanda unbuttoned her coat and handed it to the woman as she stepped out from behind the teak desk.

"I'm Caroline," she said. "If you need anything at all today, please let me know."

"A cup of coffee would be great."

"You're in luck then. Did you notice Jake's—the coffee shop on the ground floor?" As she spoke, Caroline led Amanda down a corridor, pausing to hang her coat on a rack.

"Briefly."

"Jake blends a medium roast especially for Sasha. The roaster is a firm client. I'm not much of a coffee drinker, but it's rumored to be fantastic."

"As long as it has caffeine, I'll love it," Amanda assured her.

She expected a polite chuckle, but the receptionist guffawed—a true belly laugh that didn't match her sophisticated demeanor.

"Sorry," she told Amanda, wiping her eyes. "You and Sasha are going to hit it off. I can tell."

With that, she stopped in front of a door. She gave it a quick rap before pushing it open and ushering Amanda inside. Three women sat lined up on one side of the table, and a light-skinned man with a shaved head faced off against them. They all turned toward the door.

"Ms. Teale-James is interested in a cup of coffee," Caroline said by way of introduction.

One of the woman stood and extended her hand. "I'm Sasha McCandless-Connelly."

"Amanda Teale-James," Amanda said unnecessarily as she crossed the room and shook the lawyer's hand while looking directly into her green eyes. At four feet and eleven inches tall, Amanda was rarely at eye level with anyone who wasn't in elementary school.

Sasha smiled, and Amanda wondered if she was equally disconcerted by their meeting of non-giants. If she was, she hid it, turning to gesture to the other two women.

The Black woman stood and gave Amanda a firm, cool handshake. "Naya Andrews."

"A pleasure."

Naya and Sasha eyeballed the blonde woman who'd been seated between them. She raised an eyebrow but rose to her feet.

"And you must be Ms. Farley," Amanda said.

"No flies on you," the blonde drawled, proffering her hand.

Her skin was soft, warm, and the floral scent of her lotion rose from her skin. Amanda couldn't help noticing the woman's perfect reverse French manicure. She shook Maisy's hand quickly before hiding her own ragged cuticles and chipped polish by jamming her hands into her pockets.

The lone man in the room popped up and hurried over to pump Amanda's hand. "It's great to meet you in person, Amanda."

"Likewise, Gabe."

"Come on, let's get you that coffee." WACB's employment lawyer led her to a coffee station set up on a credenza under a long, wide window.

"Do you need anything?" Caroline asked, directing the question to Sasha, who glanced at her colleague. Naya shook her head.

"Nope. We're all set. Any word on when Mickey plans to grace us with his presence?" Sasha said.

"Maureen called. He has a client who violated a gag order and gave an interview on YouTube, which promptly went viral. Mickey's getting chewed out by Judge Williams as we speak. But Maureen assures me the judge, while hot-tempered, isn't long-winded. So he should be here soon."

Sasha laughed lightly. "And I bet he'll be in a great mood."

"Splendid, no doubt," Caroline agreed before turning to leave the room.

Amanda stirred a generous dollop of cream into her coffee and rested the used spoon on a ceramic tray. She took a cautious sip, then bobbed her head, surprised and impressed. This stuff was actually decent. She probably hadn't needed to doctor it.

She turned to Gabe. "Can we peel off and talk for a minute or two, seeing as how Mr. Collins is delayed?"

Gabe looked at Naya.

"There's nobody in the breakout room next door," Naya told him, waving her hand toward her left. "Have at it."

"Thanks," Amanda said.

As she followed Gabe out of the room, she was acutely aware of Maisy Farley's eyes on her back, tracking her progress. They walked in silence the few feet to the smaller room next door, and Gabe held the door for her. Once inside, he gestured toward the table and chairs, but she shook her head.

"What's up?" he asked.

"Your Southern belle seems pretty frosty, Gabe. I thought you said she was a pushover."

He pursed his lips and drew his eyebrows together. "Did I say that? If I did, I shouldn't have. Maisy's charming—well, usually—but she's no pushover. She's sweet, but strong."

She took a sip of coffee and eyed him for a long moment. "Sounds like you're sweet on her."

Dusky color rose on Gabe's cheeks.

"Wow, you are. Noted."

He cleared his throat. "It's nothing like that, Amanda. My relationship with Maisy is strictly professional."

"Why do I sense a 'but' coming?"

"But, she's a good person and, frankly, *legally,* I don't see what the station's end game is here. You know, eventually, you're going to have to pay her."

"I'm aware," she said more testily than she'd intended.

He raised an eyebrow. "So …?"

Amanda sighed. "Look, Gabe, my client—*our* client —wants to drag this out. That's his call."

"Respectfully, my client is the station. It's not in WACB's best interest to get involved in a drawn-out battle with a woman who was once the most popular news anchor in the city and is now the darling of the podcasting set. *Your* client's interests don't seem to be taking the station's reputation into account."

He was right, and she had no valid response. So she trotted out Leith's favorite truism, even though it made her skin crawl. "He who makes the gold, makes the rules. My client pays your client's bills, including your legal fees. So he calls the shots. End of story."

Gabe scrubbed his hands over his face as if they hadn't been over this a half-dozen times on videoconferences in the past several months. Then he shrugged, resigned. "Well, I hope Mr. Delone knows what he's doing."

So do I, Amanda thought.

"Mr. Delone always knows what he's doing," she told him.

"Great. Good to know. Is there anything else we need to discuss?"

He seemed to be in a hurry to get back to the conference room, and she wondered how much of his eagerness was due to the lovely Maisy Farley's presence and how much of it was a burning desire to get away from Amanda before he said something he regretted about their questionable legal strategy.

"One more thing. You're sure this neutral mediator is neutral? It sounds like those lawyers know him pretty well."

"Mickey Collins is an extremely successful plaintiff's attorney. He made his reputation and makes most of his money doing class action work. His ex-wife is Judge Dolans—she's on the federal bench. He was a decent draw for us."

"Even though he's obviously pro-plaintiff?"

Gabe sighed. "Yes. It hardly matters anyway. The entire city of Pittsburgh is pro-Maisy Farley. But the way I hear it, Mickey and Sasha have a history. It all went down before my time—I would have been in high school then. Anyway, the year Sasha was up for partner at her former law firm, she first-chaired a class action defense that Mickey brought against an airline company that crashed a plane full of people into the side of a mountain."

"They had an associate running a case that big?"

"The partner died suddenly, I think? It was a long

time ago. Anyway, the case ended poorly for Sasha's client, and a year later, she opened her own shop. I can't imagine there's any love lost between her and Mickey."

Amanda chewed on her lower lip. The story of a bungled class action defense didn't square with Oliver's report that the lawyer had been offered and turned down partnership at Prescott & Talbot.

But did it really matter? Like Gabe said, it was ancient history. And, also like Gabe said, regardless of the mediator's feelings about McCandless, Volmer & Andrews, Maisy Farley was a sympathetic plaintiff. And Leith Delone was one of the most polarizing humans on the planet. No matter what, she had an uphill battle. Luckily, Amanda Teale-James specialized in winning uphill battles.

7

The rich flavor of Jake's dark roast worked on Sasha's nervous system like a magic elixir, warming her and filling her with optimism and energy. She let out a small, contented sigh.

Maisy broke off her conversation with Naya to lean over and whisper, "You have a serious problem."

Sasha shook her head. Her friends could joke all they wanted about her coffee habit. She knew the truth: it was her life blood, her essence.

"What are you two yammering about anyway?"

Naya painted Maisy with a look. "I was just reminding our client that she has a deep well of good-will with Gabe Parente, and she'd be smart not to squander it by taking potshots at Delone's GC or whatever that Teale-James woman is."

"In other words, she told me to pick on somebody my own size." Maisy giggled.

"Maisy, what's gotten into you? That's positively

mean-spirited. I mean, for you. It'd be the nicest thing Naya said in a week," Sasha said, trying for some levity.

Naya just rolled her eyes, but Maisy's mouth creased into a deep frown. So much for lightening the mood.

"I know, I'm just crabby. I really *like* Gabe. He's always been so kind to me, and I wish he weren't on the other side of this. But, y'all, I'm madder than a hornet that the station still hasn't given me my money. And that greedy, grubby billionaire could just pay me instead of wasting more money and enlarging his carbon footprint by flying Sasha's doppelgänger out here to snub her nose at Jake's coffee."

Sasha and Naya exchanged a wordless glance of mutual understanding. Maisy was right—she was in a mood. Not ideal for a meeting intended to bring the parties closer to a resolution.

Just then, the door opened, and Amanda and Gabe returned. Before it could swing closed, a hand reached out and held it open.

Mickey Collins appeared in the doorway. His trademark silver hair was characteristically disheveled. His bespoke suit was rumpled, and his tie was askew. He looked like he'd been through the wringer. But, then, he usually looked that way.

Too vain to forego expensive clothes, shoes, and cars, Mickey presented himself a wild-haired, wrinkled mess in an effort to appeal to the underdogs he wanted as clients and to combat the idea (accurate though it might be) that he was a wealthy lawyer. And, somehow, he made it work.

"How's my favorite mini-attorney?" he boomed as he entered the room.

He spotted Amanda Teale-James and did a double take. "Look at that, we have two mini-attorneys today!"

Sasha suppressed a smile, and Naya shook her head slowly.

"Hey, Gabe. How's it hanging?" Mickey continued, unabashed, before anyone else could get a word in.

Amanda Teale-James' eyes widened with what Sasha assumed was horror at the fact that *this* was their mediator. Having known Mickey for more than a decade, Sasha was certain the out-of-town lawyer's reaction was playing into his hands. The only question was *why?*

Mickey, for all his bluster, was a talented neutral— the federal court's term for the lawyers who oversaw alternative dispute resolution proceedings. Naya always said the descriptor made her think of a dystopian young adult movie where some characters had supernatural gifts, and others didn't. At the moment, Mickey's gift appeared to be a talent for mortifying everyone in the room.

Gabe managed to choke out a response that ignored Mickey's crassness by steering the conversation to one of their neutral's obsessions. "Hi, Mickey. Have you hit the greens lately?"

Sasha allowed their back and forth about golf to wash over her without listening to the actual conversation while she pulled her notes together. Opposing counsel did the same while her colleague described a shot out of a sand bunker in excruciating detail. Naya examined her cuticles. Maisy peeled a sticky note from the pad at Sasha's elbow and began to doodle.

Before Gabe could launch into the play-by-play, shot-by-shot retelling of his next hole, Sasha cut in.

"Do you want some coffee before we get started, Mickey? Or something else? Caroline will call down to Jake's, if you like?"

"I'm all set, and it's clear you want to get down to brass tacks. So let's get this party started." Mickey slid into the unoccupied chair at the far end of the table and clapped his hands together. "I take it the gang's all here?"

"Yes," Naya and Gabe confirmed in unison.

Mickey removed a pair of reading glasses from his breast pocket and perched them on the end of his nose, then pulled a notepad from his bag and uncapped his pen. "I assume Ms. Teale-James has decision-making authority on behalf of WACB?"

He directed the question toward Gabe, but Amanda answered it. "Yes. Well, effectively."

"Meaning what?" Mickey countered, slipping out of his good old boy routine and getting serious.

"Meaning, I have decision-making authority on behalf of Leith Delone." She glanced around the table. "I'm sure we can all agree he has the ultimate decision-making authority for all his business entities, including the news station. Ergo, I do, too."

"Taste the power," Naya mumbled the candy company slogan under her breath. Sasha aimed a gentle-ish kick at her shin.

Gabe nodded his agreement with Amanda's assessment, and Mickey turned toward Maisy. "Is that okay with you, Ms. Farley?"

"With me?" Maisy repeated, wide-eyed.

Sasha couldn't tell whether her surprise at being consulted was genuine or feigned. Maisy had met Mickey several times over the years, and Sasha was sure it hadn't been lost on her that Mickey was enthralled by her. Was that the explanation for his over-the-top performance?

Mickey smiled his encouragement. "Yes, ma'am, you."

"As long as Attorney Teale-James can authorize a seven-figure wire transfer, I'm fine with it."

The lawyer's head snapped back. "Now, wait just a minute—"

Mickey forestalled her protest before it gathered steam. "Ah, I don't think that's in the cards today, Maisy. We're here to …"—he paused to glance down at his notes—"… resolve a discovery issue." He looked up and surveyed the table. "Ugh, really? You can't all play nice? Ms. Teale-James, would you—?"

This time she cut him off. "ATJ is fine."

"I'm sorry, what?"

"Call me ATJ. It saves time."

"ATJ," Mickey repeated before turning to Sasha. "You want me to call you SMC?"

"No."

"Anybody else have a moniker they prefer, whether for efficiency or other reasons?" He waited a beat. When nobody responded, he continued, "Okay, ATJ, according to the materials Ms. Farley's attorneys submitted with their request for this meeting, back in September and October, the television station provided a series of reasons why they hadn't paid the contractually required separation bonus. Ms. Andrews and Mr. Parente met in October and reached an agreement that the station would pay Ms. Farley before the end of the calendar year—"

"But then the station learned Maisy was trying to poach its employees," Gabe interjected.

Mickey eyed the lawyer over the top of his glasses. "I was getting to that. Now, McCandless, Andrews & Volmer's timeline indicates the so-called poaching occurred in December, more than four months after Maisy was terminated and two months after you and Naya met to hammer out the details. Is that accurate?"

Gabe frowned and flipped through a small leather-bound calendar. "Yes, just before Christmas. Naya called and asked where we were on the payment, and I explained things were on hold while we investigated which of the station's employees were approached."

Sasha cleared her throat to draw Mickey's attention. "Counselor?"

"*If* Maisy approached any employees, she was within her rights. *She* wasn't in violation of her non-compete agreement. That agreement says she can't take an on-air position at another local station for a period of six months. There's not a word in it about not hiring away WACB's employees. So the argument—some might call it an excuse—WACB gave for delaying payment in December wasn't made in good faith. Everyone in this room can see it for what it is."

She paused when ATJ opened her mouth. But the other woman must've reconsidered, because she clamped her jaw shut again.

Sasha continued, "The issue then is why *is* the television station dragging its feet? Mr. Parente intimated that Mr. Delone—and, by extension, ATJ—is calling the shots. That, in and of itself, is weird. A million dollars shouldn't be enough to warrant Mr. Delone's attention. Not if the reports of his net worth are to be believed. But, maybe those reports are exaggerated. Maybe they're pure fiction. Maybe he's moon-poor the same way someone who overspends on a new residence is house-poor. We have no idea. So we requested limited financial discovery into Leith Delone's personal finances to determine why he's trying to stiff our client. And ATJ is refusing to produce it."

"ATJ, any response?" Mickey swiveled in his chair to face her directly.

She jutted her chin forward. "Yes, I have a response. If you want to talk about a bad-faith argument, the claim that Mr. Delone's television station isn't capable of paying Ms. Farley because of his personal financial situation is the height of a bad-faith argument. This financial discovery is clearly intended to harass and embarrass my client."

"For the sake of clarity, when you say your client, you mean Leith Delone, right? Not WACB," Naya said in a cool tone.

"As I've already said, I represent Mr. Delone and his business interests."

"Right, but we've initiated a proceeding against

WACB, not Mr. Delone. Sharing his financial condition won't embarrass the tv station. Right?" Naya pressed.

"You didn't seek discovery about the television station's fiscal health," ATJ shot back.

"Do we need to?" Sasha asked.

"No." Gabe Parente's voice was loud, clear, and calm. "No, you do not. Amanda, I'm sorry to do this, but I have a specific duty to WACB." He swallowed audibly, then said, "WACB has the ability to pay out the full one million dollars right now. In fact, we placed that amount in an escrow account back in August when it became clear that there was going to be a delay. We're just waiting for the go-ahead from California."

"California being Mr. Delone?" Mickey asked.

"Or ATJ."

"Sure, or ATJ," Mickey agreed.

Sasha interjected, "Assuming this escrow account is interest-bearing, our client is obviously entitled to any interest earned during this delay in payment."

"Obviously," Gabe agreed, risking an anxious glance at ATJ, whose face was a thundercloud.

Maisy hid a grin.

"I have to confess, folks, I don't understand why we're here." Mickey spread his hands wide, a gesture Sasha recognized as his 'let's be reasonable' opening gambit. "Everyone seems to agree that Maisy Farley is entitled to a million dollars. That said, there's no need for discovery into Mr. Delone's finances."

Maisy's grin thinned. Naya's eyebrow hit her hairline. And Sasha nearly did a spit-take with an ill-timed mouthful of coffee.

"Mickey—" she managed after swallowing the liquid.

But ATJ interrupted her interruption. "I came here with authority to propose a solution that I think will satisfy everyone—Ms. Farley, WACB, and Mr. Delone—without requiring any further discovery, financial or otherwise."

"We're all ears, ATJ." Mickey motioned for her to continue.

"Mr. Delone is prepared to transfer the full payout to Ms. Farley immediately on the condition that she never mention him or any of his businesses or other interests publicly again. So, not on her podcast and not if she ends up getting a real media job somewhere."

Maisy's nostrils flared, and Sasha rested a calming hand on her arm.

Mickey swiveled his chair toward them. "How's that sound?"

"No," Maisy answered instantly in a flat voice.

"No?" Naya hissed.

Sasha focused on keeping her expression neutral. "Mickey, we need a moment to discuss this new offer with our client."

"Sure thing. Let's reconvene in ten minutes." Before they were out of the room, he'd turned back to Gabe and was telling him about his latest adventure with a water hazard at Oakmont Country Club.

8

Gar was deep into the dreaded late-afternoon slump when his phone's shrill ring startled him. Okay, he was sleeping. He raised his head from the pillow he'd created with his arms and wiped the drool from his chin. He spared a wild-eyed frantic glance around the bullpen, hoping against hope that Antonia hadn't wandered by and seen him zonked out. He'd never hear the end of it.

The phone chirped again and he grabbed it.

"This is Gar." His voice was thick with sleep. Maybe his caller wouldn't notice.

"Gar, this is Brian Rosen returning your call."

Brian Rosen? Gar rubbed his eyes and tried to focus.

"Oh, right. Hi."

"Did I wake you?" Rosen laughed at the notion.

"Of course not," Gar lied. Finally, his brain shifted into gear. "I called to give you an update on the project."

"No need, pal. I reached out to Antonia last week, and she sent over the code. It looks great."

"Wait. What? No, Brian, it's nowhere near ready."

Rosen laughed at his obvious confusion. "My bosses were getting impatient, and Antonia said you can be a perfectionist, so she just sent the work in progress so I could give them a demo. Don't worry, I made it clear that the program's not finished."

Gar groaned.

"Man, Antonia's right about you. Bro, with some minor tweaks, it's there. You did it. Mjölnir put on one helluva show."

Rosen's confident, optimistic tone made zero sense.

"It's...working?" he said slowly.

"Yep," Rosen confirmed. "The investor is thrilled."

Gar raked a hand through his hair, and said in an uncertain voice, "That's good news, I guess."

"No, bro, it's phenomenal news! Just put on a bow on that puppy and ship it," he instructed, oblivious to Gar's discomfort.

He cleared his throat, hesitating, but he had to ask. "You didn't see anything strange in the demo?"

"Strange how?"

"Strange like Mjölnir predicting user tendencies toward criminal behavior."

Brian's voice dropped to a whisper. "Why would you ask that?"

"Because no matter what input I feed it, the AI doesn't just share the predictions I ask for. Like, for instance, I ask will this person be more likely to buy if they get a coupon code or free shipping? And Mjölnir spits out they're forty-seven percent more likely to buy if there's a free shipping offer and then randomly adds and there's a twenty-two percent chance she'll sell street drugs in the next six months. You didn't see anything like that? Nothing at all?"

There was a long pause on the other end. So long, that Gar wondered if the call had dropped.

"Brian?" he prompted.

"I'm still here," he said slowly. "You really are good, aren't you? That criminality modality is designed to function beneath the surface. It should be undetectable unless you know to look for it. How'd you find it?"

Gar stared at the phone in his hand, trying to make sense of what Rosen was saying. Just as Petra had suspected, Mjölnir was designed to predict criminal behavior. But nobody was supposed to find out.

"How'd you find it?" Rosen asked again, more firmly this time.

"I always poke around under the hood when I'm cleaning up code. Sometimes a program can look clean and elegant, but underneath, it's a tangled rat's nest of old functions or bloated commands. I always look for the bones."

"Well, you found them. And that's a problem. Because nobody can know about that modality."

"I don't understand. Why is an AI program designed to learn consumer buying habits built on a framework that assesses criminal tendencies in the first place?"

"You don't need to know. You already know too much, and that's a problem."

Gar didn't like the ominous tone behind his words.

"What you do mean I know too much? Who's behind Mjölnir, Brian?"

"You should stop asking questions." Rosen's voice was cold and hard.

"Are you threatening me?"

"I'm telling you to be smart. Forget what you saw. Wrap up the project and mark it complete. Move on, and don't mention your work on Mjölnir to anyone. You haven't told anyone else about what you found, have you?"

Gar thought of Petra and lied. "No."

"You're sure? Not even Antonia?"

"No, I didn't want her micromanaging me and breathing down my neck while I was figuring out how to get rid of the bug." He laughed shortly. "Guess it's not a bug, after all. But why—?"

"—It's a top-secret project. I can't go into details."

"Is it for the government?"

Rosen ignored the question. "I'll keep this quiet. You forget we ever had this conversation."

Rosen hung up without waiting for an answer. Gar flopped back in his chair and stared at the string of code on his monitor. His mind zinged and pinged, racing through the new information, trying to process it. Mjölnir was not just capable of predicting criminal behavior, it had been designed for that very purpose. The purchasing behavior program was a shield, a ruse to hide a technology that could easily be abused if it fell into the wrong hands.

He played back his conversation with Brian Rosen.

What if it was already in the wrong hands? Gar's own hands began to tremble, and he shoved them under his thighs to still them. He had to keep it together—if not for his own sake, then for Petra's.

9

Naya yanked open the door to the breakout room, and Sasha hustled Maisy inside.

"Maisy, you should take this offer," Naya told her. "You don't want to tangle with Delone in the future. He'll sue your round bottom for defamation if you so much as mention his name. So, just take the money and move on."

"No." Maisy pressed her lips together.

Sasha eyed her. "Care to elaborate? It's your call, but it would be helpful to give Mickey a reason when we reject the offer."

She pretended not to notice the daggers Naya was shooting with her eyes.

"I'm a serious journalist, regardless of what that West Coast witch thinks. If I come across something newsworthy that involves Delone or one of his stupid businesses, I'm gonna chase the story. Besides, how many pies do you think that guy has a finger in? He owns a freaking moon. I'd be afraid to say anything about anything for fear he's somehow involved in it. No. I won't do it. Mickey can't make me. Can he?"

Sasha gave Naya a look. Naya shrugged.

"No," Naya admitted. "The agreement says you get the money with no conditions, so the court won't impose one on you after the fact. Not without new consideration." She perked up at the idea.

"What's that mean?" Maisy demanded.

"More money," Sasha told her. "Would you be willing to agree to never mention him for, say, two million? Hypothetically."

"No. Not for two million. Not for ten million. I'm serious about this."

Sasha studied her friend. Maisy was bubbly, charming, and fun. She was rarely serious. But when she dug in her heels, she meant it.

"Okay, let's go tell Amanda Teale-James to pound sand."

"You mean ATJ," Naya snarked.

Sasha mimed sticking her finger down her throat. "Seriously, what is *that* about?"

As they headed for the door, Maisy's laughter faded. "You think I'll still get the one million, though, right?"

"Naya?" Sasha could get Maisy her money, but it might involve an ugly court battle. She deferred to Naya to assess their odds of getting it through a negotiation.

"Eventually, yes. Well, it would have helped if Mickey had ordered the financial discovery. You want to lower your demand?"

Maisy shook her head. "No. The station owes me a million. I want a million."

"Then let's go get your money," Naya told her.

They trooped back into the conference room with their shoulders back and their heads erect.

Mickey took note of their postures and sighed. "I'm guessing Maisy is rejecting the offer?"

"Your instincts are spot on," Sasha said. "There's an existing enforceable contract between the parties. Ms. … er, ATJ's eleventh-hour effort to impose a new obligation on Maisy *post hoc* is insulting. And everyone here knows the court would never go for it."

"This is a negotiation," ATJ spat. "I'm negotiating."

"Pro tip," Naya said. "You should offer something she's not already entitled to. That's how negotiations work."

"Does she want more money?" ATJ countered.

Mickey cocked his head, intrigued by the suggestion.

"No," Naya said. "She wants her million and no new restrictions."

"She's being intransigent." ATJ bit off each word and clenched her hands into fists.

Mickey held up a hand. "I've heard enough."

"Will you reconsider the financial discovery?" Sasha asked, taking a flyer.

He shook his head. "No. There's no need. I don't care whether WACB releases the funds from escrow or Mr. Delone finds a million bucks in a pair of trousers in his dirty clothes hamper. I'm ordering ATJ to ensure the full amount is transferred to Ms. Farley by the close of business tomorrow. Is that clear?"

ATJ's eyes bulged. "That's not feasible. I can't—"

"With interest," Naya reminded.

"Right, with interest," Mickey clarified.

ATJ's face turned red, then purple, then, finally, a sickly green color. After a long moment, she turned and spoke to Gabe in a low, furious voice. "Does an ADR neutral even have the authority to order us to pay? I mean, this is appealable, right?"

Gabe gave her a cool look. "When Thor acquired the station, you—or someone—sent out a revised employee manual. All the employees, including Ms. Farley, were required to sign a statement accepting the terms in order to keep their jobs. One of the changes was that all employment disputes are subject to the federal court's alternative dispute resolution program. No exceptions, no right to appeal. I'll note that nobody consulted the station's employment counsel, aka me. If they had, I'd have said that the change was making it almost impossible for the station to appeal unfavorable outcomes, as well as the employees."

Mickey leaned over the table. "And I'll caution the pair of you: if the station or Mr. Delone appeals this decision on frivolous grounds, I'll recommend sanctions for their attorneys. To be clear, 'Mr. Delone doesn't wanna' is a frivolous argument."

Maisy grabbed Sasha's arm. "Ask them about Thor," she whispered.

Sasha kept her focus on the back and forth between Mickey and Delone's attorneys as she answered. "What?"

"Thor. Gabe said Thor acquired the station. Can you find out—?"

Whatever Maisy was about to say was lost in the

commotion when ATJ banged down her coffee mug, pushed her chair back from the table, and stormed out of the conference room, trying and failing to slam the door behind her. Instead, it swung closed with a soft, nearly silent click.

They sat in silence, looking at the door, until Gabe wondered, "Why didn't the door slam?"

Sasha pointed at the closer installed on the top of the door frame. "Hydraulics. Really cuts down on the theatrics."

"Yeah," Naya deadpanned, "you know Will Volmer. He's a dyed-in-wool drama llama."

Their giddy laughter cut through the awkwardness of Amanda Teale-James' departure. After a moment, Gabe started to pack up his papers.

"I guess I'd better catch up with my drama llama before she takes out her rage on some innocent bystanders," he said with a heavy sigh.

"Better you than me," Mickey told him.

Gabe crossed the room and shook Sasha and Naya's hands, then told Naya he'd be in touch to arrange the wire transfer in the morning. He bent and whispered something in Maisy's ear, something that made her blush. Then he thanked Mickey for his help and headed for the door.

After he left, Mickey aimed a gentle punch at Sasha's upper arm. "You should've seen your face when I said I was denying your discovery request. How about a little faith, McCandless?"

She wrinkled her forehead. "I have a question about that, Mickey."

"Hit me."

"Aren't you the one who always says you'll know you've done your job as a neutral if everyone is equally unhappy with the outcome?"

"I say equally disgruntled, but yeah, same difference. So?"

"So, this was an unequivocal win for us. Don't get me wrong, we deserve it. Maisy's entitled to that money, full stop. How's that square with your goal of spreading the misery evenly?"

Mickey grinned. "That principle doesn't apply when a smarmy billionaire decides to mess with Pittsburgh's fan favorite. Have a little hometown pride, would ya'?"

"Fair enough." She glanced over her shoulder at Maisy, who nodded. Then she turned back to Mickey. "Naya's making us go to some buzzy new Mediterranean spot for dinner. Care to join us?"

"Saffron?"

Naya nodded.

"Excellent choice; that place is great. But avoid the ouzo. Trust me."

"That's evergreen advice," Sasha told him with a small shudder.

"Ha. You might have a point. But, as much as I appreciate the invitation, I wouldn't want anyone to get the wrong idea."

"You mean that you weren't impartial?" Maisy asked with a shadow of worry in her eyes.

Mickey scoffed. "No, that I'm off the market. I get spotted with three gorgeous women at a hot spot, and people will think I'm not available."

Naya shook her head. "You're incorrigible."

He winked, then headed for the door. He paused to look over his shoulder. "Just so you know, Maisy, there's not a mediator, judge, or jury member in the tri-state area who would've sided with Leith Delone in this dispute. Some billionaire man-baby had a temper tantrum and decided to throw his weight around. Well, now he has to pay for it. As my sainted Grandma Joyce used to say, tough titties."

10

A fter hanging their coats in the coat room behind the welcome station, the hostess led Sasha, Naya, and Maisy to the table Naya had requested: a booth tucked into an alcove near a private room in the back of the busy Mediterranean restaurant. Despite—or perhaps because of—the bustle of a popular restaurant at the height of the dinner rush, they'd be able to talk in relative privacy here. The clinking of plates and glasses, the lamb sizzling on cast iron platters, and the lively chatter from the surrounding tables all blended with the vibrant instrumental music of drums and mandolins to create something better than silence.

Sasha glanced around the cozy space. The walls were painted a warm shade of blue that reminded her of the sea and complemented the terra cotta floors. Their tabletop was inlaid with white and blue mosaic tiles. A small glass vase of snowy white flowers with bright orange stamens sat in the center.

"These are pretty." As she slid onto the bench seat, she fingered a petal and eyed Naya, who was a vast repository of horticultural trivia.

She didn't disappoint. "They're saffron crocuses. The petals are usually purple. These white ones are rarer."

"Saffron like the spice?" Maisy wanted to know.

Naya shrugged.

But the hostess smiled as she handed out the menus. "Precisely. The Greeks were the first to cultivate and harvest the stamens for their saffron threads. That's why chef named the restaurant Saffron."

"It comes from these flowers?" Sasha marveled. "No wonder it costs so much."

The hostess nodded politely. "Damon will be over to take your order in a minute."

Naya and Maisy turned to stare at Sasha when the hostess walked away.

"What?"

"How do you know how much saffron costs? Did you suddenly start doing the cooking at your house?" Maisy asked.

"Or the grocery shopping?" Naya chimed in.

"Ha ha. You know, I *do* listen when Connelly talks."

Well, usually. This morning, she had been a teensy bit distracted by the looming meeting while he yammered about Landon Lewis' documents. She'd have to make it up to him later.

"So, what's good here?" Maisy asked, directing the question to Naya, who'd chosen the spot.

"Everything."

Sasha closed her menu. "In that case, do we want to

eat tapas style? Get one of every starter and share them? I'm ravenous."

"That works," Maisy agreed.

"Sounds good," Naya seconded. "And a drink to toast to Maisy's money finally coming through."

"I'll believe it when I see it. But that won't stop me from drinking to it." She giggled.

Naya took off her suit jacket and hung it from the hook on the end of the booth. Sasha wriggled out of her cardigan and passed it to her to hang up. Maisy gathered her shoulder-length golden curls into a loose ponytail and secured it with a hair tie. They were ready to dig in.

Damon materialized to take their beverage orders and left with their meal orders as well. He returned a moment later with their drinks, a dish of bright green olives, and a stack of warm pita bread with a saucer of herbed olive oil for dipping.

Maisy sipped her white wine and then broke off a corner of a grilled pita. As she dragged it through the olive oil, she asked, "Well? What do you think Mickey made of Sasha's evil twin?"

"Evil twin?" Sasha gave her a blank look.

Naya arched a perfectly groomed eyebrow and smirked. "Be for real, Mac. You must've noticed that Amanda Teale-James is five foot nothing and weighs about a hundred pounds. Wasn't it like looking in a mirror?"

"Are you saying all White women look alike, Naya?" Sasha deadpanned in return.

Maisy choked on an olive. "I can't believe you just

said that," she muttered after Naya pounded her on the back.

Sasha raised a hand and ticked off the differences between her and Amanda Teale-James. "Exhibit A, she is obviously childless because she has the time and energy to maintain a short pixie cut with professional lowlights, whereas I just trimmed my split ends myself and have been using a colored hair pencil I picked up at the pharmacy to cover my roots until I can get into see Christos. Exhibit B, she was wearing stiletto boots. In Pittsburgh. In January. She clearly has no regard for her orthopedic health. Unlike me." She raised her foot and waggled her sensible low-heeled pumps at them. "I rest my case."

"There's nobody more annoying than a convert who's found religion," Naya told her. "Spare us your pious sensible shoe spiel. We'll be impressed when you empty your closet of five-inch heels and not before."

"Preach," Maisy said to Naya. Then she turned to Sasha. "Look down."

Sasha did as directed, and Maisy leaned over to peer at her part.

"That's not bad," she murmured. "I might have to pick up one of those pencils in honey blonde."

"What? You, of all people, have time for a salon appointment. Wait, don't tell me. Is Jordana keeping you chained to your desk?"

They were laughing when Damon returned with the first round of tapas. Steaming hot platters of mouth-watering stuffed grape leaves, creamy tzatziki, smoky baba ganoush, and tangy hummus, accompanied by another tower of fresh pita covered the table.

He refilled their wine goblets and water glasses and told them to dig in. The instruction was unnecessary. All conversation stopped while they passed plates and portioned out servings.

After several bites, Maisy returned to the question she'd been asked before the first plates arrived. "It's not that I don't have time for a hair appointment, it's just …," she dropped her voice. "Everyone knows I've been getting my hair done at Locks on Fifth for years. I've said it on the air at least a dozen times."

"Okay? And?"

"And, what if … what if whoever hired Detective Colchis and Zane Novak to kill Landon decides to come after me?"

Naya's eyes widened, and she froze, a grape leaf suspended in mid-air. "Have you gotten any weird phone calls? Noticed anyone following you? Anything like that?"

"No, nothing. I mean, not since my house was broken into. But the police think that was Colchis searching for Landon's phone and laptop."

"And Colchis is in custody," Sasha reminded her.

"I know. But realistically, a dirty cop like him is almost guaranteed to have contacts on the street. Bad people. I mean, he's the one who recruited Zane."

Sasha gnawed at her lower lip. Maisy wasn't wrong. But spending your entire life looking over your shoulder and refusing to visit your hairdresser was no way to live.

"Are you still taking that cycling class at the gym?"

"The one with the former Steeler as an instructor? What do you think?" Maisy's mood lightened and she winked.

"I think you and Mickey Collins are two peas in a pod. I also think you should skip cycling class tomorrow and come to the sparring studio with me."

"Daniel's sparring studio, you mean? So one of those musclebound guys with no necks can Krav Maga my butt into the ground? Pass."

Sasha scooped up some hummus on a triangle of bread before responding. "You can't use Krav Maga as a verb."

"I just did."

"Yeah, but it sounds dumb. And Daniel would partner you with me, not one of the former military types."

"Oh, because it's *soo* much better to get my butt Krav Magaed into the ground by a mini-attorney? Hard pass."

Naya raised her free hand. "Now, hang on. Mac's got a halfway decent idea. It wouldn't be the worst thing if you were to pick up some basic self-defense skills, especially if you're gonna be traipsing all over town solving cold cases for your true crime podcast."

Maisy bobbed her head from side to side and considered the idea.

"I'm not saying you have to break someone's nose with your forehead or choke them out or any of the wild stuff she does. But you should be able to protect yourself," Naya continued.

"Yeah, you're right. Jordana, too." Maisy's eyes lit up.

"What if I can find a class for the three of us? Would you take it with us, Naya?"

Naya shrugged. "Sure. Why not?"

"Hello. You don't need to find a class," Sasha told her. "I'm literally sitting right here. If you don't want to enroll in real Krav Maga with Daniel, I can teach you enough to get by."

"No wild stuff?" Maisy pressed.

"No wild stuff," she promised.

"We'll think about it," Maisy said.

Sasha rolled her eyes but was distracted by the sizzling plates of chicken souvlaki, grilled lamb, and moussaka that were coming their way on a large tray balanced on Damon's shoulder. Bowls of grilled vegetables rounded out the meal.

They caught up on one another's lives, sharing news as they shared the food. Sasha reported on the twins' latest escapades, Naya filled them in on a big outreach program she was running for her church to provide counseling to teens who were struggling with anxiety and depression, and Maisy regaled them with the highlights of her recent trip back home to Georgia.

11

Amanda hunched over the desk in her hotel room and cursed the dim light. Why did every hotel room have insufficient lighting at the in-room workspace?

After she'd stormed out of the conference room, she'd wandered around the little neighborhood window-shopping until she'd cooled down. Then, she did what she always did. She regrouped and developed a strategy.

Her fingers flew over her laptop keys as she searched her email archives for Landon Lewis' name. With a series of clicks, she copied all the messages and their attachments to a folder on her desktop, which she synced with her phone. She'd review them later. Right now, she had other priorities.

She took a sip of her ice water and checked her list. It was a short list—only two items—but it was a start:

Figure out Leith's connection to Landon Lewis

Call Leith and break the news about the payout

There was no point in putting it off. She had to tell him sometime. She drained the glass and rolled her neck. Then, before she could second-guess herself, she grabbed her phone and hit the entry for Leith's home number.

Raquel answered on the third ring. "Delone residence."

"What kind of mood is he in?" she asked the house manager.

"Oh, hi, ATJ. I'd say he's a solid six on a scale of one to ten. His driverless boat sank, but his longevity numbers are up."

Six wasn't too bad. It could be a heck of a lot worse.

"How's the market?"

Raquel's voice dropped. "He's lost a lot, but he doesn't know yet. If you have to deliver bad news, I'd suggest doing it now. Before he checks in with the financial team."

Amanda nodded. "Thanks, Raquel. Put me through to him, okay?"

"You got it. Hey, by the way, thanks for the shoes. They're so cute."

"I'm glad you like them. I ran into Manolo at that Luminaries of the Future symposium Leith and I went to in the U.K. last month, and he specifically suggested that pair for you."

"Oh, that's so sweet. He has the best taste."

He'd better. Those bejeweled ballerina flats had set Amanda back more than a thousand pounds. But currying favor with Raquel was worth it at any price.

"Can't wait to see you wearing them," she cooed.

"I'll snap you a pic. Okay, hold for Leith."

"ATJ?" Leith was out of breath.

"Did I catch you on the bike?"

"Yes. But I can talk. I have the lung capacity of a twenty-two-year-old man."

"That's phenomenal. When's your next longevity assessment? I bet your overall age has dropped since last time."

"Just had it, and it did."

She could hear the triumph in his voice. She wasn't sure why he was chasing immortality, but maybe he figured living forever was the only way he could spend all his money. Even then, it'd be a challenge.

"Fantastic."

"How'd it go in Pittsburgh?"

He was distracted by his workout, happy about his longevity score, and didn't yet know that he'd lost a small fortune. It was now or never. She squared her shoulders and plunged ahead.

"I'm still here. The meeting with the ADR neutral didn't go as well as I would have liked. Home cooking, you know how it—"

"No excuses."

"Of course. Never. I'm not making an excuse, Leith. I'm explaining where we are."

"And where are we?" he huffed. Whether from exertion or irritation, she couldn't tell.

The cardinal rule with Leith was to deliver the bad news first. Unlike most people, softening him up with the good news first was guaranteed to backfire.

She padded over to the window and looked out over

the downtown skyline as she explained, "The neutral ordered the station to pay Ms. Farley in full. Tomorrow."

"You're useless."

"Not quite," she countered. "I did convince him to deny the request for discovery into your personal financials."

In response, he grunted.

You're welcome, she thought. What she said was, "WACB has the money in an escrow account, so they'll handle the transfer. We don't need to involve ourselves."

"Remind me why I bought all these local television stations?"

Vanity?

"I believe you want to be able to shape the narrative in advance of the next election cycle."

"It was a rhetorical question."

"Right, sorry. I wish I had better news, but in truth, I view this as a win for us."

He snorted. "This, I have to hear."

"Aside from being an invasion of your privacy, financial discovery would have been a significant risk, Leith. Some of your investment vehicles and tax decisions are ... unusual. If Neutral Collins had granted their motion, well, there could have been wide-ranging implications. Civil, regulatory, and criminal," she added to drive the point home.

"You're supposed to insulate me from risks like those."

Great. Now he was pouting.

"And I have."

"I don't mean by convincing some clown of a mediator in a podunk town not to grant an overreaching discovery request," he snapped. "Your job is to protect me."

"Unfortunately, Leith, I can't protect you from yourself. It would've been helpful to go into this knowing why you were so interested in Maisy Farley."

"She impugned my integrity on live television, Amanda."

"Come on, Leith."

He let out a deep sigh. "She created a mess. She was instrumental in scuttling a settlement that I put into place for long-term strategic reasons. Her behavior had the potential to damage a significant business opportunity."

"Had the potential to? Does that mean it didn't actually happen?"

"That's not the point."

She pulled a face. He was veering from snappish to unreasonable. It would be a short slide into verbal abuse. It was time to do damage control, and in a hurry.

"You're absolutely right. I'm sorry. I don't know what opportunity you're referring to, but when I get back to the office, I can take a look at—"

"I don't think so."

"Pardon?"

"There's a reason I didn't involve you in this deal. Do you know what it is?"

The fact that you're an arrogant buffoon?

"No, I don't."

"I didn't think you would add any value. And you're proving my point."

His assessment stung, as it was meant to. She closed her eyes and pressed her forehead against the cold glass of the window.

After a beat, she pushed away her insecurity and humiliation and plowed forward. "I can only do my job effectively if I'm kept in the loop. I can't protect your existing interests when you have irons in the fire that I don't know about. I'd like the chance to change your mind about my value, Leith."

"You'll have to earn it, Amanda."

He hung up on her. The loud click in her ear was like a gunshot.

Earn it. How was she supposed to earn it? She pursed her lips and tried to put herself in Leith's shoes. What would he want her to do to win back his approval?

After a few moments, she scrolled through her phone and found the number for Delone Driverless Ventures' East Coast presence.

A bored male voice answered. "DDV."

"This is Amanda Teale-James. I'm Mr. Delone's personal attorney, and I have an assignment for your security chief."

12

E ven though Sasha was certain she couldn't eat another bite, she readily agreed to share an order of baklava for dessert. As the trio savored the honey-soaked film pastry, accompanied by the hot mint tea Damon had recommended, Maisy daydreamed about how she would spend her imminent fortune.

"I'm thinking I'll buy that billboard on the hill right outside the studio and plaster my big old face on it, so they can see me every single day—crow's feet and all," she cackled.

She evidently had not yet gotten over her producer's remark that station management suggested she get some "work" done—the inciting event that had started the ball rolling on Maisy's eventual separation from WACB.

"But, imagine if Preston hadn't said that?" Sasha mused. "You'd still be co-anchoring the news with awful

Chet and dreaming about being an investigative reporter."

"Mmm, true," she agreed, licking her sticky fingers. A move only she could pull off without seeming gross or sexual.

"Do you still want to start that independent news station?" Naya asked, turning serious.

She thought for a moment. "No, I don't think so. I like the podcast format. Jordana has loads of good ideas. And, to be honest, it's refreshing not to have to worry about my hair and makeup being perfect every time I want to record a segment. That's probably the biggest difference from television journalism—no primping. Do you know I recorded last week's trailer in my pajamas? My pajamas!"

"Wait until she frees herself from the tyranny of hard pants," Naya said as an aside to Sasha.

"Hard pants?"

Sasha shook her head. "The firm's very casual dress code is still too much for Naya. She's been campaigning to disallow hard pants, which is what she calls any slacks that have a button. I guess she wants to see Will in a pair of sweats."

"Scoff all you want. These new lawyers, they don't wanna be wearing hard pants. Not unless they have a court appearance. It'll make us more competitive in the job market. Come to McCandless, Volmer & Andrews and do your lawyering in yoga pants!" She cackled at her own nonsense.

Sasha was wiping the tears of laughter from her eyes when Damon appeared at their table.

"Uh-oh, are we making too much noise?" Maisy asked, still catching her breath from cracking up.

"Of course not, don't be silly. The sound of women laughing is musical."

Given that they'd been whooping and wheezing, Sasha was certain their server was being too kind. He proffered a square decanter of clear liquid.

"What's that?" Naya asked.

"Our housemade ouzo. It's very special. The gentlemen at the table near the window sent it over to aid you in your celebration. Jade will be over with the *kanoakia* glasses in just a moment." He dipped his head, stopping just short of bowing, before walking away.

Sasha sniffed the carafe and her eyes instantly watered. "Smells like paint thinner."

"Oh, live a little," Maisy scolded her.

"Remember what Mickey said," she countered.

Naya waved her hand. "Mickey, Schmickey. Where's Jade with those glasses?"

And this, Sasha thought, is the dividing line between people who need to wake up with eight-year-olds in the morning, and people who don't.

She craned her head toward the window. "Who sent it over? Some of Maisy's fans, I'll bet."

They all turned to look. But instead of a couple of besotted podcast listeners, a trio of grim-faced, suited men walked toward their table.

"Hard pants," Naya grumbled, as they approached.

"And hard everything else," Sasha responded out of the side of her mouth.

Jade appeared out of nowhere and placed three tall, skinny glasses on the tiled table.

Naya scooped up two of the glasses and gestured for Maisy to grab the carafe. "Come on, let's keep this party going." As they abandoned Sasha, she called over her shoulder, "We'll be at the bar."

Sasha sighed, took a sip of her mint tea, and eyed what was left of Prescott & Talbot's Top Five, the quintet of men who'd run Pittsburgh's oldest, most venerable law firm for decades. Suddenly, ouzo didn't sound like a half-bad idea.

Kevin Marcus, the youngest of the three by at least fifteen years, took the lead. "Sasha, we heard you ladies celebrating, and we wanted to come over and congratulate you on yet another victory. Outstanding result, and no small feat. Amanda Teale-James has a reputation as a tiger."

Ever since she'd left P&T, on the rare, but not rare enough, occasions when her former employers wanted a favor from her, they pushed Marcus out in front. He *had* been the deputy managing partner of the litigation department when she'd been an associate, so she'd known him better than the others. Whatever bond they might have had was exceedingly thin at the time. Now, more than a decade later, it was nonexistent. Still, she'd given them points for effort.

Finally, she smiled. "Thanks, Kevin. I'm surprised word spread so fast. It was only a meeting with an ADR neutral. Not exactly the most exciting fodder for the legal grapevine."

"It's been a slow week," John Porter, the oldest and dourest of the three, told her.

"And Mickey Collins gossips like my seventh-grade niece," Marco DeAngeles added.

She flashed another smile. "I'd invite you to sit and share some of your ouzo, but my colleague and client made off with the bottle, so …"

She pushed back her chair and folded her napkin over her plate.

The Top Three ignored the universal signal that she was leaving and lowered themselves onto the bench seat opposite her and squeezed into the booth.

"We need to talk to you," Porter said.

"I surmised as much."

Seeing them now, lined up shoulder to shoulder, staring at her with matching frowns, she marveled that she'd once found them intimidating. But she had.

Prescott & Talbot's Top Five—DeAngeles, Porter, Marcus, Fred Jennings (who'd died in his sleep a few years back), and, of course, Charles Anderson Prescott V (or Cinco, as he was known to both his friends and enemies), a direct descendent of the firm's founding Prescott—had once wielded almost unimaginable power in her life. The three men sitting across from her were undoubtedly as influential as ever in some spheres. But they held no sway over her. Not anymore.

"It's been a long day, and I need to get home to help get the twins ready for bed. So why don't you guys tell me what you want," she suggested.

Porter and DeAngeles exchanged a look. Then DeAngeles elbowed Marcus in the ribs.

Kevin swore under his breath, placed his hands on the table, palms down, and leaned forward. "We need you to find Cinco."

She blinked. She didn't know what she'd expected him to say, but it wasn't that. "What do you mean, find Cinco?"

Porter glared at her. "As you know, Cinco unceremoniously resigned from the firm last summer."

"I remember hearing something about that," she demurred.

"Don't be cute," he snapped. "You were in his office the morning he tendered his resignation. Uninvited and unannounced."

She gave him a level look. "You should probably let Kevin do the talking, John."

Kevin managed a tight smile. "What John means is, Cinco's departure was unexpected and somewhat chaotic. We really need to speak to him about some of the client matters he left behind, as well as some critical management issues."

"So, speak to him."

DeAngeles snorted, then pressed his hand against the table for leverage and began to rise from the seat. "This was a waste of time."

But Marcus stopped him. "Wait. She doesn't know."

DeAngeles settled back on the bench with a thud. "You really don't know?"

"Don't know what?"

"Cinco's missing. Nobody's heard from him in almost a month."

"You mean, you haven't heard from him, right?

Surely his family knows where he is." She shifted her gaze from one worried face to another and then another. "Don't they?"

"No. We spoke to his wife. Gillian admitted that she doesn't know where he is. She's as frantic as we are, if not more."

"Probably more," Sasha said.

"Don't be so sure," Marcus retorted. "You have no idea how much money's at stake for the firm if we can't find him."

There it was. In the end, it came down to money. It always did with these guys.

She gave a short laugh. "And what is it that you want from me, exactly?"

"You did something—said something—to make him quit. You must have. So the way we see it, this situation is your responsibility, Sasha," Porter told her. "You need to find him and bring him back so he can clean up his mess."

"Or what, John? Are you going to give me a bad performance review? Newsflash, I don't work for you— any of you—and I haven't in a very long time. Now, I'm going home. But I'll give you one free piece of advice as a thank you for the ouzo. You brainiacs should hire a private investigator."

She stood and snatched her sweater and Naya's jacket from the coat hook.

"Wait," Marcus said to her back.

She paused but didn't turn around. "What?"

"It's true that we came to you in part because we're

sure you were behind his sudden departure. But that's not the only reason."

She waited for a beat. Then, as they both knew it would, her curiosity won out, and she turned to face Kevin Marcus. "What's the other reason?"

"His daughter asked us to. Eleanor thinks you're the only one who can find him."

Her gut tightened, and she sucked in a breath, but she kept her face impassive. "Good night, Kevin."

She raced through the restaurant, which had mostly emptied of diners during her meeting with the Top Three. She paused at the bar to toss Naya her jacket.

"Did you settle the bill?"

She reached for her wallet, but Maisy waved her hand languidly.

"I took care of it, sugar. After all, I *am* a millionaire." She giggled and raised her ouzo glass.

"You'll be a millionaire tomorrow. Don't spend it all tonight."

In response, Maisy giggled some more.

"How much of that has she had?" Sasha asked her law partner.

Naya patted an empty stool. "Not too much. Yet. Come on, have a drink and tell us what the grim reaper brigade wanted. They looked like they'd been sucking on lemons when they walked over."

"I can't. I need to get home. I'll fill you in tomorrow." She gave them a close look. "You two better drink a lot of water before you go to bed."

After a flurry of hugs, she left them to their digestifs, grabbed her coat from the cloakroom, and hurried out of Saffron before the Prescott & Talbot lawyers could catch up with her. She passed by the valet stand and was halfway through the parking lot before she remembered her promise to Connelly. Grumbling, she returned to the entrance and pulled out her phone to order a ride share.

She waited for the car service in the shadows, far enough away from the doors that Marcus, Porter, and DeAngeles breezed by and into their waiting Lincoln Town Car without noticing her. A few moments after their car pulled away, a white SUV pulled into the lot and idled in the spot designated for rideshares and taxis.

Her app dinged to let her know her car had arrived. She stowed her phone in her purse, walked over to the SUV, and opened the rear passenger side door.

"You Sasha?" the driver asked.

"That's me."

She hopped in and settled back against the seat.

13

"Did you enjoy your dinner?" Amanda asked.

Beside her, Sasha gasped and started.

The driver met Amanda's eyes in the mirror with an uncertain expression.

"I thought you said you were supposed to meet her here." His eyes flicked toward Sasha's. "You two *are* friends, right?"

"We're not friends," Sasha said firmly, her hand on the door handle.

"Listen," Amanda said, speaking quickly. She knew she only had one shot at this. "Just hear me out. It's, what, a four-minute drive to your house? Let me plead my case while Dustin here takes you home. I won't bother you again after this. I promise."

"Sure, why not? Tonight's apparently going to be one ambush after another." Sasha flopped back against the seat with an exasperated sigh and gestured for the fretting driver to pull out.

Amanda didn't know what the ambush comment

was supposed to mean, so she ignored it. "First, I apologize for the way I left the meeting. That was unprofessional."

"It was." Sasha nodded her agreement. As Dustin eased the SUV out of the lot and into the flow of Shadyside traffic, she said, "Before you plead your case, tell me how you intercepted my ride. There's no legitimate reason for you to know where I was having dinner or that I called for a car."

Amanda arched one eyebrow. "I'm sure you can figure it out. You do remember who I work for, right?"

"It would be impossible to forget. You mention it every three seconds." She pursed her lips tighter and frowned, tapping the fingernail of her left index finger against her thumbnail as she thought. Then she leaned into the space between the front seats. "Hey, Dustin?"

"Yeah?"

"Who owns Dryve Time?"

"Leith Delone. He owns all three of the city's ride-sharing companies now. Now, you tell me, isn't that the definition of a monopoly?"

Amanda shot forward. "No, it's not. Customers haven't been harmed, and competition hasn't suffered because Le—Mr. Delone operates all three companies as separate, independent entities with their own fare structures and distinct corporate cultures."

The driver snorted. "Must just be a coincidence that all three offer the exact same crappy pay and brutal working conditions, huh?"

She was about to retort but reminded herself to stay on mission. "I'm sorry to hear that's your experience,

Dustin." He rolled his eyes, and she turned back to Sasha, who was giving her an icy look.

"So you hacked into the app?"

"*I* didn't hack into anything. I acquired information through non-public means. Listen, I'll apologize for that too, if you want me to."

"Do you not understand that your behavior is incredibly creepy?"

"I did what I had to. I *need* to talk to you." Amanda winced when she heard the desperate quaver in her own voice.

Sasha shook her head, unmoved. "So talk."

"You know that neutral, that Collins guy, home-courted me. He shouldn't have ordered us to pay your client. Not at this stage. He was supposed to help work out a freaking discovery dispute. He went far beyond the scope of his authority."

She shrugged. "So appeal."

Amanda gave her an unamused look. "Come on, you heard him. He practically dared me to appeal. He'll get the judge to impose sanctions, and that's just going to make a bad situation worse."

They both lurched forward as Dustin hit the brakes with too much force.

"Sorry. This guy in front of me slammed to a stop the minute the light turned yellow." He gave the driver ahead of them the bird.

Sasha eyed Amanda. "Let me ask you something. Why is this a bad situation? Delone is the richest man on the planet, isn't he?"

"This week, he is. You know, those rankings fluctuate with the markets. Next week, he might be number three."

"Whatever. There's no market fluctuation that would make a million dollars a meaningful sum to him. It's like a fraction of a percent of his hourly income. Why does he care at all?"

Amanda swallowed hard. This was it. This was her one chance to make this woman understand. "Leith will not stand for being humiliated. And Maisy Farley humiliated him, publicly. He's not going to just let that go. He's not capable of letting it go. Maisy has to experience a consequence. She has to pay for what she did. Do you understand what I'm saying?"

Sasha stared at her. "Do *you* understand what you're saying? She was fired. Maisy lost her job because she said something about Leith Delone that, while unflattering, was true. He did interfere with the reporting on the prosecutorial misconduct trial. If Landon Lewis hadn't died—What? Are you okay?"

Amanda had begun to shake. She *knew* she'd heard Landon Lewis' name before. Her messy situation just got infinitely more complicated.

"Amanda? ATJ? If you feel like you're going to pass out, put your head between your knees. You want your head to be lower than your heart."

She shook her head and tried to work up enough saliva to speak. "I'm not gonna pass out. Listen to me, you have to get Maisy to agree to some kind of compromise. Even if it's just three-quarters of a million instead of the full amount. That's still a lot of money to most regular people."

"It's a lot of money to all regular people, Amanda. But it's not what she's entitled to. It's not what Delone owes her."

"You're not hearing me. If WACB pays Maisy the full amount—if Gabe transfers her a million dollars tomorrow—you, and I, and Maisy, we're all going to incur Leith's wrath. And I promise you, you will wish you'd listened to me."

"You make him sound like some sort of vengeful god."

"That's an apt comparison."

Sasha scoffed. "Are you telling me he thinks he's God?"

She shook her head. "Not God. But, a god. Yeah, I'd say he considers himself a god-like figure. Thor, if I had to guess. Or, who's the god in charge of all the gods, like Zeus?"

"In Norse mythology, that's Odin," Dustin volunteered as he pulled to the side of the street and parked in front of a red brick house. "This is you, right?"

"Yeah, thanks. Amanda's going to pay you through the app. Since she can access my account through non-public means and all. Right, Amanda?"

"Sure, okay."

Sasha removed a twenty from her wallet and handed it to Dustin. "But, here's an off-the-books tip that your Norse god of a boss can't steal."

"Hey, thanks."

"Sure. Have a good night."

As Sasha reached for the door handle, Amanda dug a card out of her bag and thrust it into Sasha's hand. "This is my personal mobile number. At least think about what I said. If you can find a way to meet me—not even halfway, just somewhere shy of a total defeat for Leith—before Gabe initiates that wire, please call me. It doesn't matter what time it is."

She took the card with visible reluctance and slid it into the pocket of her cardigan. When she spoke, her voice was gentle. "Okay, but I have to tell you, that's not going to happen."

She paused, as if considering whether to say something, then continued, "You and I, we're both small women in a profession dominated by men. But also, we're both small women who live in the world. So I feel like you need to know this. The first time—the very first time—someone bullies you, infantilizes you, or tries to push you around, you have to stand your ground. Amanda, more than most people, you *have* to."

Amanda barked out a bitter laugh. "Leith isn't just some schoolyard bully or a bloviating barfly."

"Maybe not. But he's also not a Norse god. Well, maybe he is. But if he is, he's not Odin or Thor, that's for sure. He's that jerky one—Loki." Sasha gave her a wan smile and exited the SUV.

Amanda's gut twisted. Sasha was her last best hope. If she didn't come through, Amanda was going to have to make a series of hard choices.

14

Leo glanced up from the game board when the front door opened and Sasha rushed inside, bringing a burst of cold air with her. He was about to mouth *'help'* because playing Monopoly with his children was closer to being tortured than anything he'd experienced during agent training.

The main method of torment was Finn's insistence on helping his sister. He'd pay her rent, lend her cash, or give her his properties if she was losing. No matter how many times Leo explained that such charity was against the rules, Finn persisted. For her part, Fiona readily accepted the against-the-rules assistance; and when Leo objected, she'd give him a wide-eyed look and say, *'Mom says it's more important to be kind than to be right. Remember, Dad?'*

How was a person supposed to counter that?

Now, he seized on Sasha's return as his personal get-out-of-jail-free card.

"Mom's home!" he announced. "Let's have some hot

cocoa. She can tell us all about her day before baths and bed."

They abandoned the game, flung themselves at their mom for a quick welcome-home hug, and, then, with a series of whoops, raced out to the kitchen with the dog and the cat running alongside them.

He took one final look at the game in progress, gave his head a rueful shake, then turned to smile at his wife. His smile faded at the sight of her pale face and tight expression. She locked the door and secured the deadbolt with swift, efficient movements. She flipped on the motion-detecting floodlights outside and hurried to the picture window behind the couch to check the locks on the frames.

"Hey, what's going on? Is everything okay?"

She gave a short, decisive shake of her head. "No. Not really. I'll fill you in when the twins are in the bath. Let me get my coat and shoes off. Then I'll get the cocoa started and check the doors in the back of the house. Will you go upstairs and get your gun out of the safe? Please."

"Whoa, hang on. Not a chance. Give me the short version, at least."

If Sasha McCandless-Connelly was asking him to remove his Sig Sauer from the gun safe where she insisted it remain at all times, something was very, very, *very* wrong. But he couldn't assess the threat unless he knew what it was.

"Fine." She unbuttoned her coat and shrugged out of it. Then she dropped her voice low, just above a whisper. "It turns out Leith Delone's lawyer really is like a consigliere. She was waiting for me in the back of the car when I left the restaurant, and she threatened me." She paused, her coat draped over her arm. "I think it was a threat." After a moment, she nodded. "Yeah, it definitely was a threat."

He held out his hands for the coat, and she passed it to him. While he hung it in the closet near the stairs, she kicked off her shoes, aiming them toward the general vicinity of the closet. He scooped them up and placed them inside, lined up neatly next to his boots.

"She threatened you? What kind of threat?"

She dragged her hand across her mouth in an agitated gesture. "I don't know, Connelly. Mickey Collins ordered the station to pay Maisy in full, tomorrow. Delone's lawyer lost her sh … shirt—"

"—They can't hear you."

"She lost her shit. She made a huge scene. Stormed out of the conference room. It was embarrassing to watch. She was, as the kids say, cringe."

"Not everybody loses with dignity."

"This took being a poor sport to the next level. But the part where she intercepted my car? That's invasive, creepy, stalker behavior."

"How did she even do that?"

"One of Delone's companies owns Dryve Time. Actually, he owns all three of the ride-share services in town. So, I guess she was watching—or had someone watching—to see if any of us ordered a car. When she saw me using the app, she redirected the car to pick her up first and told the driver she was meeting me at Saffron. She was sitting in the shadows of the back seat when I got in. It was like something out of *The Godfather.*"

"That's disturbing," he agreed.

"It really was. And now she—not to mention Delone and who knows who else—knows where we live. So, please, go get the gun."

The hairs on Leo's arms stood up on end as the full weight of her words landed on him. They'd taken extraordinary precautions to keep their home address out of public records. Given the array of enemies they'd amassed over the years, a dollop of paranoia was advisable.

On a handful of occasions, someone had breached the fortification they'd built up around their family. Each time, Leo shored up their defenses further.

But this intrusion—someone gaining access to a mundane app—was an invasion he hadn't anticipated, and it made him wonder what other vulnerabilities existed that he hadn't considered, what other insidious threats might lie in wait. Would their paperless utility bill lead an old foe to their door? Or their digital library cards? How many ways could someone with sufficient motivation find them?

He pushed the terrifying question out of his mind, swallowed around the tightness in his throat, and took the stairs two at a time up to the home office, where his biometric gun safe sat on the highest shelf in the closet. As he removed his weapon, his gaze fell on the document safe, the safe that held Landon's perplexing note and impenetrable drive. Suddenly, their presence in his home felt like a provocation—or an invitation to danger. He needed to deal with it. Soon.

But now, he needed to find out just what kind of threat Amanda Teale-James represented to his family. He confirmed that the safety was on, grabbed a loaded magazine, and slid the magazine into the gun before holstering it at his waist and pulling his sweater down over the bulge.

WHEN CONNELLY PADDED into the kitchen in his socks, he bypassed the hot cocoa topping bar that Sasha'd set up, complete with whipping cream and sprinkles, and went straight to the back door.

"It's locked, and the lights are activated."

He shifted his head a quarter-turn to acknowledge that he'd heard her but tested the lock anyway. He peered through the window out into the dark night, scanning for some unseen threat. Then he checked the window over the sink and the one in the adjacent laundry room. She didn't try to stop him. She understood that he, like she, was trying to tamp down the fear that they'd overlooked something that would leave their little family exposed, a soft target.

When he'd satisfied himself that they were as secure as they could be, he joined them at the round kitchen table with an easy smile.

He was good at hiding his worry. Or at least better than she was. So she was glad he'd offered the twins the hot chocolate despite her feelings about too much sugar. Enthralled by the unexpected treat, they might not notice their parents' tension—or so she hoped. They weren't so easily distracted anymore. They were perceptive and attentive. Finn, in particular, was adept at picking up on other people's feelings. And as far as Fiona was concerned, no question was off limits.

"So, Maisy won? The case is over?" Connelly asked casually.

"Mmm-hmm," Sasha said, sipping her herbal tea.

"Mommy, don't you want hot cocoa?" Finn insisted, eyeing her mug with suspicion.

"No, lovebug. I had a rich dessert with Maisy and Naya to celebrate. No more sweets for me tonight."

"To celebrate what?" Finn wanted to know.

"Maisy is a *millionaire* now, Finny," Fiona explained.

His eyes widened. "She could buy Park Place!"

Fiona nodded sagely. "Or a giraffe. A real one."

Sasha choked on her tea. "I don't think Maisy's going to invest in real estate or exotic animals. She'll probably use the money for her new podcasting venture."

Fiona rolled her eyes. "Booooring. *I* would get a giraffe."

"I'd buy a railroad line," Finn said, combining his Monopoly dreams with his well-established love of trains.

Sasha waited for it. Finn didn't disappoint.

He went on, "And I would have lots of money left over to give away to people who need it."

"What would you do with a million dollars, Daddy?"

Connelly considered Fiona's question while he

topped his drink with a fluffy mountain of whipped cream. "I would buy us a castle."

"A castle?" Fiona breathed.

"Yep."

"With a throne room and a garden and space for a giraffe," Finn imagined.

Connelly's eyes met Sasha's, and she read his meaning. *And a moat, and a castle gate, and battlements with a keep. An impenetrable castle.*

Later, after the twins had bathed and brushed their teeth, Sasha read a chapter from their current book, and then tucked them into their respective beds with a kiss. Fiona pulled her unicorn eye mask down over her eyes and rolled onto her stomach. Across the hall, Finn turned on the light that projected constellations onto his ceiling and gazed up at Cassiopeia.

She changed into a pair of yoga pants and an oversized sweatshirt, finishing the outfit with a pair of slouchy, fuzzy socks. She caught a glimpse of herself in the bedroom mirror and shook her head. She looked like a twelve-year-old girl. And Naya wanted her to come to work like this.

When she crept downstairs, the house was quiet. Mocha's leash was missing from its spot near the door. She frowned. Usually, Mocha's last walk was after dinner. Before bed, they let the dog out in the fenced backyard to do whatever needed to be done.

She headed to the kitchen to clean up the remnants of the hot chocolate party. Every time the wind blew through the trees outside, her attention was pulled to the window over the sink. The rising tension wasn't helped by the presence of the cat, who'd taken up sentry duty on the windowsill and was staring unblinkingly out the same window, tail swishing like a metronome.

Java's picking up on your fear. Animals do that. And children, too. So you need to get a grip.

She was wiping down the counters when Java jumped to the floor and darted to the kitchen door, ears pointed, purring loudly.

A moment later, a key scraped in the lock, and Connelly and Mocha trouped inside, windblown and shivering.

"The wind's picked up," he told her as he unleashed the dog, who headed straight for the warm bed on the floor in front of the living room fireplace with Java trotting along behind. Mocha was no dummy.

Connelly knocked a dusting of snow off his boots, then removed them and his bright red parka. He put the boots on the shelf under the bench alongside the wall and hung the parka from the hook above.

"Don't you want to put those in the closet?"

He shook his head. "No. I might take one more walk tonight."

She eyed him closely. "You can't stay up all night and patrol the alley behind the house."

"Why don't you fill me in on this threat, and then we'll decide how to handle it?"

She nodded. He poured himself a glass of Scotch. She decided to stick with herbal tea.

They made themselves comfortable on the couch. Connelly sat at the end closest to the fireplace, ostensibly so he'd have an end table within easy reach for his glass. She couldn't help but notice, though, that the position also gave him a clear shot at the front door and a good view of the porch stairs through the window.

She wriggled in next to him and rested her head on his lap, propping her feet on the opposite arm of the couch and arranging a fleece blanket over herself. She imagined they looked like a picture of cozy domesticity. And to some extent, they were. But her vantage point allowed her to keep an eye on the kitchen, scanning for shadows outside the back door. They sat in silence for a few moments. The only sounds were the old clock ticking over the mantle and the trees creaking in the wind outside. Mocha's soft snoring cut through the quiet, and they laughed.

Sasha looked up at Connelly. "Did you delete the Dryve Time app from your phone?"

"I did. It feels like the genie's out of the bottle, though."

"I know. But at least it's *something* we can do. If you have the other two companies' apps on your phone, get rid of those, too."

He nodded. He placed his chin in his hand and cracked his jaw, a sure sign that he was thinking.

"What?" she prompted.

"Maybe we should move. Not to a castle, obviously, but someplace more secure."

Her chest tightened. She didn't want to move. She loved their house and their walkable neighborhood. But more than that, she didn't want to let fear drive her decisions. She wouldn't *allow* fear to drive her decision. Turning into someone who mistrusted her neighbors, eyed every stranger as a threat, and fortified her home with layers of security wouldn't make her safer, but it would make her a prisoner of her fears.

"No." She twisted and propped herself up on her elbow to look him directly in the eye. "We're not moving." Her voice was firm and fierce.

"It's just a suggestion. You're the one who's so freaked out."

She softened. "That's fair. But look, if the world's richest man wants to get us, any measures we take are going to be useless—short of actually holing up in a castle or a bunker somewhere. And even then …"

He finished what she couldn't. "Leith Delone's a powerful enemy, and he'll beat us in the end."

She sighed and slumped in on herself. "Right."

They sat with the unfamiliar emotion. They weren't used to feeling outmatched. Sure, they'd *been* outmatched—more than a few times—but they'd never believed they couldn't prevail. Facing down a multibillionaire with a vengeful streak felt different, though.

"So, the threat?" He took a sip of his drink.

She took a moment to organize her thoughts. "Amanda was angry at the meeting, but when she ambushed me in the car, her demeanor had changed. She was frightened, almost desperate. She told me that Maisy had humiliated Delone publicly, and he wasn't going to let that go. She said Maisy would have to pay for what she did. I thought for a minute she was going to pass out, she got so worked up."

"About Maisy criticizing Delone on the air?"

She paused, trying to recall the exact words that had

rattled the other woman. "Yeah, I countered that what Maisy said happened to be true. That Delone *did* interfere with the reporting on the case, and the disinformation he was trying to spread would have hurt my case."

"If it hadn't settled."

"Right. Which is what he wanted all along, right? A settlement. So, why does he care what Maisy said? He's Leith Freaking Delone. There are entire websites devoted to making fun of him and criticizing everything he does. He can't be *that* thin-skinned."

Connelly bobbed his head. "I mean, he *could* be. But it sounds more like Maisy's comments struck a specific nerve."

"I think that's right," Sasha said slowly. "Maisy must've really gotten under his skin. I wonder why. ATJ—"

"Who?"

She rolled her eyes. "Delone's lawyer wanted everyone to call her ATJ because it saves time. More efficient than saying her full name."

"She sounds fun. Although, think about how many more billable minutes you could squeeze out of every week if you made everyone call you SCM?"

"No, thanks. I'm not looking for peak efficiency at the risk of becoming a soulless automaton."

"Like ATJ?"

She relented, "Actually, that's not fair. She wasn't acting like a robot. She was acting like someone who was scared, really scared."

"I'm still not hearing a threat to us, to you."

She twisted her wedding band around on her finger

as she recalled the way Amanda had put it. "She wanted me to twist Maisy's arm and make her agree to a smaller payment. She said that if the full payment goes through to Maisy, we were all going to wish it hadn't. And she specified she meant herself, Maisy, and me."

"Not Naya? Not Mickey?"

She shook her head. "That's what she said. She said the three of us would, and I quote, 'incur Leith's wrath.' And she was shaken."

He twisted his lips to the side and stroked her hair as he thought. "That's definitely a threat."

"Right."

"Are you going to tell Maisy?"

She groaned. "I have to, I think. But I can't advise her to voluntarily refuse part of the money she's owed and the ADR neutral ordered the station to pay. Not even, or maybe especially not, to protect us. That's a violation of—I don't know, maybe a dozen ethical rules?"

"What about to protect her?"

"I'm not sure," she admitted. She was surprised he was pressing the issue. "You don't think we should bow to Delone, do you? You, of all people? You know you can't get rid of a tyrant by acceding to his demands. I don't see the point in letting him intimidate us. Where would it end?"

"It might end right here," he said, not unreasonably. "Delone's billionaire boy ego is assuaged, and you, Maisy, and your new friend don't have to look over your shoulders until the end of time."

She huffed.

"I know you don't want to hear that," he told her.

"You don't like being pushed around. Believe me, I get it. But I think you have to let Maisy decide for herself."

He was right. She hated it, but he was. She heaved out a long sigh. "You're right."

He smiled and pulled her closer. "Say it again. I love it when you say that."

She laughed despite the tightness in her chest at the thought of giving in. "You were right. Enjoy your moment. But don't get used to it."

She snuggled into his side. He sipped his drink.

"Are you going to call Maisy tonight?"

"No. When I left, she and Naya were most of the way through a bottle of ouzo. I'll talk to her tomorrow."

He raised his eyebrows. "Ouzo? That's a choice. Hope they drink a lot of water before bed."

"Me too. We wouldn't have ordered it. Prescott & Talbot sent it over to the table."

"Seriously?"

"Mmm-hmm. Marcus, DeAngeles, and Porter were there. Mickey told them where to find me."

"Ugh. Those three crashed your celebratory dinner? What did they want?"

She rubbed her hand over her eyes as she remembered their conversation, which had been overshadowed by her encounter with Amanda. "Apparently, Cinco's in the wind. They want me to track him down for them."

"And people in hell want ice water," he scoffed.

"That's more or less what I told them."

"Do I hear a 'but'?"

"But, tomorrow, after I deal with Maisy's money, I'm

going to drive out to Cinco's place and talk to his family."

"You don't owe Prescott & Talbot or Cinco, for that matter, anything."

"I know." She snuggled back into his side. "But I might owe his daughter."

15

Early (but not too early) the next morning, Sasha stood on the front steps of Maisy's townhouse with a glass container filled with bright green juice. She rang the bell and took a step back. The wind had died down overnight, and the day had dawned gray and cold, but somehow bright, as if the sun was up there somewhere behind the swirl of clouds beaming down on her.

Still, it wasn't exactly warm. She shifted her weight from foot to foot and muttered. "Come on, Maisy."

Finally, just as she was about to lean on the doorbell with more emphasis, she heard footsteps in the hallway. Then, the scrape of a deadbolt, and the door opened a crack. Maisy's red and bloodshot eyeball appeared in the small gap. A second later, the door swung wide open.

"For heaven's sake, what are you doin' out here in the dead of winter? Get in here."

Sasha didn't have to be asked twice. She hustled

inside, and Maisy slammed the door shut against the icy air. Sasha appraised her.

"You look awful."

"Gosh, sugar, you sure know how to make a girl's day. But I should look awful. I feel awful." Maisy groaned and clutched her temples.

"Here," Sasha thrust the neon green drink at her. "It's Connelly's hangover cure."

Maisy narrowed her eyes and studied it suspiciously. "I don't know …"

"Suit yourself. You can spend your first day as a millionaire nursing a wicked ouzo hangover if you prefer."

The prospect didn't seem to appeal to her. She stretched out her hand. "Give it here."

Sasha handed her the juice, and Maisy sniffed it.

"Don't smell it or think too much about it. Just drink it."

"Mmm," Maisy groaned. "Do I want to know what's in it?"

"Nope."

Maisy gave her a doubtful look but took a swig of the juice. "It's not that bad, actually. Come on, I made coffee, but I can't stomach it. You can have it, though."

She shuffled toward the kitchen, and Sasha followed her. She poured herself a mug of Maisy's serviceable coffee and leaned against the island, watching her friend drink Connelly's concoction dutifully. She finished and placed the glass on the counter near the sink.

"Well, thanks. Is Naya also getting a home delivery of the green stuff?"

"Nope. She's Carl's problem."

Maisy managed a weak chuckle and headed for her living room where she plopped down in an overstuffed chair. "Last night was fun. This morning, not so much. When those dour-faced lawyer dudes accosted you, I felt sorry for you. Now, I think you got the better end of the deal."

Sasha took the chair across from her. She decided not to mention that nobody forced Maisy to drink half a bottle of eighty-proof alcohol. Instead, she said, "I want to talk to you before Gabe initiates the wire transfer."

Maisy blinked at the subject change. "What's up?"

"Last night, ATJ tracked me down to try to convince me to convince *you* to agree to a smaller payout. She suggested seven hundred and fifty thousand."

She scoffed. "What difference does a quarter of a million dollars make to Leith Delone?"

"None," Sasha agreed.

"So what's her angle?" Maisy wrinkled her brow. "And why are you bringing this to me? Just tell her no."

"I did tell her no. But I'm obligated to communicate the offer to you. And ..."

"And what? What aren't you telling me?" Suddenly, Maisy was alert.

"ATJ intimated that if he's forced to pay you the full amount, Delone might hold a grudge."

"Feh. Poor little rich boy."

"I know, Mais. But I got the sense his lawyer's afraid

of him. Afraid of how he might try to, I don't know, get revenge if he feels like you've humiliated him again."

One eyebrow shot up to Maisy's forehead. "Again?"

"Evidently, his feelings were hurt after you called him out on live television for interfering with your reporting."

Her head snapped back, and the mess of blonde curls bobbed on the top of her head. "Well, for land's sake, Sasha, I can't be worrying about that. Can't he just buy another moon or somethin' to ease the pain?"

Maisy's Georgia was showing, which meant she was getting upset. Sasha sat down her coffee mug and made a 'calm down' motion with her hands. "Easy, tiger. I don't think you *should* agree to a smaller payout. But just last night, you were telling us you haven't had your hair done because you're afraid someone might be following you or out to get you. If ATJ is right about Delone's reaction, you might spend the rest of your life carrying those worries around with you. I just want you to think it through. That's all."

"Hang on, now. I've been worried that whoever wanted Landon dead might want me dead, too. It's got nothing to do with this mess with Delone. But with a million dollars, I can install a decent security system. Heck, I can hire myself a hot bodyguard to follow me around like Whitney Houston in *The Bodyguard*."

She got a faraway look in her eyes, and Sasha snapped her fingers to bring her back to the present. "Indulge in your Kevin Costner fantasies on your own time. So, are you rejecting ATJ's … it's not really an offer, I don't know what to call it … her plea?"

"Heck yeah, I am."

"Okay. I'll let her know. I don't even think she mentioned anything to Gabe, so the wire'll probably hit your account this afternoon. Naya will be in touch with the details." She drained her coffee mug and stood. "I have to run."

Maisy took the empty mug and walked her to the door. "Where are you off to?"

"Cinco Prescott's house, of all places."

"What on earth for?"

"Apparently, he's missing. That's what the terrible trio came to see me about."

Surprise, followed by disdain, flashed across Maisy's face. "That's too bad, but it's not your problem."

"I know. But, Ellie Prescott helped us out. I thought I might see if she needs my help."

Maisy's face softened. "That's fair. You're just full of good deeds today, aren't ya?"

"I try, Mais. I try."

"I'm already starting to feel more human. What's in that juice."

Sasha gave her a steady look. "Seriously, you don't want to know."

16

Gar was still in bed when his cell phone rang. He grumbled and flipped on his bedside light, then squinted at the display. *Antonia Pita.*

He chuckled at the way he'd saved his pain-in-the-ass boss' number in his contacts. Sure, it was childish, but every time she made a PITA of herself by calling or texting, it made him laugh.

"What's up, Antonia?"

"I didn't wake you, did I?"

He eyed the clock. "Well, yeah, you did. It's six-thirty in the morning."

Her voice wavered. "Oh, sorry. I just figured you must've made a New Year's resolution to turn yourself into a morning person or something. You've been getting into the office so early these past few weeks."

He rubbed the sleep from his eyes. "No, that's fair. I was getting in early, but I guess I don't need to anymore."

"That's why I'm calling. I just checked my voicemails when I woke up. I have a message from last night from Pinpoint Partners. Sounds like you've successfully debugged their project. They're thrilled!"

He winced at the naked excitement in Antonia's voice. She was no doubt imagining how good this would look for her in her annual review: a positive outcome and a happy client on the high-dollar account. Too bad it was all a big, hairy lie.

She was waiting for him to respond. He considered his words carefully.

"That's good that they're happy."

"Not just happy, ecstatic. They're sending a bonus payment over with their thanks as soon as they get the clean code. Brian Rosen is wondering when that might be."

"Uh ..." he stalled.

"I know you, Gar. You want to go over every last line one more time to make it elegant and simple. The client doesn't care. The client is satisfied. It's time to let it go."

Something about the way she said it—her lack of curiosity, maybe, or the blatant 'the customer is always right' vibe—cut through all the waffling Gar had done during the night, and he finally knew what he had to do.

He'd slept like crap, waking frequently. At one point, he'd had a nightmare in which Petra had been kidnapped and held hostage in an effort to make him cooperate. Nightmare Petra had begged him not to comply, yelling at him to do the right thing. He'd clicked on the light and written a note on the pad by his bed.

He snatched it up now and read the words he'd

scribbled down when he'd been mostly asleep: *Do the right thing, not the easy thing.* It had sounded good in the middle of the night, but in the cold light of day, the words left him unmoved. Because Garwood March knew himself. He was, at his core, a coward.

"Gar, did you hear me?"

"Yeah, sorry. I heard you. I brought the code home last night to give it one more polish. I'll go into the office in an hour or so to upload it to the secure file transfer site and let Pinpoint Partners know it's there."

"Excellent. After that, you can take the rest of the day off if you want."

"Really?"

"Sure," she said magnanimously before she ended the call.

Gar dropped his phone and the cartoonishly heroic note on his bedside table, then swung his legs over the side of the bed and dropped his head into his hands, letting the stench of his cowardice wash over him like a fetid wave.

NOT QUITE ONE HOUR LATER, he let himself into the dark and quiet office building, uploaded the code, and pinged Rosen to let him know. Then he cleared off his desktop, sweeping everything into his open backpack with one motion. Although he'd been chapped about the move from assigned workspaces to hot desks when management had announced it, now he was glad he didn't have a permanent space. He had almost nothing to remove from the office.

He grabbed the rubber ducky from its perch on his computer tower. Then he zipped up his pack and shouldered it. He removed his lanyard from around his neck and tossed it on the desk. On his way out of the bullpen, he paused to place a short note on the workstation that Petra used. As it turned out, hot-decking had been a joke. Everyone claimed a space and, being human beings with a penchant for routine, they more or less used that space exclusively.

He anchored the note with the rubber duck. To anyone other than Petra, the note would be gibberish. But they'd discussed their shared affinity for the Vigenère cipher, and he was sure she'd figure out the keyword without much trouble. Having done as much as his cowardly constitution would permit him to, Garwood March clipped his backpack straps together over his chest, pulled up his hood, and jogged down the stairs to the lobby. He pushed the door open, lowered his head against the wind, and ran to his car.

He pointed his car toward Ensenada. Canada was closer by several hours. But it was January. And Gar was tired of snow and cold, so Baja California, Mexico it was.

The last known sighting of Garwood March in the United States would be at a gas station just over the Idaho state line in Jackpot, Nevada, where security cameras showed him filling his tank before visiting the restroom and purchasing an armload of snack foods and a 32-ounce hot chocolate.

17

The private airfield in Westmoreland County outside Pittsburgh was far more utilitarian than Leith's, and thus Amanda's, home airport. Built in the middle of a literal cornfield, it lacked the breathtaking views of SVAC. Sadly, it also lacked the amenities.

Instead of a perfect espresso, Stasia greeted Amanda with a styrofoam cup of weak, microwaved instant coffee and an apology.

"Sorry. It's the best I could scare up."

"It beats a blank," Amanda told her as she accepted the cup. She took a sip and grimaced as the bitter, reheated coffee hit her throat. "Or maybe not."

"I'll make you a real mug of coffee once we're on the plane," Stasia promised. Then her blue eyes widened. "I can't believe I almost forgot. Mr. Delone wants you to call him right away."

Amanda checked the time. "At this hour?"

It was five a.m. on the West Coast, and Leith was notoriously a late riser.

"Right away," the hostess confirmed.

Amanda frowned, and her entire body stiffened. There was a zero percent possibility this was good news. She stepped away and scouted out a private corner of the wide open, charmless space. If someone had told her the airport had once been a barn, she wouldn't have been surprised. She took a breath and squared her shoulders. Putting it off would just prolong the agony. She pulled out her phone to make the call, and it rang in her hand.

Surprised, she jumped and bobbled the phone, nearly dropping it. At the last second, she recovered and kept her grip on the device. When she checked the screen, she noted that the call was being forwarded from her personal cell phone. The caller wasn't in her contacts, but they had a 412 area code. Pittsburgh.

A seedling of hope uncurled in her chest. *Please. Please be Sasha.*

"ATJ."

"Hi, Amanda. It's Sasha McCandless. I hope it's okay to call this early."

"Yes, it's fine. I'm at the airport about to head back home."

Sasha's voice sounded distant, and faint traffic sounds filtered through the handset.

"Am I on speaker?"

"I'm driving, so I'm connected through my Bluetooth, but there's nobody else in the car. This call is private."

"Okay." Amanda hated to have to take her word for it, but what choice did she have? "Did you speak to your client?"

"I did. I just left her house. That's why I'm calling."

The seedling sprouted and stood up taller. "And?" Her leg jittered with nervous anticipation.

"She's not interested in reducing the amount of the payout." Sasha pulled the Band-Aid off with dispassionate efficiency.

Amanda's hope plant withered and died in her mind's eye. She swallowed and tried to form a response. "Oh," she croaked.

"I wanted to let you know before Gabe initiates the wire transfer. It seemed like the courteous thing to do."

"Yeah, of course," Amanda mumbled numbly. "Thanks for trying."

In her mounting panic, she didn't hear what Sasha said next. "I'm sorry. Could you repeat that?"

"I said, if you're in danger—if you're legitimately afraid of Leith Delone—I know people. People who can help you."

The concern in Sasha's tone was genuine. Amanda could hear it. And for a fraction of a heartbeat, she almost gave herself over to it. She considered saying, 'Yes, I need help.' But the moment passed, and she straightened her spine and infused her own voice with ice water. "I'm not afraid of my client, Ms. McCandless-Connelly. I'm not sure where you got that misapprehension."

Amanda's frosty tone must have set the other

woman back on her heels because it took her a moment to respond.

"I see. My apologies for my confusion. Have a safe flight." The call clicked off.

Amanda removed the phone from her ear and stared down at it. Sasha had been her last hope for a graceful solution to her problem. Instead, things were about to get messy, very messy.

She inhaled deeply and then exhaled. After letting out a long, slow breath, she reviewed everything she knew as calmly as she could.

One, Leith's reaction to Maisy Farley's allegation that he was interfering with reporting on the Milltown case had been undeniably extreme—even given his infamous mercurial temper.

Two, Landon Lewis was involved in that misconduct case as a witness.

Three, one of Leith's companies had paid a pretty price for the AI program that the police were alleged to have misused in the case. She knew she'd recognized that name, and five minutes of digging through her old emails had refreshed her recollection.

Four, whatever Leith had planned for Landon's technology, at best, skirted the law, but more likely was blatantly illegal.

And five, the most logical explanation for his obsession with making Maisy's life miserable was to dissuade her from digging any further into the Landon Lewis story.

There was a sixth issue, but she couldn't fairly call it

a fact. While she had her suspicions about Lewis' death, she had no proof.

Amanda was many things, but a coward wasn't one of them. She'd learned long ago that despite her physical size, nobody could make her feel small without her permission. And while she deferred to Leith, she had more leverage in their relationship than anyone knew—Leith included.

Although she'd hoped this day would never come, she'd planned for it. She'd had to. She knew too many of Leith Delone's secrets to do otherwise.

She'd socked away sizable sums of money in multiple off-shore accounts that would be difficult, although not impossible, to trace to her. She had a file full of damaging information about Leith and his various business interests. She'd had the foresight to wear sturdy, low-heeled shoes this morning rather than her sexy boots. And, most importantly, she had a head start.

She turned back toward Stasia and waved her arms. Once Amanda had the woman's attention, she pointed toward the restroom near the entrance to the barn-turned-airport. The attendant nodded her understanding.

Amanda powered down her phone as she strolled toward the bathrooms. She casually dropped the phone into a trash bin, swung the strap of her bag across her chest diagonally, and darted past the bathrooms and out the front door. As soon as the cold air hit her face, she dropped her chin and started to sprint, making a beeline toward the cornfield.

It wouldn't take long for Stasia to realize Amanda had done a runner. She needed to put as much distance between her and the hostess as she could. Because among the many things Amanda knew about Leith's businesses was that Stasia was not just a former super-model and not just Leith's sometimes-mistress. She'd been a Mossad agent, and after she'd left the Israeli intelligence agency, she'd worked in private security until Amanda lured her away to work for Leith.

Amanda ran as fast as she could, as far as she could. When she spotted a dilapidated tool shed, she kicked at the rotting door until it splintered and then burst inside. She collapsed onto an old tarp that smelled of motor oil and mold and lay on her back, panting until she caught her breath.

When her heart rate had slowed to normal, she sat up and took stock. She'd abandoned her suitcase and laptop at the airport. She had no phone, no computer, and no clothes. What she did have was four hundred dollars in cash and her wits.

She pulled her wallet from her bag and plucked out the credit cards. She looked around the dim, musty shed and spotted an old compost bin. Holding her breath to block the smell, she opened the bin and tossed the cards into the pile of decomposing vegetables and grass, then she cranked the handle to turn the compost, shifting her cards to the bottom of the muck. She eyed her driver's license through the plastic window. It had to go, too. She plucked it out, tossed it into the bin, and gave it another turn. Amanda Teale-Jones was now decompos-ing, just as surely as if her physical body had been buried beneath the earth. She thought she'd feel a certain way about her symbolic death, but she didn't feel much of anything.

She stretched up onto her toes to peer out the small dirt-streaked window set into the shed's back wall. She spotted a large farmhouse in the distance, with smoke curling from its chimney. The easy play would be to head for the house, present herself at the door with a story of woe, and ask to use a phone. But she wasn't sure she'd covered enough ground. This farm might be too close to the airport. She couldn't risk it.

She dropped her heels to the dirt floor and paced through the cramped shed slowly, studying the farm implements and assorted broken junk, looking for something that would help her. She saw nothing useful. She blew out a breath. She could make her way to the highway and stick out her thumb. Hope for the best.

She dismissed the idea. Not yet.

She oriented herself and tried to recall the location of the nearest town. Her Dryve Time driver had made an offhand remark on the way to the airport, pointing out a twenty-four-hour diner that purportedly served the best apple pie in the county. If she continued to make her way across the fields diagonally, she should hit the road into town eventually. Maybe.

Spurred on by the promise of a mug of hot coffee and a slice of warm pie, she slipped out of the shed and resumed running.

18

S asha ended her call with Delone's prickly attorney and wove through the concentric circle of tree-lined streets that made up the Foxwood Manor neighborhood. By the time she entered the long looping driveway that led to the Prescott family's mansion, she was moderately dizzy. As she continued up the drive, she eyed the massive fountain in the middle of the circle. Cinco was nothing if not ostentatious.

Be fair, she chided herself. The home had been in the Prescott family for generations. Cinco hadn't designed the landscaping. If he had, there'd certainly be a Cubist sculpture where the fountain sat.

She rounded the circle and took the dogleg that led to a drive-through *porte-cochère,* then continued on to a carriage house turned detached six-car garage behind the house. She brought her none-too-clean SUV to a stop in the *porte-cochère.* She didn't know why the Prescotts couldn't just call the structure a carport like normal people, but the last time she'd been here, more than a decade ago, she'd made that mistake, and Cinco had let her know it. The term *porte-cochère* had been seared in her brain ever since, uselessly taking up space until today.

She turned the key in the ignition, killed the engine, and walked across the flagstone patio to the servants' entrance, where she'd been told to present herself.

Eight A.M. was on the early side for a social call. But when she'd texted Cinco's daughter, Ellie had suggested the time. It suited Sasha fine. She wanted to get this over with and get on with her day.

Connelly had once told her that Mark Twain famously said, *"If it's your job to eat a frog, it's best to do it first thing in the morning. And if it's your job to eat two frogs, it's best to eat the biggest one first."* She wasn't sure whether ATJ or the Prescotts was the bigger frog, but having them both knocked off her list would certainly improve her day.

She stared at the door. There was a doorbell, but Ellie had made it clear that it would be better if her mother didn't know about Sasha's visit. At least, not yet. It seemed Mrs. Prescott blamed Sasha for Cinco's recent rash decisions.

Come on, Ellie.

As if Sasha'd summoned the younger woman, her face appeared in the pane of glass set into the door. A moment later, the door opened, and Ellie stepped outside, wriggling into a parka as she did so. She pulled up her hood and yanked the door shut behind her.

"Hi."

"Hi."

They stood in awkward silence, eyeing one another.

"Thanks for agreeing to see me." It was a bit cold for a standoff, so Sasha tried to put Cinco's daughter at ease. Maybe they could go inside once she relaxed a bit.

Ellie's eyes went huge. "Are you kidding me? Your text was a godsend. Mom and I've been flailing since he stopped communicating with us. We don't know what to do. You're a lifesaver. And, once I've had a chance to get Mom on board, she'll think so, too."

Sasha wasn't so sure that Gillian Prescott would ever become a fan, but she let that pass without comment. She was more interested in getting an answer to a question that had been nagging her since her run-in with the P&T lawyers at the restaurant.

"You said your dad went to stay at an artists' colony in upstate New York at the beginning of August and planned to come home for the new year."

"Right, in the Hudson Valley. Mom was going to spend Christmas with my Aunt Rhiannon because Uncle Simon just died. But Mom and Dad had plans to celebrate New Year's Eve together. He never showed up, and we haven't heard from him since."

"But until then, through the fall, he was in contact?"

"Not a ton, but some. The last communication was a package. He sent Mom some charcoal sketches through the mail just before Christmas. After that, it was radio silence. Then John Porter showed up at the house asking a lot of questions about where Dad was and how to reach him. Mom said he was very insistent. Pushy, is how she put it."

Sasha tried, and failed, to imagine someone pushing Gillian around. Ellie must have read her mind because she laughed.

"Right. Mom sent him packing."

"Did she tell him where your Dad was?"

"I doubt it."

That tracked. If the partnership knew about the artists' colony, she imagined they'd have given her that lead when they asked for her help.

"Did she let your Dad know about Porter's visit?"

"She called and left a vague message, but he never called her back. We don't know if he got it."

"You haven't reached out to the artists' colony again? Or visited?"

Ellie frowned. "My mom is in some sort of frozen denial state. And I'm not sure it's my place to make those decisions for her. That's one reason I'm glad the firm went to you. If you do it ... I don't have to get into it with my mom."

Sasha understood. Mother-adult-daughter dynamics could be tricky, even in the absence of a crisis.

"Is there a reason you haven't called the police?" She kept her tone gentle and nonjudgmental, even though it was an absolute no-brainer to report a missing person to the authorities.

Ellie snorted. "Oh, there are lots of reasons. How much time do you have?"

"As much time as it takes."

"Well, the main one is we're not sure he didn't do anything unethical before he left the firm. Like siphon off client funds or take documents he wasn't supposed to take or ... I don't know, something shady."

"Why would you suspect that? Did he say something?"

"Not exactly. But we wondered. Especially after he sent those sketches home."

"Really? Why?"

"You should see them for yourself. We're storing them in Dad's studio," Ellie told her.

She pointed across the courtyard to a stone structure that looked like it might be a pool house. But unless Sasha's memory was failing her, the pool house and the pool were behind Gillian's English garden on the far side of the house. She fell into step beside Ellie.

"What was the studio originally?"

"A summer kitchen." She ducked her head, as if she thought the grandeur of her parents' estate was off-putting.

"So the house must be very old. It predates central air conditioning?"

"Oh, yeah. The buildings were all built between 1886 and 1894."

They hurried through the courtyard toward what Sasha hoped would be the warmth of the studio. They reached the small stone structure, and Ellie dug a keyring out of her pocket, unlocked the door, and stepped inside.

Sasha followed, curious to see the inside of Cinco's studio. She looked around wide-eyed while Ellie closed the door, turned on the lights, and adjusted the temperature on a thermostat on the wall.

"We keep it on just high enough that the pipes won't freeze. But it'll warm up fast," Ellie assured her.

Sasha nodded, barely registering Ellie's words. She'd never been inside a professional artist's studio before. But she imagined Cinco's hobbyist space would put most of them to shame.

The studio was one large, open room. Tall windows, left bare to let in the sunlight, covered three walls. Recessed lights dotting the ceiling supplemented the natural light, and gleaming white walls reflected it back. Floor-to-ceiling shelving had been installed along the fourth wall. The shelves were filled with an array of art supplies. Stacks of sketchpads, tubes of paint, pencils, brushes, crayons, palettes, and everything in between sat lined up, waiting to be pulled off the shelf and put into service. In one corner, a small stainless steel utility sink sparkled. In the opposite corner, a tidy stack of drop cloths waited to cover the light pine floor. Beside them, blank stretched canvases stood at attention next to a pair of empty easels.

"Wow. I had no idea your dad was so serious. I mean, I know he loves art—everyone knows that. But, this is quite a setup." She turned to gauge Ellie's reaction.

Ellie shrugged. "It's his greatest regret, I think. Did you know he was accepted into the master's program in painting at the Royal College of Art in London? It's apparently the best in the world. But my grandpa said no way—go to law school or lose his trust fund. He should have told the bastard where to shove the trust fund."

Sasha noted the bitterness in the younger woman's

voice but was curious to see how Ellie'd respond to being challenged. "You mean, like you did? Oh, wait ..."

She bristled. "That's different. I *want* to be a lawyer."

"Just like your dad and all those other Charles Anderson Prescotts—Uno through Quatro?"

"No, just like *you!*"

Sasha blinked. "What?"

Ellie yanked down her hood and ran her fingers through her short blonde hair. Somehow, the result was slightly tousled layers. If Sasha tried that, she'd look like she'd been electrocuted.

"True story. Do you remember busting me trying to steal whipped cream at a summer associate event the year before you left the firm?"

Sasha furrowed her brow and searched her memory. The innumerable Prescott & Talbot events had blurred together in one indistinct mess, but she managed to call up a fuzzy image of a teenaged Ellie in a frilly pastel sundress trying to palm a canister of whipped cream from a buffet table.

"The ice cream sundae bar?" she ventured.

"Right. Nico DeAngeles dared me to take it. You saw me, and you were so cool about it. You treated me like I had a brain, like I mattered. You told me I wasn't going to be able to grow up and kick ass if I had brain damage from doing whippets. I was so sheltered, I didn't even know what whippets *were* or why Nico wanted it. But, I never forgot the way you talked to me. Then, like a year later, you were all over the news for the Hemisphere Air thing, kicking ass. And I knew then—*that's* what I wanted to do, too. Dad just assumed I'd follow in his footsteps because of the trust fund and be as miserable as he is. But I love practicing law. Or, well, I did." Her face crumpled.

"You're not working?"

For all of Ellie's sneering at her trust fund, it must be nice not to have to work for six months after quitting a job.

Ellie shook her head. "I didn't want to jump at the first big firm that dangled an offer under my nose. I'm not stupid. I know most lawyers would want me because of my name and connections. But, I'm not sure I'm big firm material."

Privately, Sasha thought that most humans weren't big firm material, but she kept that opinion to herself for the moment. "That's smart. Take your time and find something that'll be a good fit."

"Yeah. I was thinking about working for an advocacy group. I had an interview lined up with the Innocence Project at the beginning of the month. But, then Dad went radio silent on us, and my mom freaked out. So … I thought I better stick around here, at least for now."

Right. Cinco was missing. Back to business.

"You wanted me to see some paintings?" She scanned the room.

Ellie moved the stack of canvases to reveal a door set into the wall. "They're back here. In this little room where my dad sometimes rests when he's in the middle of a piece."

19

Sasha followed Ellie into a room that had undoubtedly started life as a closet. A cot was crammed against one wall and a straight-backed chair was shoved up against the opposite wall. Ellie flicked on an overhead light and pulled a thin stack of large, heavyweight papers from a high shelf.

She removed her parka and dropped it down onto the cot, then perched on the bed beside it. Sasha shed her coat and took the chair. Their knees nearly touched. The open door let in light and air and kept the tight space from becoming claustrophobic. Ellie held the pages on her lap and passed them to Sasha one at a time. She sat in silence as Sasha studied them one by one then placed them on the edge of the cot. After Sasha finished with the final image—a large hammer splitting the Earth into two, she rubbed her finger over the textured paper and squinted at the title scrawled on the bottom of the page in Cinco's minuscule printing. 'Unintended Consequences.'

"So what's your impression?" Ellie asked in a quiet voice.

"Um, there's definitely a theme." The sketches were dark in visual tone and in subject matter: the destruction of the world; a man plummeting from a window to his almost certain death; a graveyard with stacks of cash protruding from the ground in the place of headstones; and, most distressing, a self-portrait of Cinco as a sad clown.

Ellie laughed without humor. "Yeah. And if you've seen any of my dad's stuff, it's all vibrant and colorful. Personally, I think it verges on chaotic, but at least it's joyful."

Sasha considered. "Do you think he was trying to tell your mom something?"

She shrugged. "Sure seems that way. But whatever he thought he was communicating went right over her head—at least that's what she claims."

"You don't believe her?"

"I don't know. These drawings are obviously related to the Milltown case."

Sasha's eyebrows shot up in surprise, and she glanced back down at the one she still held. "You think so?"

"Yeah, I do. And I think you know more than you're letting on." Ellie flushed as she said the words.

Sasha eyed her calmly, wondering how much she knew. "Why's that?"

The young lawyer pushed through whatever discomfort she was feeling. "After you visited Dad at the office, he resigned immediately. Or at least, that's what I was told. I'd quit the day before."

"Mmm-hmm. That's right."

Ellie eyed her. "Did you have anything to do with his decision to resign?"

Sasha gave her a level look. "No comment."

"It might be related to what happened later," Ellie pressed.

"Why don't you tell me what did happen, and we'll take it from there?"

She frowned but acquiesced. "I heard this all second-hand, from Lettie, who got it from the Prescott & Talbot rumor mill. After you left, Dad called an emergency meeting of the Management Committee and told the other three that he was stepping down effective immediately. They tried to talk him out of it, but he was insistent. That night, on the news, Maisy broke the story of the settlement and called Leith Delone out for interfering with her reporting. At that point, I think the firm was probably glad Dad had up and quit."

Sasha cocked her head. "Probably?"

"Yeah, probably. I don't know for sure what the brain trust thought after they saw the reporting. Remember, I had just quit the day before. I wasn't talking to anyone at the office, and I didn't dare show up at the house. Dad and I weren't exactly on the best of terms. But I do know he shoved the Leith Delone representation down their throats."

Sasha choked. "You knew Delone was funding the settlement?"

She nodded. "That's why Dad wanted me on the

case. He thought he could trust me to keep my mouth shut. He was so blinded by the prospect of being Leith Delone's lawyer that the small amount of sound legal judgment he possesses went right out the window."

Sasha thought of Amanda Teale-James and nodded her understanding. "I'm sure the prospect of working for someone with so much power is tempting—seductive, even."

"That, and the money," Ellie said sourly.

Something about the way Ellie had worded her explanation of why she'd been assigned to the Milltown defense was poking at Sasha's brain. "Hang on. You said your dad *thought* he could trust you to stay quiet."

"Yeah, so?"

"You didn't say he *knew* you'd keep quiet."

"Okay, and?"

A knowing smile crept across Sasha's face. "You didn't keep quiet, did you? *You* were the anonymous tipster who emailed Maisy the documents she needed to connect Delone to the settlement."

Ellie shrugged. "No reason to deny it now. Unless you're going to turn me in to the bar association on an ethics violation. Yeah, that was me." She wrinkled her forehead. "Only, the weird thing is, I didn't email Maisy. I sent them to that Summer woman. But, whatever. Maisy responded, and I sent her the trust documents."

"That was a bold move."

Another shrug. "I guess. I had to do something."

"Why? Sure, you were representing an unpleasant person. But that can't be the only reason. I worked at

Prescott & Talbot, remember? We used to say that if the devil himself needed a lawyer, he'd retain P&T."

Ellie made a face as if she were nauseous. In fact, she did look a bit green.

After a long moment, she sighed. "Yeah, I know. Believe me, I grew up hearing about how every client, no matter how repugnant, deserved representation. But two things happened that I couldn't stomach. First, when he told me Landon Lewis was dead, he was a total simp about it."

Despite years of exposure to Jordana, Sasha was not fluent in Gen Z. She took a wild guess. "A simp, like sympathetic?"

To Ellie's credit, she didn't roll her eyes. "No. He was fan-boying all over the place because Leith Delone himself called to share the news. That's being a simp. It was cringe." She gave Sasha a sidelong glance.

"I know what cringe means," she confirmed. "Okay, that's unseemly. But Landon's death *was* good for your case."

"I know, but the man was dead, and my father was celebrating. It was gross. Plus, Delone knew before it hit the news. He knew before anybody. Well, I guess he didn't know before you and your husband. But he called the next morning from freaking South America to tell Dad."

That *was* strange. She filed the tidbit away for later consideration. But, then, Delone was the richest person on the planet. Surely he had all sorts of information at his fingertips.

"What's the second thing?"

This time, there was an eye roll. "Remember that conference with Judge Cook?"

"Of course. Your dad showed up late, but you did an impressive job until he got there."

She watched Ellie brighten at the compliment, and her wheels began to turn.

"Thanks. Well, you said you were going to be at a party with your client and told me to call you there if we could get the district attorney to agree to a court-appointed monitor as a condition of settlement."

"I remember. You said you'd see what you could do."

"After we left, Dad went off on me for overstepping or whatever. And he said it wasn't even up to the district attorney. Delone was calling the shots."

"Completely unethical, but probably true," Sasha observed.

Ellie cleared her throat and dropped her gaze to her lap. "Yeah, but when he called the DA … he told him about the party and that you'd be leaving around nine o'clock. And …" She lifted her chin and met Sasha's eyes. "And he asked DA Botta to have the cops pull you over and intimidate you on your way home. I'm so sorry. I did try to talk him out of it, but he told me if I didn't want to know how sausage was made, I shouldn't have become a butcher." She barked out a bitter laugh. "I hadn't realized I was a butcher. Here, I thought I was a lawyer. So I got back to the office, sent Maisy the documents, and quit. I'm sorry I didn't warn you. I was a total coward." Tears shone in her eyes.

"That's why you quit? Because your dad set the corrupt Milltown cops on me?"

Ellie swallowed and nodded miserably.

Sasha gave her a long look. "Eleanor, think for a minute. I've known your dad for over a decade. I know what kind of man he is. Right?"

Another nod.

"I shared a lot of information about where I was going to be and when I'd be leaving, didn't I?"

"Yeah?"

"Much of which wasn't strictly necessary. Unless …"

Understanding sparked in Ellie's eyes. "Unless you wanted him to act on it. You *baited* him?"

"I did."

"I quit my job. I've felt like a piece of human poo for six months because of what he did, and you lured him into it? But why? Why would you do that?"

"Tell you what. If you can tell me why I did it, there's a job for you at McCandless, Volmer & Andrews—if you want it."

Ellie was quiet for a moment. Then she spoke, slowly and uncertainly at first. "You used the interaction with the cops as leverage. Maybe you recorded it."

Sasha nodded, and Ellie went on, more confident now. "Then, the next morning, you sent Maisy to see District Attorney Botta. She probably played the video, and he knew he was screwed, so he agreed to the settlement and to record a statement for the news. And knowing Ron Botta, he told her it was all my dad's idea—which you already knew."

"I did. But Maisy got the confirmation I needed."

Ellie shook her head and laughed. "Damn, that's

elegant. You forced him to resign or else be exposed for what he'd done."

"So, when do you want to start?"

Her eyes widened. "Wait. That was a serious job offer?"

"If you want it to be. Yes."

20

L eo rapped his knuckles on Naya's doorframe. She shifted her gaze from her computer monitor to her office doorway. A smile lit her face when she saw her visitor.

"Flyboy, this is a surprise." She gestured for him to come in.

He plopped down into the chair closest to the door with a laugh. "You do know I haven't worked as an air marshal in over a decade, right?"

"You'll always be flyboy to me. Top-secret-could-tell-you-but-then-I'd-have-to-kill-you-boy doesn't exactly roll off the tongue."

"Fair point. So big day for you and Maisy, huh?" He grinned at her.

"Long overdue, but yeah. The wire transfer should come through in the next hour. Maisy's on her way in with mimosas and bagels for the whole office if you want to stick around to celebrate."

"Mimosas, huh? You two didn't learn any lessons last night?"

That earned him a grimace. "Yeah, I learned that ouzo is the devil's own spit. But luckily, Carl remembered your disgusting green hangover cure and made me drink it first thing this morning. Man, that works like a charm. Maisy said your wife delivered a glass to her this morning. Good thinking on her part. What's in it, anyway?"

"You don't want to know," he assured her.

She gave him a skeptical look. "Probably a placebo, anyway."

"Sure. You should believe that."

"Are you looking for Sasha? I don't know where she is. Maisy said she left her place over an hour ago, but she hasn't turned up."

"She had to go out to Cinco Prescott's house. It's a long story. I'm sure she'll fill you in when she gets here. I'm actually looking for Maisy. Or Jordana," he told her.

"Oh? Why?"

Here, Leo paused to think. He was more than willing to obfuscate, mislead, or outright lie for Uncle Sam. But this side project was off the books, and, as a rule, he didn't lie in his personal life. Especially not to his friends. He could, as all these lawyers loved to say, shape the narrative, though. Tell the truth, but in a way to make her want to help him.

"I have some time on my hands," he began.

"Well, that's good. The busier you and Hank are, the scarier the world is. Right?"

"Something like that. Anyway, with all this free time,

I thought I could help Maisy and Jordana go through Lewis' papers. The ones the firm's been storing for his ex-wife."

She pursed her lips and eyeballed him. "That's a weird way to spend your down time. Why don't you, I don't know, go skiing or something?"

He leaned forward and gave her an earnest look. "There are a lot of unanswered questions surrounding Lewis' death. Some of them are eating at me. I have a skill set that, no offense, Jordana and Maisy don't. I could be useful."

Naya's response was lost to the chaos of Maisy's arrival at the office. Her southern accent floated down the hallway from Caroline's reception desk and through Naya's open door as she trilled, "It's party time, y'all."

Naya stood. "Come on, let's toast Maisy's million-airedom and you can talk to her about it."

They followed the chatter and laughter to the large conference room, the one they seemed to use mainly for parties. Most of the office had already gathered. Leo scanned the faces, looking for McCandless, Volmer & Andrews' IT wizard, August.

Just as Leo spotted August and started to head toward him, Will Volmer intercepted Leo, handed him a champagne flute, and launched into a lament about the Steelers' failure to secure a spot in the playoffs. Leo'd lived in Pittsburgh long enough to know that one didn't simply walk away from a conversation about football—especially not one as raw as this one. August would have to wait.

"Listen up, y'all," Maisy said, her musical voice

somehow cutting through the conversation. "I just want to thank everyone for helping me hold the station's feet to the fire, especially Naya and Sasha." She paused and surveyed the room. "Where is she?"

"Right here, Mais," Sasha said as she breezed into the conference room, still wearing her coat and clutching a sheaf of papers in her hands.

A tall woman with blonde hair and an angular face trailed Sasha. She looked vaguely familiar. Maybe a new legal intern? She seemed uncertain about being there, and she was young. Not as young as Jordana, but young enough to make Leo realize he was turning into a geezer. Just last week, he'd asked his dentist if she was even old enough to drive a car, let alone poke at his mouth with a sharp implement. She'd just poked him harder.

Caroline offered Sasha and the young woman champagne flutes.

Sasha waved her off. "Let me dump my coat and these papers in my office. I'll be right back. In the meantime, everyone make our newest litigation associate feel welcome. Everyone, this is Eleanor Prescott. Eleanor, this is everyone."

Will blinked in surprise but recovered quickly and raised his glass. "Welcome, Eleanor. We're delighted to have you join us," he said smoothly.

"Um, thanks. Call me Ellie." She raised her glass in return.

Leo thought she looked even more shell-shocked than Will did. He suspected his indomitable wife had consulted absolutely nobody about her new hire and had sprung the job on Ellie just this morning. As if to prove him right, he caught Sasha mouthing *'sorry'* to Will with a sheepish smile. Then she met Leo's eyes and gave him a puzzled look.

"No, she's not," Will said in an undertone.

"Nope, not even a little," Leo agreed. "Excuse me, would you?"

Will nodded. "Sure. Tell her she made a good hire, but remind her that there's a process, would you?"

"No way. At work, she's your problem, not mine." Leo clapped him on the shoulder.

Will laughed good-naturedly and made his way over to Ellie while Leo sought out his wife.

She greeted him with a quick kiss. "What are you doing here? Is everything okay?"

"Yeah. Come on, I'll walk you to your office." He glanced down at the papers she held rolled up in a loose scroll. "What's this?"

They headed down the hallway, and she passed them to him. He unrolled them and raised an eyebrow at a charcoal sketch of a man wearing clown makeup and a bereft expression.

"New art for the office? It's … uh … different."

"Check the title." She pushed open her door, hit the lights, and slipped her coat off, letting it fall on her guest chair.

He picked up the coat, shook it out, and hung it from the hook on the back of her door. Then he read the title. "The Artist Realizes He's a Fool." He narrowed his eyes and took a closer look at the sad clown. "Is this Cinco?"

"Mmm-hmm. He did a series of these and mailed

them to his wife from some artists' colony in New York. Then, he fell off the radar. Nobody's heard from him since before Christmas."

He studied the Cinco clown's expression. The eyes held defeat, pain, and shame. "It's a weird picture. But it really is evocative, isn't it? He's talented."

"And troubled." She spread the rest of the sketches across her desk, and he frowned down at them.

"Do you think he hurt himself? This one with the graveyard is really disturbing."

She lifted one shoulder. "I don't know, Connelly. His daughter thinks he was trying to say something about Landon's death. Maybe. I can see that—especially with the guy falling from the window. But what's with this hammer one?"

He leaned over and read the title. "'*Unintended Conse-quences.*' I don't know. But it sure looks like he was having a crisis of conscience when he drew these."

"Right. Which is surprising. Because, frankly, I didn't think Cinco Prescott *had* a conscience."

She shook her head, and her loose updo bobbed. A wavy tendril of hair escaped. He tucked it behind her ear and trailed his finger down her neck.

"Mmm … Hey, I'm at work." She slapped his hand away playfully. "I do need to get back to Maisy's party, but you never told me—what *are* you doing here?"

"I wanted to get started going through Landon's papers, assuming you cleared it with Maisy and Jordana."

A guilty expression flashed across her face, which was perfect. He figured she'd forget in all the drama of the past twenty-four hours, but now she'd be extra motivated to get him the go-ahead.

"I'm so sorry."

"It's okay. I don't want to interrupt the celebration. I'll come back later."

"No, that's silly." She rolled open her top desk drawer and removed a single gold key on a small ring. "You know which room the documents are in, right?"

"Yep."

She dropped the key into his open palm. "Knock yourself out. I'll let Maisy know. She's not going to object and, to be honest, I probably need to take a look at them, too. If Ellie's right, and her dad's disappearance has something to do with Landon Lewis, maybe there's something helpful in there."

"Sounds like a plan. You want to grab lunch in a few hours?"

She flipped her desk calendar open and scanned her schedule. "I might be able to. Pop your head in when you're ready to eat, and I'll let you know."

He gave her a quick kiss. "Okay. Have a good morning."

"Uh-huh, you, too." Her attention had drifted away from her calendar and back to Cinco's drawings.

When he left, she was still staring down at them with a perplexed look.

THE METAL DOOR banged shut behind Stasia as she barged into the airport bathroom. She crouched and checked under all three stall doors. No shoes. Still, she shouted Amanda's name. Her voice echoed off the tile walls and came back to her as a taunt.

"Sonofa—." She drove her fist into the mirror hanging over the sink with an explosive punch.

The glass shattered and blood dripped from her hand. She hardly noticed. Leith's lawyer had run, and Stasia was going to have to be the one to break the news to him.

Her nostrils flared as a swell of rage broke over her like a wave. When she caught up to ATJ, she'd enjoy making the little lawyer pay.

For now, though, she had to switch into damage control mode. She wrapped a rough, unbleached paper towel around her bleeding hand and steadied her breath.

When she had herself under control, she bumped the restroom door open with her hip and opened the trashcan just outside to drop the bloodied towel inside. She'd use the first aid kit on the plane to treat her injury properly. As the lid swung open, a glint of shiny metal caught her eye. She scanned the mostly empty space before she reached inside. She retrieved Amanda's cell phone, then wadded up the paper towel and tossed it into the refuse container.

She tucked the phone into the pocket of her fitted dress and smoothed the fabric over her hips. She returned to the counter and removed her own mobile device from the shelf. She powered it up and placed the call to Leith's home.

"Delone residence."

"It's Stasia. Put me through," she instructed the house manager.

Raquel complied immediately, and a moment later, Leith's voice sounded in Stasia's ear.

"What is it?"

She ignored the tone. "Your lawyer ran."

"What?"

"When ATJ arrived at the airport this morning, I told her to call you, as you wanted. She spoke to *someone* on the phone. Was it you?"

"It was not."

She took Amanda's phone out of her pocket and powered it on.

"She ended her call and indicated she needed to use the restroom. She never returned to the boarding area, so I went looking for her. I found her mobile in a trash-can. She left her suitcase and computer here. So she's on foot with nothing more than what she has in her pockets," Stasia told him.

"This is unacceptable. Who did she speak to?"

Stasia rolled her eyes heavenward. "Tell me her PIN, and we'll find out."

Leith required his inner circle to share their PINs and passwords with Raquel. Updating or changing them without reporting the new one to his house manager was grounds for termination and banishment.

"Raquel, get in here," he barked on the other end of the phone.

A few moments later, Raquel rattled off the digits, Leith repeated them into the phone, and Stasia keyed them into Amanda's device. The screen came to life, and she navigated to the call log.

"She took an incoming call. The number comes up as McCandless, Volmer & Andrews, and it's listed in her contacts as SMC," Stasia reported.

"It's the lawyer she met with yesterday," Leith told her as if she didn't already know that. "She must have told ATJ that her client wasn't budging and rather than face the music for her failure, ATJ decided to run."

There was a heavy silence. Then Delone said, "Raquel, get out."

After a pause, he spoke again. "What do you think?"

She told him what they both already knew. "What I think is, she wouldn't have done that unless she had a contingency plan."

"Take care of it," he ordered through clenched teeth. "Call me when it's done."

"With pleasure," she said even though he'd already disconnected the call.

21

When Sasha returned to the conference room, she located Naya and Will in the sea of people and pulled them over to a relatively quiet corner.

"Sorry I didn't consult with you about hiring Ellie—"

Will cut her off with a wave of his hand. "Don't be. She'll be an asset to the firm. I have no doubt."

"Yeah, don't sweat it," Naya assured her. "You did good."

She stared at her partners. If either of them had dared to bring on a new associate without getting her input, she'd have been irritated, to put it mildly. And they were just *fine* with it?

"Look at her," Will said to Naya. "She's befuddled."

Naya laughed. "Mac, you're a control freak. Will and I? Not control freaks. We're not upset. Now, if you're done wringing your hands about something you're not even actually sorry about, I'm gonna get a bagel."

Sasha watched her walk away.

"Huh. Wonder what that's like?"

"Not wanting to control the universe?" Will asked. "It's delightful. You should give it a try. You might find it refreshing."

She arched an eyebrow. "You think?"

He reconsidered. "Yeah, no. I don't think it's for you." He chuckled, then jerked his chin toward Ellie, who was chatting with Jordana. "Do we have an office for her?"

"Um … not exactly. Although Jordana doesn't technically work here anymore—not that you could tell. I thought they might double up, at least for now."

"That could work. Do you have a case in mind for Ellie's first assignment?"

"About that."

"Oh, boy. Let me guess, you also took a representation without running it past anyone?"

"Mmm. Yes? But, no. Not a representation. A project."

"A project," he echoed.

It sounded right, so she nodded. "Yep, a project."

"Are we being paid for this project?"

She looked at him for a long moment before responding. "Cinco's missing."

He furrowed his brow. "I thought he was at an artists' colony in the Hudson Valley."

"How do you know these things?"

"I can't recall who told me. Probably someone at one of the bar association luncheons that you're so fond of skipping."

She let that comment pass without a response.

"That's where he went after he resigned. He headed up to Light on the River, I think it's called. But he was supposed to come home for the new year and didn't. And Ellie and Gillian haven't heard from him."

"Wait. Ellie asked you to find her father, and you offered her a job?"

"Nope. Marcus, DeAngeles, and Porter asked me to find Ellie's father, and I told them to bugger off."

Will choked on his drink but managed not to do a spit take. "Not in so many words, I hope?"

"Eh … Anyway, I texted Ellie, and she invited me to come out to the house this morning. She thinks his vanishing act has something to do with Landon Lewis."

"Of course, she does," he muttered. He did that thing where he pinched his index finger on the outer corner of one eye and his thumb on the outer corner of the other and scrunched up his face like he was in pain. Caroline, who'd worked with Will since the dawn of time, called it his 'Calgon, take me away' face.

"Why do you say that?"

He took his hand away from his eyes and sighed. "Haven't you noticed that Landon's like a bad penny? He keeps turning up. First, he unleashes his diabolical program on the community, and you get it shut down. Then, he agrees to testify for you at trial and gets himself murdered."

"That one probably wasn't his fault," she pointed out.

"Perhaps not. But, here you are again, about to go off on a wild goose chase because of Landon Lewis."

"We don't know that it's a wild goose chase," she protested.

"We do know that's not the practice of law, Sasha. If Cinco's missing, his wife should call the authorities. Or Prescott & Talbot could do it if the powers-to-be are so concerned. You're not a private investigator. You're a litigator."

Although his tone was mild, this was as close as Will Volmer came to ranting. And his scolding was fair. So she didn't react to being chastised. Instead, she nodded.

"I hear you, Will. I do. And believe me, I don't care how worked up P&T's Top Three are about Cinco's disappearance—"

"I hear a *but* coming."

"But, let's just say, I forced Cinco's hand to resign. And I owe Ellie a favor."

"So you hired her?"

"No, I hired her because you're right. She'll be an asset. She's a damn good lawyer."

He took a breath. When he spoke, his voice was heavy with resignation. "But because you owe her a favor, you're traipsing off to the Hudson Valley to look for her father."

"Exactly. And I'm bringing her with me." She smiled brightly.

One down, one to go. Now she just had to tell her husband.

22

L eo commandeered a table from an empty conference room and dragged it into the storage room to use as a work surface. He began paging through Landon's documents, giving the contents of each box a quick once-over to get a sense of the universe of information. Once he understood the scope of what he had to work with, he'd go through each set of papers more methodically.

He was most of the way through his first pass when the door opened and Maisy strolled into the small room, a champagne flute in hand. Jordana was half a step behind her, munching on a pumpernickel bagel as if it were an apple.

"Sasha told us we'd find you in here," Maisy informed him.

"She said you wouldn't mind."

"We don't," Jordana said immediately around a mouthful of bagel. She swallowed. "Sorry, shouldn't talk with my mouth full. Are you kidding? There are a billion documents in here. Not only do we have the stuff Landon's ex-wife gave us, Sasha gave us copies of all the Milltown files that relate in any way to Landon. We need all the help we can get."

Maisy took the last sip of her mimosa and nodded her agreement. "If there's a clue as to who killed Landon buried in all this stuff, we haven't found it. Maybe your fresh eyes will see something we missed."

"Have you? Found anything, I mean?" Jordana asked.

He grinned, relieved that he wasn't going to have to pull rank on them. He'd been prepared to invent an issue of national security if they'd put up a fuss, but he really hadn't wanted to. This way was much easier. And better. Three sets of hands were better than one.

He gestured for them to pull over two of the chairs stacked against the wall. "Not yet, but I do know something you don't. Maybe we can agree to share our information?"

He leaned back and watched them consider his offer. Maisy, he knew, would jump at it. She was a journalist. Information was her life's blood. Jordana, on the other hand, rubbed her chin and studied him. Her expression was lawyerly and knowing—eerily similar to a look Sasha gave him when she was calculating a response.

"Of course, sugar," Maisy agreed.

"It depends," Jordana interjected, shooting Maisy a cautioning look.

Leo wondered who was calling the shots here. Maisy paid Jordana's salary. But Jordana was the podcast's producer. Heaven help him if Jordana was in charge.

Maisy waved a hand at Jordana's warning. "Oh,

come on. We've been banging our heads against the wall for weeks, and you know it. I'm going crossed-eyed looking at financial records. It couldn't hurt to pool our resources with a real ... whatever Leo is."

Jordana twisted her mouth skeptically. "Sure it could." She eyed Leo. "Does Sasha know about this information you have?"

Maisy's eyes went wide. "Oooh, good point. Does she?"

It was the one question he didn't want to have to answer. But he had to answer it honestly because they'd never trust him again if they found out.

"No."

A long silence stretched over the room. The two women waited. He raised both hands as if in surrender.

"I'm going to level with you and ask you not to mention any of this to Sasha."

Maisy opened her mouth, and he cut off her objection before she gave voice to it.

"I'm going to tell her. I've been meaning to tell her. But I didn't say anything back in July, and now I'm just waiting for the right time."

"There's never going to be a good time to tell your wife you've been keeping a secret from her for six months, Leo."

He accepted Maisy's point. "Probably not. But *I* will tell her. Not you. Got it?" He shifted his gaze from Maisy to Jordana, who nodded with clear reluctance.

"Sure thing. If you think we're gonna fall all over ourselves to let her know, you've lost the plot," Maisy told him.

"Good. Now that we've got that out of the way, do you want me to fill you in or what?"

They leaned forward in unison, their eyes gleaming with anticipation. There was nothing either of them loved more than the hunt. It was why their true crime podcast had become an instant success. He started at the beginning—well, near the beginning—with the unexpected delivery of a package from Landon Lewis after his fatal tumble from a window.

"How did Landon know where you live?" Jordana demanded. As Sasha and Leo's favorite babysitter, she was well aware of their hyper-vigilance about protecting their privacy.

"He didn't." Leo explained that the package had been addressed to the office that he and Hank maintained, mainly as a cover and a mail drop.

"Was the letter opener in this package?" Maisy asked.

Jordana gave her a confused frown. "The letter opener?"

"Remember how Landon had two matching letter opener and pen sets—one at home and one at his office?"

"Yeah, one had his son's date of birth inscribed on it, and the other had the date he was murdered." Jordana shuddered. "Kind of morbid."

"Right, and the one from his office was missing."

"But you found it somewhere because I saw you give it to Deanne. Where was it?"

Maisy lowered her chin and fixed her gaze on Leo.

He coughed. He hadn't planned to put *all* his cards on the table, but what the hell. "It wasn't in the package.

The night Landon died, Sasha and I just happened to be in the alley—"

"Mmm-hmm. After you *happened* to hear a call over the police radio," Maisy interjected.

"Oh, so she told you that much. Did she mention that while I was identifying Landon's body, she sneaked into an active police scene and snooped through his office?"

Maisy gasped. "No."

But Jordana snorted. "That's so on brand."

"In any case, she knew not to touch anything and risk leaving fingerprints, but she wanted to read the back of the note on his desk, so she used his letter opener to flip it over. Then, of course, her prints were on the letter opener, so …." He trailed off.

"She *stole* it?"

"Stole is a strong word." It wasn't the wrong word, but he wasn't about to say so.

"The note was his fake suicide note, right?" Jordana asked.

"We have this theory whoever killed him forced him to write the note first."

"A decent theory, but wrong," he informed them.

Maisy bristled. "How could you possibly know that?"

"Because that note was a draft of the note in the package he sent me. The version I got was addressed to me, more detailed, and gave me some indecipherable marching orders."

Her eyes widened. "Can we see it?"

"It's in my safe, but I have a picture of it on my phone." He pulled up the photo and handed his device over the table to Maisy. As they huddled together over it, Maisy's mess of blonde curls nearly touching Jordana's half-black/half-red dyed hair, he returned to the stack of Landon's journals that he'd been about to tackle when the pair had come into the room.

Maisy had started to go through the diaries the week after Christmas, but she'd set them aside for the more exciting pursuit of tracking down a dirty police officer. As he paged through them, he understood why. Landon's writing was dry and his subject was drier still.

Maisy slid his phone back across the table to him. "Wow. Okay. So what—or who—is Mjölnir? What are you supposed to stop it or them from doing?"

"If I knew the answers to those two questions, I wouldn't be here. I'd be stopping Mjölnir."

"It's been six months. It might be too late," Jordana, ever the beam of sunshine, pointed out.

"Well, the world hasn't turned into a dystopian hellscape yet, so I'm operating under the assumption there's still time."

"That's fair," she allowed. Then she twitched her nose like a rabbit. "Isn't Mjölnir the name of Thor's hammer in Norse mythology."

"Yes. But I assume Landon hasn't literally tasked me with stopping a god from using his mighty hammer. I'd hope to go into battle with Thor armed with more than a thumb drive."

"He sent you a thumb drive?"

"Yeah. I imagine the program to stop Mjölnir is on it, which makes me think it's a thing, not a person."

"You imagine? You mean you haven't looked at the

drive yet?" Jordana's eyes bulged in disbelief.

Leo removed the drive in question from his pocket. "This thing is serious business. It's protected by a PIN, the data on it is encrypted, and the case is coated with epoxy. I don't have the PIN, so I can't open it to access the stick. Even if I could—which I can't—I don't have the correct password or whatever I'll need to decode the information, and I'm pretty sure the data will self-destruct without that key. Finally, the physical defenses mean that if I try to physically remove the data chips, a destruction process will initiate and wipe out that data. So, no, I haven't looked at it."

He placed the aluminum rectangle on the table, and they stared at it with an inexplicable air of expectation. Like they were expecting an alarm to go off or a small explosion to detonate. He knew the feeling. For such a small item, it had an outsized impact.

Suddenly, Jordana jerked her head up. "I'll be right back."

She pushed back her chair and ran out of the room. He turned to Maisy, who shrugged.

"How is it that this never came up with Sasha?"

He shrugged. "To be fair, it was a hectic time. You two ambushed the DA and Cinco in the morning, the package came in the afternoon, and then you went off on your rant about Delone on live television and got yourself fired. Plus, it was slime camp week for the kids. Look, we were busy. And then, as time wore on, I decided to handle it myself. After all, Landon sent the package to me, not Sasha. There was no reason to involve her."

"Not even when I started investigating his death last month, and we found out he'd been murdered? That didn't seem like the time to say, oh, by the way, Landon's last request on this earth was for me to prevent Armageddon?"

"You're being melodramatic, now. Armageddon? I don't think he's foretold the final battle between good and evil."

"I do. Read your note again."

"He was unhinged."

She gave him a thoughtful look. "You're scared."

"I'm not *scared*," he scoffed.

"No? You should be. I am. I've had a glimpse into how Landon's mind worked. And maybe he wasn't the most mentally balanced person. But he was smart, and, more important, he had a high tolerance for risk and viewed unintended consequences as an acceptable outcome if it meant making the world incrementally safer. So, if he was scared—and it sure sounds like he was—you should be, too."

She sat back, crossed her ankles, and pressed her lips together as if to indicate she'd said her piece and she was done. He turned his attention away from her, staring down at the leather-bound journal in his hands. There was nothing to say to her. Not because she was wrong, but because she was right.

She cleared her throat, but he kept his gaze locked on the page.

A moment later, Jordana burst into the room with August in tow.

23

The crappy little town with the amazing apple pies was further from the airport than Amanda had estimated. Or she'd gotten lost in those freaking dormant cornfields as she'd thwacked through dead cornstalks. Or both.

She guessed she'd been running for well over two hours. Maybe three. There was every likelihood she was going in circles. She hadn't passed by the shed at the farm where she'd first sought shelter, which was encouraging. But then again, she hadn't seen any other structures either, and every field looked identical to the last.

She stumbled across a gully and sat down heavily on a tree stump to catch her breath. Raw blisters had formed on her big toes and rubbed against her socks with every stride. Her warm thigh-length coat had been more than sufficient for her short trips outside the hotel and office building yesterday, but it wasn't up to the job today. The cold had seeped into her bones so thoroughly that she no longer shivered.

Is it possible to be too cold to shiver?

The entirety of her survival experience had come from a wilderness leadership program her parents had shipped her off to one summer when she was in high school. She had a vague memory of the stages of hypothermia and thought the lack of shivering might be a sign that she was moving from the first stage to the second. Or she could be entirely wrong.

Pie.

She *really* wanted that pie. She could taste it. The promise of mouth-watering apple pie had become her new primary goal. Forget starting a new life, free of Leith Delone and his skeletons. She wanted pie.

Just another fifteen minutes, she promised herself as she massaged her sore feet through her socks. If she didn't come across the town after fifteen minutes, she'd take shelter in the first spot she found. Even if that meant digging a hole and crawling into it. She was pretty sure she'd seen that in a movie.

If Amanda hadn't been experiencing symptoms of moderate hypothermia, she would have had the mental acuity to remember that confused thinking was, like the cessation of shivering, a symptom of moderate hypothermia. But how does a person recognize a decline in her own cognitive ability? If she'd realized her situation, she'd have appreciated the irony of it.

Instead, she trudged, zombie-like, down another hill and up a crest. She thought she heard the rumble of trucks driving at speed, and hope flickered in her chest.

A few moments later, she spotted the tall, lighted sign for *Erma's Diner* towering over a long low aluminum-sided structure.

She raised her fist in triumph and whooped. From its perch in a bare tree, a fat crow squawked in response. Amanda's body reached deep into some reserve that it should have exhausted hours ago and produced a final glucose-fueled burst of energy. She laughed as she sprinted down the hill and out of the field.

When she reached the berm along the side of the highway, she stopped and stared across at the diner to confirm that it was really real. Her lungs burned and her legs shook, but she'd done what she'd set out to do. Just as she always did.

Amanda turned her head to the left, then the right, and then back to the left to confirm there was a break in the flow of traffic before she darted out to cross the two-lane highway. She'd almost made it to the dividing line when the eighteen-wheeler barreled around the blind curve on the opposite side of the road.

Later, the driver, Seb Boardman out of Dayton, Ohio, would swear she stutter-stepped forward, which is what caused him to swerve off the road and onto the strip of grass in front of Erma's Diner. He explained at the inquest that he'd avoided slamming on his brakes because he was hauling a full load of washers and dryers, which might've shifted, possibly toppling his big rig onto its side. His vantage point from the narrow shoulder gave him a front-row seat to the carnage that occurred when the small woman—who, at first glance, he'd taken for a little girl—jerked back into the west-bound lane and was hit at full speed by a dark subcompact.

The force of the impact launched the woman airborne. She flew across the eastbound lane and bounced off the windshield of Seb's truck, leaving a large red smear down the front when she crumpled to the ground. Through the blood, he watched the car that had hit her accelerate and career out of sight. He knew before he even climbed out of his cab that there was no way the victim had survived, and he was right.

Shaken, Seb wasn't certain about the make and model—maybe a Honda Fit, maybe a Chevy Sonic—or the color—might have been dark gray, might have been black. He'd managed to get a partial plate that the state police would be unable to run down and had caught a glimpse of blonde hair on the driver. But the one thing Seb Boardman knew for sure was the driver had made no attempt to stop after hitting the Jane Doe and possibly had even sped up before the impact, not after.

More than a year later, a navy blue Ford Fiesta with significant front-end damage and West Virginia plates matching the partial provided by the truck driver would be found by engineers draining a lake in a state park over the Maryland border. The car would be traced back to a stolen vehicle report filed the day of the accident by a worker at a service station two towns over from where the hit-and-run happened.

It's possible that trace blood or DNA evidence might have survived the lengthy submersion in fresh water. But by then, what was left of Amanda Teale-James (which wasn't much at all) had been buried at county expense in the nondenominational cemetery just three miles from the cornfields where she'd spent her last hours. The commissioners didn't see the point in exhuming her, and so she remained a Jane Doe.

ugust handed the drive back to Leo with a disappointed expression. "Man, I'd love to help you, but you're right. If we try to brute force crack into that thing, the data on it will self-destruct. You're sure you don't even have a guess at what the PIN would be?"

Leo shook his head. "No clue."

The IT guy spread his hands wide and made a 'can't help you' gesture.

As he turned to walk out of the room, Maisy said, "Hang on."

He stopped and looked over his shoulder. "Yeah?"

"How many tries do you think we have at the PIN? If you had to guess, I mean. Like, he wouldn't have set it up so you only get one try, right?"

He scratched his forehead. "Most of these secure drives give you a surprising number of attempts. Up to twenty, sometimes. But I wouldn't risk doing that many if I were you."

Maisy was nodding eagerly. "What about two?"

"Two ought to be safe," he answered slowly, clearly unhappy about having to opine.

"Do you have an idea?" Leo asked.

Maisy grinned. "I have two."

"Even if we get in, we'll still have a password to deal with," Jordana reminded them.

Maisy waved a hand. "I got into his phone and laptop, didn't I?"

August wheeled around and returned to the table. "Can I stick around and watch?"

"Sure," Leo told him. "If she does manage to get into the files or whatever's on here, we'll need you to tell us what we're dealing with."

He passed the drive to Maisy.

She took it hesitantly, her confidence apparently already deflating. "Are you sure you're okay with this?"

After a moment's thought, Leo nodded. "Yeah, I'm sure. I definitely don't know the PIN. So unless you give it a shot, my only options are to take as many wild guesses as I can or toss this thing back into the safe and wait for the end of the world."

She turned her head and gave him a searching look. "And you promise you're not going to be mad at me if I accidentally destroy it?"

"Hell, Maisy, we're out of options. I promise I won't be mad."

"Okay, then. After all, as my Aunt Alice always says, 'Cain't never could.'"

Cain't never could?

Leo looked at Jordana, who shrugged, then at August, who shook his head.

"Um, what?"

"You know, the saying, 'cain't never could.'"

They stared at her with blank faces. Finally, Jordana said, "That's not a saying."

Maisy *tsked* at them. "Come on, y'all. It means you'll never do it if you don't try."

"How does that remotely mean—?"

Leo cut August off and gestured toward the drive. "Let's focus, people. Maisy, do the honors."

She took a deep breath, positioned her right index finger over the number pad, and said each digit aloud as she pressed it. "Zero-three-one-one-nine-zero." She blinked down at the drive. "How will we know if it worked?"

"Hit the green icon of an open lock," Jordana told her.

"That's right," August confirmed. "How'd you know that?"

"I don't know? Because I'm sentient?"

"That's enough out of you. Here goes."

She pressed the icon. Nothing happened. They let out the collective breath that they'd been holding.

"Well, shoot," Maisy huffed.

"That was Josh's birthday, right?" Jordana asked.

"That's right." She turned and explained to Leo, "Our tech genius reused the same password for sixteen years —the date his son was born."

August groaned and pulled his hands through his

hair. "Don't tell me that," he moaned dramatically. "It'll give me nightmares."

"I'm sorry, Leo. It opened his laptop right up. And his cell phone, too."

August emitted another pained grunt.

Jordana shushed him before Leo had to. "Quiet. Maisy, didn't Landon's ex-wife say he knew the password was easily guessed, but he didn't really care if anything on either device was secure?"

"She did."

"But he *did* care about protecting whatever the heck's on this drive. Otherwise, he could have put it on any old drive he had lying around. Not this encrypted-self-destructing-super-spy thing."

"True," Maisy mused, slowly. "He'd want to make it harder to guess, but not *too* hard. It could be …" She reached for the keypad, then hesitated. "I don't know if I should. What if I'm wrong again?"

"Two failed attempts isn't going to lock us out. Do it," August urged.

She met Leo's eyes. He nodded.

"Okay. One-zero-one-three-zero-seven."

Leo wrinkled his forehead. He recognized that series of numbers. But why?

She pressed the icon. For a millisecond, nothing happened.

Leo heard the disappointed sigh rising in his throat. But then, the button lit up and flashed green. She gasped. August and Jordana spontaneously clapped their hands.

"I can't believe you did it. How'd you know the PIN?" Leo asked.

"Funny thing is you had the PIN. At least until December, when you gave it back to me."

He dropped his head back against the wall. "Ten-oh three-oh seven. It was engraved on the letter opener. The date of Josh's murder." In retrospect, it seemed obvious.

Maisy bounced on her seat and turned toward August. "So, can you look at it now?"

"I can. But if it's encrypted and password-protected, this might take a while," he cautioned.

Leo shook his head. "No. He wouldn't do that. He wanted me to be able to use this program or whatever it is. Sure, he locked the drive. That's a basic precaution. But my gut says that's all he did."

August shrugged. "Let me grab a laptop that's not connected to the network, and we'll find out."

SASHA PUSHED OPEN the door to the storage room to find her husband peering over August's shoulder at a computer screen. Maisy and Jordana hovered behind him.

"What are you kids up to?"

At the sound of her voice, the IT guy slammed the laptop closed, and the other three jumped back.

"Nothing," Maisy squeaked.

"Very believable," Sasha told her dryly.

A brief, but awkward, silence followed.

She rolled her eyes. "I don't actually care. Connelly, I need to talk to you for a minute."

"Is everything okay?"

"Yep." She tilted her head toward the hallway, and he got the message.

He followed her outside and lowered his head. "What's up?"

"I need to go to New York for a day, maybe two. Are you good with the kids or should I get my parents on standby?"

"We'll be fine," he assured her.

She twisted her mouth and looked up at him. "Are you sure?"

He caressed her stiff shoulders with his open palms and lowered his chin so he could look her in the eye. "I'm positive."

She felt her shoulders soften, but the tightness in her gut remained. "Okay, thank you. We can do a video call tonight, okay? I don't like leaving without saying goodbye to the twins, but if I stop by their classroom, it'll only be disruptive."

"They'll be fine. We'll do pizza with homemade dough for dinner. That'll keep them busy until you can call."

She managed a small smile. "Thanks," she said, before stretching up on her toes to kiss him lightly.

"Be safe," he murmured against her mouth.

"Always," she breathed back.

The door creaked, and Maisy's face appeared in the opening. "Um, should we wait for you?"

Sasha answered before Connelly could, "He's all yours. Ellie's waiting for me in the car."

"You're taking her with you?"

"She's gotta earn her keep somehow. Chauffeuring me around is a good start," she joked.

He grabbed her hand and squeezed it before he went back into the storage room.

"Take care of him," she told Maisy.

"You got it," Maisy promised before pulling the door closed.

Before she walked away, she listened for a moment to their indistinct voices. Although she couldn't decipher the words, she could detect an unmistakable undercurrent of excitement, as if they'd made a breakthrough in their search for answers about Landon.

She only hoped she and Ellie would have similar luck in their search for the younger woman's missing father.

25

Stasia hopped out of the car, slammed the door shut, and leaned in through the open passenger side window. The handsy pervert who'd picked her up on the side of the road in Maryland smiled expectantly.

"Change your mind?" he asked.

"No." She breathed out through her nose, reminding herself to keep a handle on her temper. "I'm definitely getting out here. I appreciate the lift, Frank. But I have some advice for you."

"Yeah? What's that, honey?" He leered at her.

She reached over and grabbed his t-shirt collar, bunching the fabric into a tight knot at his throat. His face turned red and his eyes bulged. He wheezed indistinctly.

"The next time you pick up a woman—or God forbid, a girl—it'd be a good idea to keep your hands to yourself. You never know if the hitchhiker in your passenger seat has been trained to kill a man with one clean snap of his neck."

His eyes grew wider still. She tightened her grip.

"Do you understand?"

He tried to nod.

She released his shirt, and he fell back against the seat, panting and choking. "Now, get the hell out of my sight before I do change my mind and put you out of your misery."

He hit the gas, and the car lurched forward. She stepped back and watched him speed out of sight before she took out her phone and punched in Leith's number.

He must have been waiting for her call, because he answered the line himself. "Hello?"

"It's done."

"How?"

"Are you sure you want to know?"

"No," he said quickly. "You're right. Don't tell me. Where are you?"

"I'm about a mile and a half from the airport, maybe two. I should be back there in half an hour or less." She planned to avoid the roads and cut through the endless farmland to return to the airfield.

"Don't file a return flight plan. There's been another development. I may need you to handle something else."

She blew out a long breath. Leith was lucky she was an adrenaline junkie—because neither his paltry salary nor his flaccid member was enough incentive for her to stay in this job. But the constant excitement made up for his cheapness and his impotence.

"What is it?"

"Rosen called me. The developer who debugged Mjölnir sent over the finished file and then apparently quit with no notice. Just left his lanyard on his desk and walked out."

"This guy worked at Pinpoint Partners?"

"No, Rosen contracted the project out. According to Rosen, it's probably nothing. Just some Gen Z douchebag who doesn't want to work. But, I want you on standby while I have his background checked out. I'll let you know later tonight."

"Understood."

He ended the call, and she stowed her phone in her pocket. A slight frisson of disappointment ran through her. If she'd known she was going to have time to kill, she would have toyed with Frank longer and taught him a proper lesson.

She loped across the field as the sun began to fade.

26

The sun was just beginning to set over the Hudson River when Sasha and Ellie neared the little town nestled along its banks.

"Pull over," Sasha said.

Ellie eased the car off the narrow street and parked alongside the river. "Is here good?"

"Yes, hurry," Sasha said, scrambling out of the passenger seat.

Ellie killed the engine and jogged around to join her. "Is something wrong?" she panted.

Sasha tugged on Ellie's sleeve, pulling her toward the wooden walkway to the right. "No, but we're going to miss it if we don't hustle."

"Miss what?"

A moment later they reached the end of the walkway and stepped out onto a small octagonal deck that jutted over the river. Built-in benches dotted the perimeter of the platform, but Sasha and Ellie walked past them, right up to the edge of the railing.

"This," Sasha said.

They stood in silence, transfixed by the sight of the sun slipping into the river. The entire sky was banded by streaks of dark purple and golden yellow-orange as the light reflected off the water. On the opposite bank, a pale evening mist settled over the deep blue hills.

"It's like a painting," Ellie murmured.

It was. "It probably is. Lots of them," Sasha told her.

Ellie gave her a confused look.

"It's the name of the art colony—Light on the River. I'm sure dozens of artists have tried to capture this moment."

"Right. Of course." She turned in a slow circle. "It must be nearby. But I don't see any buildings."

They were still on the very outskirts of the hamlet proper, but Sasha also pivoted, looking for signs of life.

"Let's ask him." She pointed back toward the riverbank, about forty yards from a station wagon. A man in a puffy winter coat and a jaunty hat was packing up an easel and painting supplies.

They jogged up the walkway and cut through the frozen grass to intercept the artist before he reached his car.

"Hi, there," Sasha called as they approached. Her warm breath made a small cloud in the cold air.

He turned quickly toward the sound of her voice and blinked when he spotted them.

"Evening. Didn't know anybody else was out here."

"I'm surprised that display doesn't draw a crowd every night," Sasha told him.

"She does put on a show," he agreed.

"She?" Ellie asked.

"The sun. I suppose you could say the Creator puts on the show, depending on your beliefs."

Sasha pointed her chin at his easel. "Looks like you're a creator, too."

"I dabble."

"May we see?" Ellie asked.

"You ladies want to stand out here in the cold and look at a painting by some grizzled old grump?"

"Ellie here comes from an artistic family," Sasha told him.

"Oh?"

"My father paints. I'd love to see your work." She gave him a warm smile.

He softened and turned his canvas toward them. "I'm doing a series. This is the third one."

To Sasha's surprise, he hadn't painted the brilliant sunset over the river. Instead, his subject was the hills beyond the river. He'd captured the mist creeping up from the water and the shadows stretching down from above.

Ellie considered the painting for a long moment, her expression intent and thoughtful. "I like the way you create movement in the rolling mists and the spreading shadow."

A pleased grin lit his craggy face. "You have a good eye. What's your dad's name? Maybe I know him."

"Oh, I doubt it. We're not local—we drove up from Pittsburgh." Ellie reconsidered. "Although, Dad *is* in town right now. He's been in residence at Light on the River since August."

The painter nodded. "You're Chuck's daughter?"

Sasha was about to correct him when she remembered Cinco's given name *was* Charles. She wouldn't have pegged him as a '*Chuck*,' but maybe there was another side to Cinco that she knew nothing about. Based on the cough that Ellie choked out, she also wasn't acquainted with her father's inner Chuck.

"Um, yeah. He's my dad."

He stuck out his right hand. "Pleased to meet you Chuck's daughter. I'm Vern."

"Hi, Vern. Ellie Prescott, and this is my … um, boss, Sasha."

Vern pumped Sasha's hand. "Pleased to meet you both. You ladies here to visit with Chuck?"

"Right. It's a surprise," Sasha told Vern. "We're in the area for work so we thought we'd pop in. We got rooms in town for the night. Isn't the artist colony near here, though? Maybe we'll stop in to say hi before we check in at the inn."

He chewed on his lower lip. "Well, now. Light on the River is just yonder, over that rise." He jerked a thumb behind him. "But I hope you didn't detour too far out of your way, because I don't think Chuck's there."

Ellie frowned. "Where else would he be?"

"I don't rightly know. But I haven't seen him around in, let's see, it's been several weeks, if I recall correctly." He thought for a moment. "Yeah. Last time I saw him was before the new year. He was buying oils at Russell's Art Supply in town. Haven't laid eyes on him since. Tell you the truth, I assumed he'd moved on."

"Back to Pittsburgh, you mean?" Sasha asked. 'Moved on' struck her as an odd way to say 'went home.'

"For some reason, I have it in my mind that he might be heading to Stratford after this."

"Stratford?"

"Little town a lot like this one up in Ontario."

"He told you he was going to Canada?"

After she asked the question, she flicked her eyes toward Ellie to gauge her reaction to this suggestion. Her face was taut with tension.

Vern grimaced. "I can't say for sure. He might've or I might've picked it up from someone at the tavern. There's a pub in town—Cole's—caters to us artistic sorts. Chuck was a regular." Vern chuckled at a memory. "Your dad's quite particular about his martinis. He about drove Leona mad before she finally started making them to his liking."

"Up, extra dry, two olives," Ellie recited.

"Yep, that's it, all right. It was the extra dry bit that kept tripping Leona up. No matter how little vermouth she put in, it was too much." Vern leaned in and stage whispered, "Shouldn't tell you this, but Leona confessed she started just pretending to add a splash. Once she left it out, then he declared it perfect."

Now, this sounded more like the Cinco Sasha knew.

Ellie giggled. "I'll have to pass that tip along to my mom." Then her face fell, and Sasha knew she was wondering if Gillian would ever have use for that knowledge.

Sasha turned to Vern. "I think we've held you up long enough, Vern. It sure gets cold fast up here after

186 | MELISSA F. MILLER

the sun goes down. Thanks for sharing your work with us."

"It's my pleasure. Sorry you may have made the trip for nothing, but check in at the colony before you head into town. They might know if he's coming back here." He glanced at his watch and frowned. "Poppy's probably working reception this time of the evening. She can be prickly. If she gives you a hard time, go grab a bite and try again after nine. Pete works the night shift. He's a good egg."

"I appreciate the inside info," Sasha told him.

"Of course. Oh, and if you're looking for dinner, Cole's serves food, too. Nothing fancy, but it's good." He touched his fingers to the brim of his felt hat in an old-fashioned gesture, then started to load his supplies into the station wagon.

Sasha and Ellie turned and ran to their car, their heads lowered against the biting wind. They raced inside and slammed the doors closed. Ellie started the engine while Sasha checked the GPS directions to the art colony. Once the air from the heater was blowing warm, she cranked up the temperature and held her bare hands in front of the vent. Ellie watched out of the corner of her eye and then followed suit.

"We should've worn gloves," Sasha said.

"Or snowsuits. I think the temperature must've dropped by twenty degrees once the sun went down. Vern's brave to paint out there in this weather.

"Brave or foolish."

"Or both." Ellie fell silent for a moment before

saying in a soft voice, "This trip was probably a waste of time."

"Why? Because some random guy we met on the river bank said your dad went to Canada? Let's not declare defeat prematurely. The first rule of working with me is: it's not over until I say it's over."

Ellie arched an eyebrow, but a faint smile bloomed on her lips. "Fair enough. So, are we going to take a run at Poppy?"

"I don't know that I have the energy for prickly right now. Let's check-in and get settled at the inn, hit Cole's for dinner, and then go to the art colony while Pete's on duty."

The hint of a smile faded. "We're just putting off the inevitable. If my dad's gone, he's gone. Whether the receptionist is cranky or not won't change that."

"No, it won't. But a cranky receptionist isn't going to bend the rules to let us into his room. Besides, we might pick up some scuttlebutt at the tavern. And, importantly, the second rule of working with me is: Eat when you have the opportunity; sleep when you can. A nourished, rested brain and body are sharp weapons."

"Yes, ma'am." Ellie's shoulders straightened, and she gripped the steering wheel. "Just tell me where to go."

"Head east on this road."

As she eased the car off the shoulder and onto the road, she said, "Out of curiosity, how many of these rules are there?"

"So many," Sasha told her. "So, so many."

27

Leo leaned against the back wall of August's dimly lit office and watched the fingers of the computer guy's left hand fly over the keyboard while his right hand manipulated a complicated-looking mouse so quickly that the movements blurred.

"Is this legal?"

He didn't necessarily care—or, at least, he wouldn't have cared if they weren't using his wife's law firm resources. But Sasha would have his head if McCandless, Volmer & Andrews was charged with cyber-espionage.

August's hands paused. "Define legal," he said without looking away from his screen.

"Spoken like a man who works with a bunch of lawyers."

The IT expert laughed. Then he turned to meet Leo's eyes, "Seriously, though. It's a gray area, at best. I'm using a VPN to mask my location, but it's a risk. Are you sure you want to go forward?"

"You said the thing on the drive is a worm, right?"

He nodded and cracked his chewing gum. "That's right."

"And the only way to deploy it is to stick this thing into a USB drive connected to the system where Cesare is running?"

August drew his eyebrows together. "What's Cesare? This program is the Mjölnir Killer, remember?"

He remembered. "Cesare is the original Mjölnir. It's the AI Landon Lewis was using with the Milltown Police to predict criminality."

"You mean, to racially profile law-abiding Black men?"

"That, too."

Landon had helpfully included a short text file on the drive with the more explicit marching orders that Leo had been wishing for. Unlike the flowery hand-written note, the note on the drive was brief and pointed:

Landon had sold his reviled artificial intelligence program. An outfit named Pinpoint Partners was working to turn it into Mjölnir, an algorithm that would be sold to online retailers, social media sites, and other commercial enterprises with a virtual presence. Each copy of Mjölnir would communicate with every other copy, building a composite picture of every person who wandered into its path online. Landon's terse note described the program as "an insidious threat, lying in wait to destroy longstanding concepts of privacy, free will, and agency." Per Landon, "Mjölnir must be stopped, or the unintended consequences will wreak unimaginable damage."

According to August, the Killer program was a worm virus. Once loaded onto a computer that was connected to a network where Mjölnir resided, the worm would infect Mjölnir. Because Cesare—and, thus, Mjölnir—was designed to replicate itself and share input with each copy of itself, as soon as Leo infected a single copy of Mjölnir, the program would do the rest. It would infect and reinfect itself until it self-destructed.

"And all I have to do is insert the USB stick into a port on a computer running a copy of Mjölnir?" The task sounded almost too easy.

"Yes, but don't get excited, yet. If I were running the show, I'd be very careful to keep Mjölnir un-networked until I was ready to deploy it. And unless Pinpoint Partners is entirely incompetent, they'll have sandbox detection set up."

Leo cocked his head. "It's weird, August. You'll go for extended periods of time speaking English and then, bam, it all falls apart. What in the world is sandbox detection?"

"Sorry. A sandbox is a virtual environment where you can run a program and analyze its behavior to determine if it's malicious before you allow it anywhere near your actual programs."

"But, if I find a physical machine and plug the drive into it, how can the sandbox stop the virus from infecting the box?"

"It can't. Which is why Pinpoint Partners will make

absolutely sure there's no way to access a machine running Mjölnir until it's too late to stop it."

The task suddenly seemed a hundred percent less easy. "So what are you doing now?"

"I'm probing Pinpoint Partners' network to see if there are any unprotected access points."

"And?"

August raised his hand and gave the skin above his lip a vigorous rub. Leo'd had enough training in reading body language to know August was hesitant to speak and uncertain about his answer. "I don't see any vulnerabilities."

Leo studied his face. "But you don't believe that's true, do you?"

"Every network has *some* vulnerability. With enough time, maybe I could find it. But this isn't really what I do. I said it's a gray area, but that's not quite right. You probably need a red hat."

"Come again?"

"You've heard of white hat, black hat, and gray hat hackers, right?"

"Sure. White hats are ethical hackers who work to help improve cybersecurity by exposing vulnerabilities. Black hats exploit those vulnerabilities for their own illegal gain, and gray hats are in between. They might be technically breaking the law, but they don't have malicious intent. Right?"

"That's close enough for our purposes. A red hat hacker is a hacktivist, someone who hacks to send a message. Like a vigilante."

"Like Anonymous?"

August snapped his fingers together. "Exactly like Anonymous."

They were silent for a long moment. Then, Leo asked the obvious question. "Do you know any red hat hackers?"

August's silence stretched out further. Then he pursed his lips. "I know one."

"Can you put me in touch with him?"

"Her. And that's not how it works. I'll reach out to her. If she's willing to help you, I'll let you know."

Leo clapped him on the shoulder. "Listen, I know I'm putting you in a touchy spot. I appreciate the help. If Lewis was right, and this program's as dangerous as he said—"

"I know. We need to kill it. I'll be in touch after I talk to her." August slid the drive toward Leo.

He pocketed it and left August's office, pulling his coat on as he headed for the exit. Jordana had offered to pick the twins up from school, but he needed to relieve her and get some food into their bellies, and his own.

28

G ar hit traffic outside Los Angeles. Of course, he did. He still had four-and-half to five hours of driving before he crossed the border and started his new life. He wanted to put as much distance between himself and Sun Valley as he could, as fast as he could. But he'd used the long hours in the car to rubber ducky his situation.

Any programmer or coder worth their salt knew the famous debugging technique. It was a method of working through a problem by verbally processing it. The coder would literally talk to a rubber ducky, pet, stuffed animal—it didn't really matter—saying the code aloud, line by line, to find the bugs. It was a viral meme because it worked.

And while Gar didn't have a rubber ducky with him, he did have his vintage hula dancer toy mounted to his dashboard. So as the miles unspooled and the plastic hula girl bobbed and danced, Gar talked out his problem.

He needed to disappear. Possibly forever. But he'd need money of some kind.

The money was the easy part. With a cheap laptop and an internet connection, he'd be able to find free-lance debugging work, anonymously and quickly. The disappearing was trickier. He needed to get rid of his car. But when, and how? Crossing the border in it seemed like a dangerously stupid move.

He didn't know how exactly powerful the person behind Mjölnir was, but he knew how powerful the program was so he knew enough to be terrified. Rich, powerful people didn't like loose ends. Every billion-aire-adjacent schlub who 'committed suicide' in prison, 'fell out a window,' or 'got hit by a car' was proof enough of that.

His chat with the dashboard dancer convinced him to ditch the car in San Diego and take the trolley to San Ysidro, where he could cross the border into Tijuana on foot, then rent a car for cash.

He'd need a fake passport, but if he'd learned nothing else during his time as an undergrad at UCSD, he knew those were plentiful around the trolley station. They were terrible, obvious forgeries but readily avail-able in parking lots and back alleys throughout the neighborhood. Good enough for underaged drinkers to get into bars and coders on the run to flee the country. Besides, nobody really checked that closely when a U.S. citizen was crossing into Mexico. Getting back over the border would be tougher, but he didn't plan to ever set foot on U.S. soil again.

Once he was on the other side of LA, the traffic thinned, and he made up some time. Two and a half hours later, he parked on a side street behind the trolley station, yanked the hula dancer off the dashboard and shoved it in his pocket. He left the keys in the ignition. The car would be long gone before he got on the trolley.

He bought a passport on the loading dock behind a big box hardware store for three hundred dollars even and assumed his new life as Rodrigo Pablo Roberto. He removed the rest of the cash from his wallet and dropped the billfold into a fetid dumpster two streets away.

He bought a street taco from a truck outside the station and demolished it while he walked inside to purchase a one-way ticket to San Ysidro. The woman behind the counter didn't even glance at his passport.

"Thanks," he said, taking his ticket. "Do I have time to use the bathroom?"

She looked at him over the top of her glasses. "Suppose that depends on how fast you can go. You have eight minutes."

He nodded, headed for the bathroom, and stood at the sink. He ran the water over his hands and watched in the mirror as people entered and exited the restroom. Finally, the door swung open and the guy he'd been waiting for walked in. A slim, wiry man wearing a trolley company uniform and pushing a cleaning cart, entered. The custodian nodded in greeting and headed into a stall. Gar dropped his gaze to the sink.

He turned off the water and pulled his phone out of

his pocket and dropped it into the mop bucket, where it sank to the bottom, submerged in gray, sudsy water. Then he dried his hands and walked out leaving the last traces of Garwood March behind.

29

Cole's Tavern took its name from Thomas Cole, the father of the Hudson River School of painting, but—as Leona was quick to explain—he was no relation to her uncle, Daniel Cole, who established the bar.

"Uncle Dan was a fan of the painting style, and especially of Mr. Cole, who captured the beauty of the natural landscape better than just about anyone else in Uncle Dan's opinion." She pointed to the reproduction on the front of the menus she placed down on the table in front of Sasha and Ellie. "This one here was my uncle's favorite. It's from a series he did of Catskill Creek, but Uncle Dan and I think it looks a lot like the view of the river from the little deck the hamlet built."

"It does," Ellie agreed.

The tavern owner blinked in surprise. "You've been already? I thought you two just got into town."

It was Sasha's turn to show surprise. "Word travels fast, I guess."

Leona laughed. "Oh, The Luminist Inn and I have a little arrangement. Rhonda calls me when new guests check-in and directs them my way, and if I have a patron who over-imbibes, I send them to Rhonda's to sleep it off."

"Ah, a little quid pro quo."

"Just two small businesswomen looking out for one another," Leona said stiffly, as if she wasn't sure whether quid pro quo was good or bad.

"Of course," Sasha said quickly. "As you should. Although, in this case, you owe our patronage to a gentleman named Vern. We met him at the river when we stopped to see the sunset, and he sent us here. But, don't worry, Rhonda also recommended we come here when we checked in."

Leona relaxed. "Vern's an old fool. He's gonna catch his death of cold painting those hills in the dead of winter. I told him, Vern, get a camera and work off a reference photo. That's how most of these painters do it nowadays, you know. But Vern just blathered on about the light and the movement of the air and such." She shook her head. "Speaking of blathering on, listen to me. What can I get you ladies to drink?"

Sasha studied the cocktail menu for a few seconds. "Oh, this spiced gin warmer sounds perfect."

"It's good," Leona told her, "like a hot toddy but with spiced apples and gin, of course." She turned to Ellie, "I'm gonna have to card you, honey."

Ellie laughed and handed over her ID. Sasha tried to remember the last time she was carded.

"Thanks. So what'll it be?"

Leona placed Ellie's driver's license on the table in front of her. Ellie left it there.

"I'll have a vodka martini. Up, extra dry, two olives." Ellie watched for Leona's reaction.

Leona's eyes grew huge. She leaned over and read Ellie's name off the ID card. "Eleanor Anderson Prescott. You're Chuck's girl?"

Ellie nodded. "I am. I go by Ellie."

"Yeah, your dad told me."

"He talks about me?" Her voice cracked.

Leona waved a hand. "All the time. You know how fathers are. He's so proud of you. A very fine lawyer, he says."

Ellie's lip quivered, and Sasha gave her a small smile of encouragement. If she had to guess, she'd bet the twins' college fund that Cinco had never once told his daughter that he was proud of her.

"So, Leona, Ellie and I work together. We're in the area for a case." They were, sorta. "We thought we'd surprise Ch—" She couldn't bring herself to call Cinco Chuck. "—Ellie's dad. But Vern told us he may have left the area."

"Well, now, I think he must've. He was in here just about every night for months on end, but I haven't seen him since some time in December. One of the fellas said he went to Canada."

"Do you remember who?"

Leona tapped her finger against her lips, then shook her head. "Can't say for sure. Tell you what, you look over the menu while I fix your drinks. Decide what you want to eat, and then I'll take you over to the motley crew of painters and shabby writers he pals around with. They might be able to tell you more about his plans. How's that sound?"

"That sounds like an excellent idea," Sasha told her.

The barkeep met her gaze over the top of Ellie's bent head. They both seemed to realize that the younger woman was pretending to study the menu to hide the tears swimming in her eyes. She gave Sasha a small nod of understanding.

When Leona headed over to the bar, Sasha placed her hand on Ellie's forearm. "Rule number three: Emotionally mature people express their emotions."

Ellie sniffed and nodded, but didn't look up.

"So, you can fight back those tears if you want to. But you might feel better if you go to the ladies' room and cry. Just come back here ready to move on, because rule number four is we don't declare preemptive victory *or* preemptive defeat."

Ellie raised her chin and swallowed hard. "I don't need to cry," she insisted fiercely.

"Suit yourself," Sasha told her. "Just know that there's no big prize for stoicism at the end of your life."

It was a lesson that had taken her twenty years of practicing law, a decade of marriage, and eight years of motherhood to learn. She hoped Ellie Prescott would be a faster study.

∾

SASHA AND ELLIE were polishing off their sandwiches and the plate of fries they'd split, when Leona appeared at the table, wiping her hands on her green apron.

"Do you need anything else?"

"I think we're set."

She laid the bill facedown on the table. "No rush, take your time finishing up. But when you're ready, I'll introduce you to some fellas who know Chuck."

She nodded toward the fireplace, where a cluster of men, most of whom appeared to be middle-aged or older, was engaged in a boisterous conversation. A young couple with their heads bent over a chessboard sat off to the group's left, shooting them the occasional dirty look when a roar of laughter or a raucous shout rose up. Sasha wasn't sure the collection of artists was in the right frame of mind for a serious chat, but given the determined set of Ellie's chin, they were about to find out one way or another.

"Let's do it now." Ellie wiped her mouth, dropped her napkin on the table, and pushed back her chair.

Sasha handed Leona her credit card along with the check and drank the last gulp of water from her glass. "Lead the way."

The tavern owner wove a serpentine path between tables, and Sasha and Ellie followed her from the dining room to the cozy seating area in the front of the bar. Four overstuffed chairs and two well-used couches formed a loose semi-circle around the hearth. All the chairs were occupied, and two men sat on the sofa closest to the fireplace. The hum of overlapping conversations died as Leona approached.

"Ah, heck, did the lovebirds playing chess complain?" A dark-skinned man in a tweed cap asked.

"No, Barnaby. But give them time," Leona said. "I'm sure it's coming."

Someone in the group gave a small hoot of laughter. Leona shot the collective group the stink-eye, then gestured toward Sasha and Ellie, standing behind her.

"This is Chuck's daughter, Eleanor," she explained.

Ellie turned her lips up into the approximation of a smile and raised her hand in a wave. "Everyone calls me Ellie—well, except my dad."

"And this is Sasha."

"Hi," Sasha said.

Several of the assembled men nodded in greeting.

Leona continued, "Sasha and Ellie are up our way for work, so they stopped here to see Chuck. But I told them that unless I'm mistaken, he's moved on. So I thought this collection of artistic geniuses and reprobate drinkers might be able to shed some light."

"Don't forget Clark—there's a failed writer here, too," Barnaby cracked.

"Good point. Didn't mean to overlook our resident Hemingway. Anyway, can you gentlemen help these ladies while I settle their bill?"

The men exchanged glances. Sasha wasn't sure exactly what wordless communication was passing back and forth, but she suspected they were trying to decide how much to say. Ordinarily, she'd draw them into conversation and let them dribble out information piecemeal without realizing they'd done it. But, tonight, she didn't have that kind of time. And, to be frank, she didn't have the patience.

"Leona, before you run my card, buy a round of whatever these guys are drinking."

A chorus of cheers went up, drawing the ire of the chess couple. Leona smirked at Sasha to let her know she saw what Sasha was doing. That was fine by Sasha, she wasn't trying to be subtle. She was trying to be efficient. She gestured for Ellie to sit on the unoccupied sofa, then she perched alongside her. She leaned forward so the heat from the flames in the fireplace could warm her hands and scanned the circle of men.

Clark, the hapless writer, met her gaze levelly and held it. He had something to say.

So she didn't look away as she said, "We met Vern at the river. He said he'd heard Ellie's dad may have gone to Stratford, in Ontario. Did any of you hear the same?"

Clark shook his head but didn't speak.

Barnaby volunteered, "Chuck mentioned wanting to check it out. The town has a reputation for being a haven for artists, not unlike this place. But I didn't get the sense that he planned to go any time soon. For one thing, he complained about the cold *here.* Why go to Canada in the dead of winter if you don't like the cold?"

It was a valid point.

"Indeed," a smooth, melodic voice chimed in. "I'm certain he's not in Stratford."

Sasha craned her neck to see the speaker. It was the guy in the velvet armchair. He wore a paisley-patterned silk cravat and had on little wire-rimmed glasses that reflected the flames. He had his legs crossed, and one loafer dangled from his heel as he swung his foot back and forth. She knew she shouldn't stereotype, but this guy looked like the sort of person Cinco would've been comfortable socializing with.

"Why are you so sure?" Ellie piped up.

"He mentioned visiting, yes, but he planned to go while the Shakespeare Festival was running, which is from April to October—decidedly not in January. He said his wife is an aficionada of the Bard so he'd like to take her along."

Yeah, this dude was definitely Cinco's kind. They were two peas in a pod.

Ellie nodded. "Mom is a Shakespeare fan," she confirmed.

"I'm sorry, what's your name?" Sasha asked.

Leona returned, trailed by a teenager bearing a large round tray laden with drinks. "That's Fig."

"Fig?" Sasha echoed.

"Fitzgerald Isaac Grant," the man sniffed. "Which has resulted in my being saddled with the ridiculous moniker 'Fig.'"

She was beginning to realize that Cinco might not have introduced himself as Chuck. "What should I call you?"

He gave a sigh of resignation. "You might as well call me Fig. Everyone else does."

"Okay … Fig. If Mr. Prescott didn't go to Canada, do you have any idea where he *did* go?"

Fig sucked in his cheeks. "Until tonight, I would have guessed back to Pittsburgh. I know he was meeting his wife in Manhattan for New Year's Eve. He'd planned to return here afterward, but I assumed his plans changed and he realized he missed his home." He turned his searching gaze on Ellie. "But the fact that you two are here from Pittsburgh suggests he did not. I don't know where else he would have gone. Maybe he stayed in Manhattan?"

"He never showed up. My mom went up to NYC, but Dad was a no-show," Ellie explained.

The air took on an electric charge. The men around the fire put down their drinks and sat up straighter.

"He's missing?" Barnaby asked.

"Apparently," Sasha answered. "Can we go back through the weeks leading up to New Year's Eve? When's the last time anyone remembers definitely seeing him?"

Several of the men began to talk at once. Others chimed in to contradict them. Ellie made a small, frustrated sound in the back of her throat.

Sasha leaned over and whispered, "No, this is good. Let them hash it out."

She nodded and relaxed her shoulders.

Sasha stared into the fire until Barnaby cleared his throat, drawing her attention back to the group.

"Okay," he announced. "We're pretty sure the last time anyone saw Chuck would have been on December twenty-first, the week before Christmas. He was at the post office mailing out a tube that he said had some sketches he was sending home. Glen here is dating the postmaster, so he was mooning around the counter waiting to take Bill to lunch." He pointed to a portly, bearded man.

Glen objected, "I wasn't mooning around. You make me sound like a lovesick preteen girl. But, yeah, the rest of that is right. I know it was the twenty-first because Bill mentioned that it was the Winter Solstice."

Sasha glanced at Ellie. "Does that timing track with when your mom got the sketches?"

She nodded.

"And nobody saw him after that? Everyone just assumed he left town?"

Barnaby shrugged. "Well, yeah. We come here every night that Leona's open. So if he didn't leave town, he'd be sitting right here right now."

Sasha tilted her head toward the door, and Ellie stood up.

"Thanks for your help," Sasha said. She handed Barnaby her card. "If anyone thinks of anything else, please call me."

He tucked it into his shirt pocket. "We will," he promised.

"Excuse me, Ellie?" Fig interjected.

She turned toward him. "Yes?"

"I'm awfully sorry to hear that your father's gone missing. When you find him, will you tell him that Fig would appreciate knowing that he's okay?"

"I will." She managed a small smile.

They collected their coats from Leona and bundled up for the short walk back to the inn. They'd just stepped outside and were standing on the sidewalk in front of the tavern, getting their bearings, when Clark burst through the door behind them. He wound a long, knit scarf around his neck and rubbed his hands together.

"There's one more thing," he said. "I don't know if it's important, but Chuck had a visitor, maybe a day or two before Glen saw him in the post office."

"A visitor?" Sasha echoed. "Do you know who?"

"Well, I assumed she was his wife, but I guess not." He shifted his weight and gave Ellie an uncomfortable look. "She was an attractive woman, about his age. And very polished-looking. Her hair and nails were done. She was lovely, really. I was in Sleepy Hollow Used Books, just perusing the shelves and she came in and asked the girl behind the counter for directions to Light on the River. The girl, Jessie—she's the owner's niece, and she can't be a day over fourteen—had no idea what she was talking about, so I stepped in. I offered to take her there because it can be tricky to find, off in the woods. She was charmingly polite but assured me that wouldn't be necessary. So, I gave her directions and asked if she was an artist planning to stay there. She said no, she was visiting someone and volunteered that it was Charles Prescott." He kicked at the ground with the toe of his shoe. "That's all I know."

"Thanks, Clark," Sasha said warmly. "We appreciate the information."

"Like I said, it may be nothing." He threw another glance at Ellie.

"It may. But it may be helpful. You should go inside before you freeze," Sasha told him.

Then she linked her arm through Ellie's and pulled her down the street.

"Do you think my dad was having an affair?"

"Ellie, I have no idea. But I do know jumping to conclusions isn't going to help us find him. Let's go back to the inn. I need to call and say good night to my kids. Then we can drive over to Light on the River and see if Pete can help us. Okay?"

Ellie mumbled something indistinct. Sasha decided to take it as agreement.

She'd told Ellie the truth. She had no clue if Cinco was cheating on Gillian. But so help her, if it turned out he'd pulled his disappearing act to hole up with his mistress somewhere, Sasha would strangle him herself.

30

The video chat icon on the family tablet came to life, chirping and blinking, just as Finn and Fiona were finishing up drying the dishes after their pizza dinner.

"Dad!" Finn called from the kitchen. "It's Mommy."

Leo was gathering the recycling to take it out to the curb. He turned to Jordana, who'd stayed to eat with them. "Would you mind?"

"No problem."

She jogged out to the kitchen, and he heard her accept the video call and greet Sasha, explaining that she'd picked the kids up from school and had, of course, not been able to pass up homemade pizza. He hurried to get the rest of the bins and bags and ran down the porch stairs to leave them for pickup in the morning.

By the time he came back into the house, Jordana was sitting on the couch with the tablet on her lap, Fiona on her left, and Finn snuggled into her right side.

Mocha was curled up on the rug at her feet, and Java was sprawled along the back of the couch.

"Isn't this the picture of cozy domesticity?" he teased her while he unlaced his boots and removed his winter coat.

"Domesticity?" Finn parroted, his eyebrows coming together in wonder.

"Daddy's showing his age," Sasha explained from the square on the screen. "It's an archaic word for 'hominess.'"

Before he could retort, Fiona sprang into action to defend him. "And 'archaic' is an archaic word for old, *Mom.*"

Sasha laughed, and Jordana stage-whispered, "Fiona's almost perfected her eye roll. You two better look out."

Leo leaned into the camera's frame. "How's the Hudson River Valley?"

"Cold," she told him.

"Any luck finding Cinco?"

She bobbed her head from side to side. "Yes, and no. He *was* here. Half the town seems to know him. But they said he left before Christmas."

He frowned. "Nobody knows where he went?"

"There was a rumor he headed to Canada, but we're pretty sure that's not right. We're headed over to the art colony when I hang up. I hope we'll get some answers there." She changed the subject. "So I heard the pizza was perfect tonight. Crispy, but not burnt, and Finn got a slice with a bubble in the crust just the way he likes it."

"You weren't here, so it wasn't completely perfect. Pretty close, though." He winked at her.

Fiona launched into a story about an albino squirrel they'd seen on the walk home from school, which Jordana confirmed as fact. While Sasha was marveling over the sighting of the rare squirrel, the doorbell rang.

Sasha stopped mid-oooh. "Who's there at this hour?"

Leo shrugged. "No idea."

Jordana lifted the tablet from her lap. "Here, you sit and talk. I'll deal with whoever it is. It's too late to be going door to door selling stuff."

Before he could object, she was halfway to the door. "She's the best babysitter," he told Sasha.

"Agreed."

"Agreed!" Finn chimed in.

"She's pretty good," Fiona said. High marks from Fiona.

"Did you and Maisy find anything new in Landon's boxes?" Sasha asked out of the blue.

Leo pressed his lips together. He needed to tell her about the package Landon had sent. The conversation was way overdue. But breaking the news over a video chat with a pair of eight-year olds interrupting every thirty-seven seconds wasn't ideal.

He hemmed. "Sort of. I have a lot to fill you in on. Do you think you'll be home tomorrow?"

"Maybe. Probably. If Cinco's not here, and it looks like he's not, Ellie and I will come back and regroup."

"Then why don't I see if Jordana can babysit again tomorrow? I'll make a reservation at Hearth, and we can catch up."

From four hundred miles away, her grin lit up the room. "Sounds great. And then after that, I declare a family game night. Monopoly and popcorn!"

The twins cheered. Leo groaned.

"How about Risk and popcorn instead? Or Clue, Jr.?"

"We'll see," Sasha hedged. "I should go. Tell Jordana I said goodbye. I love you all. Sleep tight."

After a chorus of goodbyes and 'I love yous,' Fiona pressed the icon to end the video call.

Leo turned around to find Jordana and August standing in the doorway.

"Sorry to bother you at home," August began.

"Don't be. I assume you're here because you have news. Did you hear from the hacktivist?"

August shifted his gaze to the kids, who were listening intently and making no effort to hide it. "Um …"

"Hey, why don't I help you two brush your teeth and get ready for bed while your dad talks to August? August is *verrrry booooooring*," Jordana said in a dramatic voice designed to make the twins giggle.

It had the desired effect, and Finn and Fiona scampered up the stairs laughing and shouting.

Once they were out of earshot and the water was running in the upstairs bathroom, August said, "She doesn't trust you. Because, you know."

"No, I actually don't know. She doesn't know me. How could she trust or not trust me?"

August scratched his neck just under his left ear. "See, that's probably my fault. I told her you used to work for the Department of Homeland Security, but now you work for some top-secret organization. And I couldn't give her any details because, uh, I don't know any."

"Couldn't you have just said I'm a stay-at-home dad?"

"Yeah, that would have been better."

Leo fisted his hands and willed himself not to snap at August. It took every iota of his self-control. He'd pinned all his hopes on this red hat hacker. He needed her to help him find Mjölnir and then help him deploy the virus that would destroy it. He didn't have any other good options. Scratch that, he didn't have any other options at all—good, bad, or otherwise.

"So that's it? She won't help me?"

"Not exactly."

August gave Leo a look that was clearly meant to communicate something. Whatever that something might be, it was lost on Leo.

"So she *will* help me?"

"Maybe."

"Could you be more specific?"

He cleared his throat. "She wants to meet with you in person. She said once she looks you in the eye and hears what you have to say, she'll know whether you're trustworthy."

"Sure, let's go see her." He could be persuasive. Charming, even.

August shook his head. "Not us. Just you. There are only maybe three people in hacking circles who know her real identity, and I'm not one of them."

"Okay. That's fine. Where does she want to meet?"

"Idaho."

"What?" Leo cocked his head. He must've misheard.

"You need to go to Idaho. She'll be at this coffee shop at ten a.m." August pulled a crumpled sticky note from his pocket and handed it to Leo.

31

The Light on the River artist colony was, for lack of a better word, a compound. The lanterns hanging from the entrance gate revealed a large stone farmhouse with candles glowing in the windows, a warm light illuminating a wide, graceful wraparound porch, and a curl of smoke rising from the chimney. Eight to ten small stone cabins fronted by rustic wood porches were situated in an arc around the main house. An old-growth orchard towered behind the structures, the trees' bare branches outstretched and reaching skyward like elegant ballet dancers raising their arms.

The scene was picturesque and welcoming—or should have been. But as Sasha and Ellie sat in the car waiting for the clock on the dashboard to tick over to nine o'clock and the start of Pete's shift, a deep, bone-chilling dread gripped Sasha. She shivered despite the hot air blasting from the car's vents. The setting reminded her of another compound and a harrowing run-in with a Doomsday prepper cult on a similarly dark and starless winter night years ago.

"Are you okay? I can turn the heat up."

She shook her head. "I'm not cold. Just a bad memory."

"Someone walked over your grave."

"Pardon?"

Ellie made a face. "Sorry. It's a superstition. Grandmother Anderson used to say it."

Sasha glanced at the clock. "It's nine-oh-three. Are you ready?"

Ellie nodded.

They exited the car, then ran across the gravel lot and up the stairs to the porch. Sasha tried the door. Locked. She rang the bell. A moment later, they were buzzed inside. They approached a gleaming mahogany reception desk lit by flickering wall sconces. As she reached the desk, Sasha pasted a broad smile on her face for Pete.

Unfortunately, instead of the friendly night manager she'd been promised, a sour-faced woman with her hair scraped back into a tight ponytail and deep bags under her eyes stood behind the desk. Sasha glanced at the name badge pinned to her wrinkled white blouse: Poppy.

"Can I help you?" Poppy's voice held neither warmth nor any hint that she wanted to help them in the least bit.

Change of plans.

Sasha smoothed the smile into a serious, expectant

expression. "I was told to speak to Pete when we arrived."

"Well, Pete's not here."

Sasha waited.

After a heavy pause, Poppy explained, "He called off with the flu. Did you reserve a cabin?"

"No, no. We have a delivery for one of your artists. A Charles Prescott."

She felt Ellie's eyes on her and willed the younger woman to play along.

"I'll take it for him."

"I'm sorry, our instructions were very clear. We need to hand it directly to Mr. Prescott. Right, Ellie?" She glanced over her shoulder.

"Um, right."

"Well, then you're out of luck because Mr. Prescott isn't here right now." Poppy crossed her arms in front of her chest and stared hard at Sasha.

"That *is* a problem," Sasha agreed. "Our employer is going to be most unhappy to hear that we weren't able to give the artist the contract for a showing at our gallery. And, of course, Mr. Prescott will be upset to miss out on this opportunity."

Sasha hoped her bluff made sense. Her knowledge about the art world was limited and mostly gained from watching heist films. She gave Ellie a meaningful look.

Ellie jumped in smoothly. "Mr. Prescott's been offered a career-making one-man showing at *Faux-Semblant.* It's incredible for an artist at his stage in his career, to be honest. And, what a coup for Light on the River that the work that brought him to the gallery's attention is one he created while in residency here. Truly amazing. I'm sure you'll see quite an uptick in applications after the show opens."

Poppy's tired eyes widened. Sasha could almost see the tourist dollars dancing in her mind's eye.

"Unless, of course, Jonathan becomes impatient and invites that woman who does those paintings with her ferret's tail as a brush. Jonathan can be capricious," Sasha explained to Poppy.

"I'm sure Mr. Prescott would want you to leave the contract with me. I promise to get it to him as soon as I see him."

"I don't know …" Sasha pretended to waffle. "When will he be back? Perhaps we'll wait for him."

Poppy looked trapped. Like a rat. Or a painting ferret.

"Well, to be completely honest, I'm not sure when he'll be back," she confessed with a tight expression.

"Oh, this won't do at all. He's checked out? Jonathan will be apoplectic." Sasha raised her voice an octave.

"No, no. He didn't check out. He's just … gone for a few days. He's rented the cabin through the end of March. He'll definitely be back. Please, you can leave the papers with me."

Ellie shook her head and sighed deeply. "That won't work. We need to drop off the contract *and* pick up a painting that Mr. Prescott promised to Jonathan. Oh, this is no good."

Poppy dithered. "I don't know what to do."

"Perhaps you could call Charles," Sasha suggested. "If he gives you permission, you could let us into his cabin. We'll leave the agreement and take the painting."

Sasha watched the reception manager consider the idea. Then she watched her work through what would happen if she tried to call him and he didn't answer.

"Why don't I just lend you ladies a key? I would accompany you, but I can't leave the desk unattended."

"That should be fine, don't you think, Sasha?" Ellie asked, barely containing her glee.

Sasha sighed heavily. "I suppose."

She held out her hand for the key to Cabin Number 6, The Frederic Edwin Church Cabin, as if she were doing Poppy a favor.

As Poppy pressed it into her palm, Sasha heard her murmur to herself, "And here I thought his sketches were rubbish."

Sasha and Ellie rushed out of the farmhouse before their giggles overtook them. Once they were safely out of earshot, Sasha fixed Ellie with a look. "*Faux-Semblant*, really? You named our fake art gallery 'pretense' in French?"

"A woman who uses her ferret's tail as a paintbrush?" Ellie shot back.

"It could happen. Didn't Andy Warhol have his assistants pee on the canvases?"

"Among other bodily fluids," Ellie told her. "How do you know that?"

"Took my nieces and nephews to the Warhol Museum on a snow day. It was an adventure. We got kicked out after an incident in the mylar balloon room."

"Andy would be proud," Ellie declared.

They were still giggling when they reached the cabin Cinco had rented.

Sasha knocked on the oak door—two heavy raps—and waited for a beat before she inserted the key into the lock. *Please, please, don't let us find Cinco's dead body.*

They did not find Cinco's dead body. What they did find was Cinco, very much alive and cowering in the closet under a pile of blankets.

32

I t was after nine p.m. by the time Leith finally called Stasia back. She'd showered, eaten dinner, and taken a refreshing nap in the comfortable bed in the rear cabin of Leith's plane. The mattress was a touch too soft for her liking, but otherwise, she had no complaints about the accommodations.

"Where's your pilot?" Leith asked when she grabbed the phone from the nightstand.

"He went to try his luck at the casino."

"Get him back. It turns out I do need you."

He sounded agitated. She sat up and grabbed her dress from the hanger she'd placed it on. She pulled it over her head and wriggled into it.

"I'll text him when we hang up," she told Leith.

"He'd better be sober."

"He will be. And if I need to, I can fly this thing myself. What's going on?"

"Rosen lied to me."

Uh-oh.

"Oh? About the programmer?"

"Right. The guy—his name is Garwood March— uncovered the algorithm hidden in Mjölnir's DNA. He thought it was a bug. He called Pinpoint Partners to ask about it, and freaking Rosen told him to send over the final product and pretend he never found the criminality prediction."

"But he didn't?"

"No, he did. He uploaded the program to the FTP site, and then he took off. We've tracked him as far as Nevada."

"So, you want me to get rid of March?"

"No. Rosen assured me there's no way Garwood March could tie the work he did back to me, and I think that's likely correct. Besides, at this point, he's had a big head start."

"I assure you I can find him, Leith."

"I have no doubt. But you have other priorities."

"Let me guess. You want me to deal with Rosen."

"Yes, eventually. But first I need you to make sure March didn't tell anyone else at his company what he found. Rosen is sure March didn't tell his supervisor, and he swears the guy wouldn't have told anyone else either. But—"

"But Brian Rosen's proved that you can't trust him anymore."

"Precisely. So you're going to go to Idaho and confirm that nobody else knows what Mjölnir is capable of."

She wrinkled her nose. "Idaho?"

"Yes. Raquel will send you the address."

"And you're sure Rosen won't skip out on you, the way ATJ tried to?"

Leith's voice was tight. "He knows better. Besides, he thinks that by coming clean after the fact he's stayed in my good graces. He doesn't know what's coming."

Stasia wasn't so sure about that. She'd met Brian Rosen. He wasn't an idiot. He knew what Amanda had known and what this developer seemed to know, too: Once Leith Delone determined you were a threat (no matter how remote), or disloyal, or incompetent, you became expendable. If she were in Rosen's shoes, she would run.

But there was no point in arguing with Leith when he was in a mood—or any time, really. He wanted her to go to Idaho, so she'd go to Idaho. She said goodbye, retrieved the text from Raquel, filed the flight plan to Sun Valley, then called Bruce, the pilot, and instructed him to return to the airport and prepare to be wheels up as soon as they got clearance.

Then she poured a large glass of wine, popped two melatonin tablets, and removed her dress again. She crawled into the bed, pulled the heavy comforter up over her, and fell into a deep sleep. Once Bruce had the Airbus in the air, they would be airborne for four hours and ten minutes. She would sleep through the flight and stay asleep until morning. She would wake naturally, work out, and begin her day with a sharp mind and a rested body. Her discipline and adherence to routine had served her well thus far. She trusted they would see her through whatever lay ahead.

33

Cinco was shaking. While Sasha closed and locked the door to the small cabin, Ellie pulled her father out of the closet, settled him in the sole chair, and draped a blanket over his knees. Then she crouched in front of him and looked up into his pale, blank face.

"Dad, are you okay?"

Cinco didn't react.

Sasha walked back to the closet and surveyed the pile of wrappers that littered the floor. She stooped and picked one up.

"Have you been living on packaged peanut butter on wheat crackers for an entire month?" she asked.

From the chair, Cinco blinked. "I don't know. What's today's date?"

"January eighteenth," Ellie told him.

"Then, yes. I guess I have."

"Wait. You've been hiding in this closet since before Christmas?"

He nodded.

"But why?" Ellie asked, her voice cracking with emotion.

Cinco shifted his gaze to Sasha. "What is she doing here?" He frowned in confusion at his daughter. "For that matter, what are *you* doing here?"

"Dad, don't change the subject. Please. Are you in some kind of trouble?"

It was obvious he was. But Sasha held her tongue and watched the father-daughter dynamic play out.

"Yes, Eleanor, I am. I'm in trouble of the worst kind."

"Mom is sick with worry. So are the partners at P&T. And now all your new artist friends in town are, too. Why did you vanish?"

"It's not safe for you to be here."

"Why not?"

"I can't tell you. I thought everyone would assume I left the country. I told Poppy and Pete I was going out of town for a while, then I hid the car in the woods and sneaked back in here. I didn't know what else to do."

Sasha narrowed her eyes. "Who came to see you in December?"

"I don't … what are you talking about?" Cinco stammered.

"Do we really have to do this? I could be home with my family, curled up with a glass of merlot and a good book. But I'm not. I'm here with Ellie to help you. So instead of pretending you're not terrified of someone or something, just tell us what's going on. Please." At the last second, Sasha tacked on the *please* to soften her words because Cinco looked like he might burst into tears.

He crumpled, folding his arms over his torso and hanging his head. "Her name is Bella Steptoe," he whispered.

"Why do I recognize that name?" Sasha wondered.

Ellie pulled out her phone and thumbed out a quick search. "She's that real estate agent who was arrested last month. You know, the one who tried to kill Maisy."

"She's in jail?" Cinco straightened perceptibly.

"She's on house arrest, actually," Sasha told him absently. "Wouldn't do for a rich, White middle-aged woman to be imprisoned awaiting trial, now would it?"

"Why'd she come here to see you, Dad?"

He answered her question with one of his own. "Did your mother get my sketches?"

Ellie and Sasha exchanged a look.

"Yes," his daughter told her.

"Well, those explain everything."

Sasha frowned. She wasn't *entirely* sure what effect a month-long diet of packaged snack crackers, no exposure to sunlight, and no human interaction had on a person's cognitive function, but it wasn't a net positive. That much was clear.

Ellie reached into her oversized tote bag and removed the rolled-up pictures. She laid them out on the floor and smoothed the pages. "Can you tell me the story of these drawings, Dad?"

He lowered himself to his knees to study the sketches.

Ellie glanced at Sasha over his head and said in an undertone, "He used to do that when I was little. Sketch several pictures then string them together to make a bedtime story for me. Maybe this will get through to him."

"It's worth a try," Sasha agreed. "But I think he probably needs to be checked out by a medical professional sooner rather than later. Even for your dad, he's …"

"Spacey. I know."

"Before you start story time, let me ask him one direct question, okay?"

Ellie bit her lower lip and gave Sasha an uncertain look. "Okay."

Sasha crouched beside Cinco, who was mumbling to himself and switching the order of the drawings. "Hey, Cinco?"

"Chuck," he muttered.

Ellie arched an eyebrow.

Sasha rolled with it. "Chuck, did Bella threaten you?"

He looked at her wide-eyed. "She warned me."

"What did she warn you about?"

"That Leith would be very mad if I told anybody what happened to Landon. That he'd take it out on Gillian and Eleanor." Cinco rocked back on his heels and began to sob and babble at the same time.

While Ellie settled her father down, Sasha stepped out onto the porch to place a phone call. Maisy answered on the third ring.

"Hey, sugar, how's your trip going?"

"It's been … interesting so far."

"Did y'all find Ellie's daddy?"

"We did. And he appears to have had a psychotic break or, at least, some sort of trauma response."

"Good gravy. What's got him traumatized?"

"Bella Steptoe."

The line went completely silent.

"Maisy?"

"I'm here. I'm just stunned."

"That makes two of us. With the caveat that I'm not sure how much of what he's said it reality-based. Cinco claims that a day or two before Landon died, Leith Delone called and asked Cinco to find someone who could pressure Landon."

"Pressure him to do what? Back out of his deal to testify for you?"

"That's what I thought, too, but Cinco says no. According to Cinco, Landon had entered into an agreement to sell his wretched Cesare program to one of Delone's companies, and suddenly, Landon was getting cold feet. Delone's guy in Silicon Valley was worried that Landon wouldn't hold up his end of the bargain. Delone wanted Cinco to find someone to intimidate Landon. To convince him to go through with the deal."

"It kind of weird to ask your lawyer to find you muscle. I mean, isn't it?"

"For normal people, yeah. But Delone seems to consider himself almost like a Mafia don or something. You'll never guess who Cinco found to do it."

"Tim Colchis."

"Gold star for you."

"Well, here's something *you* probably don't know. Detective Colchis died today."

Sasha's breath caught in her throat. "What?"

"According to my source at the county arraignment court, he was alone in his cell when he slipped and fell, striking his head on the cement floor."

She sucked in a breath. "Good Lord."

"He lost consciousness. They did emergency brain surgery to relieve the pressure on his cranium, but he didn't survive the procedure."

"So, they're calling this an accidental death?"

"They are."

"That's convenient."

"That's what I thought. And get this, the prosecutor's office had just given Zane Novak's widow an update on the murder case against Colchis. Apparently, Colchis was about to plead guilty to murdering Zane and turn state's evidence. He was going to tell them everything he knew about Landon's murder."

It was Sasha's turn to fall silent for a long spell. "And now he can't," she finally said.

"And now he can't."

"Maybe Cinco wasn't crazy to hide in his closet." She peered through the window. Ellie had managed to get her father to his feet and back into the chair.

"He did what now?"

"It's a long story."

"Listen, Maisy, you still have Landon's phone, right?"

"Yeah, but I told you, he didn't text or save his emails."

"What about a call log? Can you see if there are any calls to the San Francisco area code in the day or two before he died?"

"Yeah, sure. But Jordana and Jenna went through all that stuff and showed Landon's ex-wife. Deanne said nothing stood out."

"Will you do it again for me, though? As a favor."

"Of course, I will. I'll do it right now and call you back. I have the phone and laptop here. I brought them home because I've got a meeting with Deanne next week and I wanted to go over everything again, anyway."

"You're a peach," Sasha told her.

"I know I am, sugar. A genuine Georgia peach. I'll call you back in two shakes of a lamb's tail."

"Thanks, Maisy."

She ended the call and steeled herself to return to the cabin. Ellie had found a can of soup in the small galley kitchen and was heating it on the single-burner stove. She turned when Sasha came back in.

"I figured getting something besides peanut butter crackers into his stomach couldn't hurt," she said.

"How is he?"

"About the same."

"Will you be okay to stay with him if I go back to reception to tell Poppy he's actually here? I thought I'd say he has the same flu her coworker came down with. I doubt she'll come within a hundred yards of the cabin if she thinks he's contagious."

Ellie nodded, but her forehead was wrinkled with concern. "But, Sasha, what are we gonna do? If what he's saying is true, he might be in danger. But I think he needs mental health services. And probably we need to tell the authorities. He may have facilitated a murder."

Her loud whisper drew a curious glance from her father. Sasha pulled her over to the far corner of the kitchen area and spoke to her in a low, measured voice. "The most important thing is you have to remain calm. If you can't do that, then our options shrink down to almost nothing. I know it's asking a lot, and if you can't do it, there's no shame in it. Can you stay calm, Ellie?"

Ellie took a deep, shuddering breath. "Yes."

Sasha locked eyes with her. "Good. All you need to do is keep him safe. Don't worry about trying to get a coherent story out of him right now. Feed him some soup. Maybe read a book with him. I'm going to put the sketches away because they seem to upset him."

She nodded. "What's the plan, though? You're going to buy time with Poppy, and then what?"

"Maisy's checking on something for me. If I can find out who Landon spoke to in Silicon Valley, we can present the district attorney with a case against someone other than your dad and get him a solid cooperation deal, probably with no jail time. He didn't realize what he'd put into motion, Ellie. I'm not exactly your dad's biggest fan, and even I can see that. He's going to come out of this fine—as long as he can keep it together for a little while longer. That's why I need you—"

"To stay calm. I understand." She lifted her chin. "I can do it, Sasha."

She smiled. "I have no doubt."

She snatched up the charcoal drawings and shoved them into her bag then grabbed her coat and phone and ran outside.

34

As soon as Leo shut the door behind August and secured the deadbolt, he called Hank. Hank Richards was not only Leo's best friend, and not only his boss. He was also the third-highest-ranking official in the shadow agency that kept the United States safe from the most domestic of enemies: those within its own government. It was a new role for Hank, and he'd brought Leo along as his deputy.

In truth, Leo wasn't quite sure what his responsibilities were in this new role. Nor did he know exactly how much pull Hank had. But he was about to find out.

"What's up?" Hank answered.

In the background, Leo heard the basketball game playing at low volume on Hank's television. A moderate fan of Pittsburgh's three professional sports teams, Hank scratched his basketball itch by following the Washington Wizards. He claimed rooting *for* someone in the nation's capitol made for a refreshing change of pace.

"How are the Wizards doing?"

Hank grunted.

"That good, huh?"

"I know you didn't call to talk basketball."

"Are your kids sleeping?"

"If not, they're being quiet, so same difference. What about the twins?"

"Jordana's reading to them now."

"Jordana? Where's Sasha?"

"She had to go to upstate New York for a work matter. That's why I'm calling. I need a favor. Two, actually."

"Hit me." The sounds of the game vanished as Hank muted the volume.

"I need to get on a flight to Sun Valley, Idaho. It's an emergency. I need to be there by nine o'clock a.m. local time. How much pull do we have with the TSA?"

"You mean officially? I have no idea. But we both know enough people at DHS to get you on a plane."

"Can I make some calls? I'm not sure what's okay and what's not in the new gig and I don't want to jam you up."

"Then don't. Let me make the calls. I'll make it happen. There's no way there's a direct flight from Pittsburgh International. So it's probably going to be a messy, overnight zigzag across the country. You sure you have to be there in the morning? You can't get there tomorrow afternoon?"

"I have to meet a source at ten o'clock local."

"A source?"

"Not a source in the traditional sense. You don't want to know."

Hank groaned. "Is it illegal?"

"Probably."

"Does it involve your tiny trouble-magnet wife?"

"No, for a change. Not only is she not involved, she doesn't even know it's happening."

Hank snorted. "Oddly, I don't think that makes me feel better about it. She may be trouble, but she's handy to have on your side in a fight."

"Pretty sure I can hold my own, Hank."

"Hmph. Okay, I'll arrange the flight. You said there were two favors."

"Yeah. I'm going to ask Jordana to stay with Finn and Fiona. And she's more than competent to take care of them. But … this probably not legal thing I'm about to do … I'm not sure there won't be fallout."

"Fallout," Hank repeated.

"Right."

"Someone knows where you live?"

"Unfortunately."

"How long are you going to be gone?"

"One day."

"I'll send a team to sit on the house overnight. Tell Jordana to let the kids know Uncle Hank will be over in the morning to walk them to school. If you're not back in time to pick them up, I'll bring them back to my place in the afternoon. My kids will be thrilled to see them, anyway."

"I owe you."

"And I'll probably collect. Now, the fourth quarter is starting so let me go make these calls."

"Yeah, sure. Thanks, Hank."

"No problem. Do you want to be armed on the plane?"

"If you can arrange it, it would be good."

"Bring your Sig. I'll make it happen."

Leo ended the call and went upstairs to talk to Jordana, who was more than happy to help him out.

Twenty minutes later, he threw a change of clothes into a duffle bag, removed his Sig Sauer and ammunition from the safe, and kissed his sleeping children on their sweaty little foreheads. He tiptoed down the stairs and gave Jordana a close look.

"Are you sure you don't want to have Maisy or someone come to stay with you?"

She arched one pierced eyebrow. "I'm positive. I *am* the babysitter. I don't *need* a babysitter. I have Mocha, Java, and the streaming password. And I know where Sasha hides the good ice cream."

He did a double-take. "The salted caramel stuff she buys at the fancy European store? Where does she stash it?"

"As if I'd tell you."

"Lock the door behind me."

"And leave the motion-sensing lights on for Hank's guys, I know. I've got this. Will you leave already? Go save the world. And remember, Maisy gets the exclusive for the Farley Files."

"Like you two would let me forget." He laughed, then grew serious. "Really though, thank you for doing this."

"You're welcome. Just promise you'll tell Sasha as soon as you see her."

He gave her a somber look. "You can't imagine how much this is weighing on me. I can't wait to come clean with her."

"Good."

He ruffled the cat's fur and rubbed the sleeping dog's head, then let himself out into the cold night. As he pulled up the flight itinerary he groaned. Pittsburgh to Philadelphia to Denver to Sun Valley. Two stops and a plane change. The trip would take eight and a half hours, assuming no delays. He'd be dead on his feet when he met this red hat hacker.

35

Sasha had filled Poppy in on her guest's flu and had received a mask and a bottle of hand sanitizer for her troubles. She was crossing the dark courtyard to Cinco's cabin, when Maisy called.

"Can you talk?"

"Yes." So long as she kept one eye on the path so she didn't trip over a root or rock and go flying across the gravel lot.

"So there was a call to a number in San Jose. Deanne didn't think it was important. Landon worked in Silicon Valley for years. He knows a lot of people there."

"I hear a but."

"But, I did an Internet search and this San Jose phone number belongs to an outfit called Pinpoint Partners."

"Okay?"

"Which is a fully owned subsidiary of NTI, Inc. NTI stands for Norse Technological Innovations, a privately owned company that lists Leith Delone as its sole shareholder."

"So, Delone owns Pinpoint Partners."

"Seems like."

"Huh."

"There was another call, right after that one. This one was to a number in Sun Valley, Idaho."

"Ski resort?"

"Another tech company. As far as I can tell, Delone doesn't own this one, but it specializes in providing third-party solutions to cutting-edge emerging technologies."

"Wonder what that means in English?"

"Helping fix a crappy racist artificial intelligence program, maybe?"

"Yeah, maybe."

"The first call was pretty short. The second one to this outfit in Idaho was longer."

"Is that all you have?"

"Yes, and no. Remember I started to ask you to find out about Thor during the meeting with Mickey?"

"Sure. But then ATJ threw her fit, and we never finished the conversation."

"Right. So the name Thor just keeps coming up."

"In what context?"

"Well, Gabe said Thor acquired WACB. The money that was wired into Landon's account the day he died was from something called Thor Trust International."

"That's funny. ATJ compared Delone to a Norse god last night."

"Yeah, so when you put it all together, it's obvious that Delone has been behind all of this the whole time."

Sasha's breath caught in her throat as she recalled the fear on Amanda Teale-James' face when she begged Sasha to appease the billionaire.

"Your wire did go through, right?"

"Oh, yeah. I have the money. But all the Norse mythology was ringing bells, so I also went back through the corporate trail I used to tie Delone to the settlement fund for your case. One of the intermediate entities was called Thor's Hammer Funding ... oh no. Oh, no."

The sudden note of panic in Maisy's voice sent a chill running along Sasha's spine. "What is it?"

"Mjölnir."

"What?"

"I just pieced it together. Mjölnir. It's Thor's hammer. Like in mythology."

"Oh-kaaay?"

"Sasha?"

"Yeah?"

"You need to talk to Leo. Like right now."

Sasha blinked, confused by the change in subject. She glanced at her watch. "It's getting kind of late. I'll call him in the morning."

"No. Call him now. He has something he needs to tell you. Something about Landon. I think y'all are in over your heads. Actually, all of y'all are in over your heads. Cinco and Ellie included."

"You're freaking me out. Why don't you just tell me what you know?"

"Please promise me you'll call Leo. He and August can explain it better than I could."

"August? Maisy, don't be cute. I'll call Connelly as soon we hang up, but please, tell me what's going on."

Maisy groaned. "Leo figured out that Landon had given someone access to his old program, renamed Mjölnir. As far as I know, Leo doesn't realize that someone is Leith Delone, but he's got this idea that he has to stop the program from being disseminated."

"Stop it? Stop it how? Is he going to arrest it? Shoot it? You're not making any sense."

"Just talk to your husband, okay? Colchis is dead. Cinco is apparently a hot mess. This whole thing is spiraling out of control, and I'm worried about the unintended consequences."

"What did you just say?"

"I said talk to Leo."

"No, not that part. The spiraling out of control part."

"The unintended consequences of what Leo's trying to do could be very bad."

"Unintended consequences," Sasha repeated. The charcoal drawing of the large hammer destroying the world flashed in her mind. That's what Cinco had been trying to tell them. "I need the name and address of the company in Idaho."

Maisy hesitated. "But you're going to call Leo first?"

"Yes, I promise."

"Okay, then. I'll text it to you."

"Thanks, Maisy."

"Of course. Whatever you're about to do, please be careful."

"I will."

"And, Sasha?"

"Yeah."

"I want an exclusive."

Sasha was laughing despite herself when she ended the call with Maisy and dialed Caroline Master's home number.

"Sasha? Is everything okay?"

"I'm sorry to call you at home, especially this late, but I need you to work your travel agency sources for me."

"Where do you need to go?" The firm's office manager sprang into instant efficient action.

"Sun Valley, Idaho. I need to leave tonight."

"Flying out of Pittsburgh International, I assume?"

"No, departing from … shoot … the closest airport to Peekskill, New York."

"Probably Westchester County," Caroline mused to herself. "Okay, I've got this. I'll text you the itinerary when it's set. Client number?"

"Firm charge."

Caroline sighed. "Does this mean you found Cinco?"

"How did—?"

"The network."

"Yeah, I found him."

"Is he okay?" Caroline's voice held genuine concern for her former boss.

"I don't know," Sasha told her honestly. "I'm doing everything I can. This trip might help."

"I'm on it."

"Thanks." Sasha ended the call and rapped on the cabin door.

Ellie pulled it open, and Sasha handed over the hand sanitizer. "I need the car keys."

"Why?"

"I need to get my stuff from the inn and drive to the airport."

"The airport? But …"

"I'll fill you in tomorrow. For now, you stay put. Tomorrow, you can get his car from the woods and drive into town. Check us out of the inn, get some groceries, and come back here until you hear from me."

Ellie dropped the keys into Sasha's outstretched palm. "But where are you going?"

"Idaho."

"Idaho?"

"You trust me, right?"

Ellie considered her response for a long moment. "Yeah, I do."

"Good. Take care of your dad. I'll take care of this. How's he doing, anyway?"

"He's sleeping."

"It wouldn't hurt if you got some sleep, too."

Ellie cracked a small smile. "Yeah, I know. It's the second rule."

36

10:20 P.M.
Pittsburgh International Airport

L eo kept his attention laser-focused on the emailed instructions from August while pretending not to notice the flight attendant looming over him with a frown. Finally, the man tapped him on the shoulder.

"Sir, I understand you're traveling on special business, but I'm going to have to ask you to turn off your device." The man lowered his gravelly voice.

Leo wondered what sort of *'special business'* Hank had coded his ticket for. Did this man think Leo was an air marshal? Secret Service? He supposed it didn't much matter. Either way, the guy had a job to do.

"Sorry. I was just getting my marching orders." He

made a point of putting his phone on airplane mode and then showed the flight attendant.

"Thank you, sir. I appreciate your understanding." He leaned down. "And just between us, it's a silly rule. Cell phones don't interfere with the cockpit equipment."

"Maybe not anymore," Leo told him. "It may have been before your time, but back in the day, they did."

The flight attendant flashed him a baffled smile. Leo suddenly felt every year of his age, plus some. He turned off his overhead light, leaned back his head, and closed his eyes. By the time he fell asleep, the first leg of his trip would be almost over, and he'd be jarred awake to the noise and lights of Philadelphia's airport. But, he might as well try to catch a catnap.

~

10:40 pm
Westchester County Airport

SASHA SAT on the very edge of the molded plastic chair at her departure gate. She'd made the mistake of leaning back earlier and her sweater had stuck to the seat back. She didn't want to think too hard about what substance might have caused the adhesion.

Instead, she dialed Connelly's mobile number for the fourth time since her arrival at the airport. And for the fourth time, the call rolled straight to voicemail. For the fourth time, she didn't leave a message. If she weren't afraid of waking the twins, she'd have tried the home landline. But at this hour, that was too dangerous.

She settled for thumbing out a quick text:

> Hey, when you get this, please give me a call. Hope you're already sleeping. If so, ping me in the AM. Just need to touch base about something. Love you, S

I tried, Maisy. I really did try.

She eyed the closed coffee kiosk through the locked gate with unabashed ire. Caroline had worked a miracle to get her to Idaho, but it wasn't going to be pretty: Westchester to O'Hare to Denver to Sun Valley. Two stops, two plane changes, and just under ten hours of travel time—if every single thing broke her way. And what were the odds of that?

She knew she should obey her own rule and sleep now. She could get a cardboard cup of crappy coffee on the plane. She turned off her phone to conserve the battery because, of course, there was one lone outlet at the gate and a road warrior shouting financial buzzwords into his headset had claimed it for his laptop. She almost rested her head against the back of the chair and closed her eyes, but at the last second, she remembered the stickiness. She popped to her feet and took an aimless walk around the terminal until she found two empty seats with no armrest between them—a perfectly serviceable makeshift bed.

She smiled at her good luck and went to claim her

napping spot. Then she saw the harried young mother, traveling alone with a toddler clinging to one hand and a baby in an infant carrier hanging over the crook of her free elbow. The woman was making a beeline for the seats. At the same moment, the finance bro strode purposefully toward the pair of seats.

There was only one thing to do. She nodded to the mom, then stepped directly into the guy's path. He moved to his left. She stepped to her right. He juked right. She bobbed left. She wondered if they looked more like dance partners or boxing opponents to anyone who might be watching. He grunted in frustration. She craned her neck to see the mom settling her little one on the seats with a travel pillow and a fleece blanket. Then she took the baby out of the seat and, cradling the infant against her chest, eased herself onto the seat next to her toddler.

'Thank you,' she mouthed when she caught Sasha's eye.

Sasha nodded. She could sleep on the plane—probably. It would be fine. How much sleep did a person really need in order to converse intelligently with a bunch of computer geniuses, anyway?

37

7:45 AM local time
Sun Valley, Idaho

The shops, restaurants, and cafes that made up the charming business district were dark and quiet. Soft pools of light illuminated the empty sidewalks from above. Dark, snow-dotted mountains crouched behind the town like protective parents. A pale purple sky hinted at dawn.

Stasia ran. She started at a slow jog. Then as her muscles warmed and awoke, she stretched her legs and increased her speed. She filled her lungs with the cold, crisp air and ran faster yet. The world was coming alive along with her. The light in the sky spread and intensified. She ran across the street and entered a public park with a groomed trail that even at this early hour had been shoveled clear of snow.

She rolled her neck from left to right, checked her pace on her fitness watch, then poured it on. She sprinted as fast and hard as she could for as long as she could. Then she slowed her pace, turned around, and jogged back to the private air hanger just twenty minutes from town. The airfield was ideally located so that robber barons pressed for time could jet in, squeeze in a handful of runs on the world-famous ski slopes, then fly back to their offices in time to impose the latest round of right-sizing cost-cutting measures and institute layoffs by locking their employees out of their email accounts. It also made a convenient base of operations for her purposes.

Securing an overpriced hotel room at the height of the winter season would have been an exercise in frustration. On the plane, she had every creature comfort and, most important to her, privacy. Working for Leith had its perks, there was no denying that. Even if it sometimes meant going on wild goose chases like this one.

She reached the gate, slowed her pace to a brisk walk, and raised a hand in greeting to the sleepy-eyed guard. He lifted his coffee mug in salute. She pretended not to notice the way his gaze traced the length of her body and lingered on the snug running tights that emphasized her taut butt and long lean legs. Stasia had learned to choose her battles with care. If she tangled with every random man who sexualized her in the course of her day, she'd do nothing else.

She wiped the sweat off the back of her neck. At least her meeting this morning was with another woman. Antonia Glass had been Garwood March's direct supervisor, and, at least statistically, she was unlikely to leer at Stasia for the duration of their meeting.

Stasia entered the plane, nodded hello to Bruce, who sat at the table doing the crossword puzzle, and grabbed a bottle of mineral water from the fridge.

"I made coffee," he said without looking up.

"Great. I'll have some after I shower."

"Any idea when you want to be in the air today?"

She chugged the water and calculated. "My meeting's at ten o'clock. After that, I'll want to poke around the building myself for a bit. Assuming I find nothing—which I think is a fair assumption—we could be out of here by mid-afternoon. I'll know more after this meeting."

"Okay if I head out for a few hours then?"

She eyed him. "Is there a poker room here?"

Bruce was a good pilot and an even better travel companion—quiet, easygoing, and he never left the coffeepot empty. But the gambling was a concern. He needed to be kept on a short leash. That long weekend in Monaco had been a disaster; the authorities had been closing in, and he'd been too drunk to fly. It was the closest she'd come to being apprehended. Ever since that trip, she'd made Bruce pre-clear his free-time activities with her.

Now, he shrugged. "I don't know. I thought I'd hit the slopes."

"You ski?"

He shook his head. "Snowboard."

"Knock yourself out."

She tossed the empty water bottle into the recycling bin and headed into the bathroom. She was running the water to get it as hot as possible when he called out a goodbye. She heard the clatter of his shoes on the steps as he left the plane. Then she peeled off her sweat-soaked running clothes and stepped into the steamy shower.

38

9:58 AM

L eo stopped in front of the coffee shop, rubbed his bleary eyes, and tried to focus on the letters that swam in the sign in the window to confirm he was in the right place. He was, and with two minutes to spare. He shuffled inside and glanced around the cavernous space.

The coffeehouse was buzzing with caffeinated energy. A row of men and women hunched over laptops filled the high bar in the front window. The keyboard warriors wore earphones, drowning out the very sounds they were paying to experience—the hum of conversation, clatter of dishes, and cool functional music engineered to increase focus and productivity.

He turned toward the back of the cafe, driving his thigh into the corner of the laptop bar in the process.

The sharp contact sent a jolt of pain through his nervous system and, with it, a spark of alertness. He was really dragging. The delay in Denver to change out the crew had been an unexpected hiccup. The pilot and cabin crew had timed out and had to go off duty, which meant the plane and passengers sat at the gate for nearly three hours while a new crew was called in to work the flight to Sun Valley. He'd tried to nap, but it had been futile.

So now, he'd been awake for twenty-eight straight hours, had changed time zones twice, and, in lieu of a shower, had stuck his face into a stream of cold water in a public restroom sink.

He trudged to the counter and ordered a large coffee.

"What kind?"

He eyed the barista. "Regular coffee. Black. Strong." He almost laughed at his words. He sounded like he was channeling Sasha.

A tap on his shoulder drew his attention as he was swiping his credit card. He turned and found himself face to face with a very young woman with jet-black hair and matching lipstick.

"You Leo?"

He nodded.

"I'm Rock."

The barista slid a ceramic mug down the counter, and Leo grabbed it. He inhaled deeply, letting the aroma tickle his brain before the first sip even hit his bloodstream. He stuffed a handful of dollars into the tip jar, then followed the woman to a table in the corner across from a small bookshelf labeled "Leave a Book, Take a Book" that sagged under the weight of airport hardbacks and dog-eared paperbacks.

The hacker took her seat and picked up a mug of tea, then gestured for him to sit, too. Leo sat across from her and gathered his thoughts.

"So, I should call you Rock?"

"You shouldn't call me anything," she told him, shrugging out of her plaid fleece shirt to reveal a black ribbed tank top and well-defined arms.

"Okay. Well, thanks for meeting me. I'm not sure how much Au—my friend—told you."

"Enough to know that you work for the feds."

"This isn't related to my work."

She sipped her tea and pressed a button on her watch. "You have three minutes to convince me to help you. Go."

Leo pushed back the irritation that bloomed to life in his chest. It went against his nature to beg, hat in hand, for help. But the truth was he needed this woman. So, he exhaled slowly and modulated his voice. "Several months ago, I received this flash drive."

He removed Landon's drive from his duffle bag's zippered inner pocket and placed it on the table between them. He noted the spark of interest in her eyes.

"This is military-grade protection," she said.

He nodded. "The information was secured by a PIN and, of course, the epoxy provided a physical barrier to accessing it without the PIN."

"But you got in?"

"Finally figured out the PIN."

She raised one eyebrow. "Impressive."

"Don't be too impressed. I got in, but I can't get any further without help. The virus on this drive is a worm. It's designed to destroy an algorithm."

"What kind of algorithm?"

He sighed. "Here's the thing. I can't tell you unless you're going to help me."

She made a clucking sound with her tongue. "Here's my thing, though. I'm not going to agree to help you unless I know what I'm helping you do. I believe this is called an impasse."

"It's a dangerous program that has the capacity to destroy society."

"Melodramatic much?"

"I'm serious," he told her. He lowered his voice. "The program is some sort of commercial consumer behavior predictor. I know, I know, that sounds crassly capitalistic but not particularly frightening. But, it is. I don't know enough to understand the details, but the program is built on an artificial intelligence program that predicts whether someone will commit a crime. It's a flawed, problematic program to begin with. The Justice Department got a consent decree to prevent it from being used for law enforcement purposes, but by masking it with this other program, this private company is going to be able to spread it everywhere. I need to destroy it. That's where you come in. If you agree to help me, I'll give you all the details. I promise."

He sat back and looked at her with a level gaze.

She shook her head no. A rapid, decisive motion. "No way, dude. I don't know who you really are or how you know about Mjölnir. But this is a setup. I'm out of here."

She grabbed her shirt and pushed back her chair with a metallic screech.

"Wait. Did you just say Mjölnir?" He leaped to his feet and grabbed her arm.

"Get off me," she hissed from between clenched teeth.

He relaxed his grip but didn't release her arm. "Please, just don't go. You know about Mjölnir? You have to help me."

"I don't have to do a blasted thing, and if you don't let go of my arm right now, I'm going to scream."

He could see from her expression that she meant it, so he removed his hand from her forearm and raised both of his hands up near his face, palms forward to show her that he meant her no harm. Unfortunately, the motion also caused his sweater to ride up, exposing the butt of his holstered gun.

"Oh my God, you have a gun?!"

Her voice cut through the coffeehouse noise and drew several curious glances.

"It's government-issued," he told her. "I'm licensed to carry."

"I don't freaking care, dude. Anyway, I thought you said this wasn't about your work? You're a liar. I'm leaving. Do not follow me. If I see you anywhere, I'm going to cause a scene like you wouldn't believe."

She wheeled around and ran smack into a very small

woman who was clutching a very large coffee. "Oh, sorry."

"No worries. Are you okay?"

The hacker gestured toward Leo. "This guy was just bothering me. I'm fine. Thanks." She smiled tightly.

"Connelly?"

Leo dragged a hand over his tired eyes. "Sasha? What the hell are you doing here?"

"Funny, I was just about to ask you the same thing."

39

For a moment, Sasha was certain she was hallucinating. After all, she'd been awake for nearly thirty hours. She'd been traveling all night. She couldn't remember the last time she'd been so desperate for coffee. In what was surely a violation of international human rights laws, the flight from O'Hare to Denver had had no beverage service, and then the Denver to Sun Valley leg had served decaf only. Decaf. She could only imagine that the FAA was testing some new torture regime at the request of the government.

So when she'd finally made her way to Sun Valley's cute little business district, she'd had one singular objective: to find the biggest cup of coffee she could. Now, she stood, gripping said enormous coffee tightly and staring at her husband, who absolutely should not be in Idaho. More than that, he shouldn't be in Idaho manhandling a goth-looking woman in her early twenties. Sasha had so many questions that her exhausted brain couldn't even process them all. So she settled for the most important one:

"Where are the kids?"

The woman with the cut arms and black dye job widened her eyes. "Kids?"

Connelly raked his fingers through his hair and gave her a tired look. "They're safe. Jordana stayed with them. Hank has a team sitting on the house, and he's going to take them to school today. What are you doing here? You're supposed to be in New York."

"And you're supposed to be in Pittsburgh," she hissed. "Do you ever check your messages?"

A guilty expression splashed over his entire face.

His victim—or whatever she was—cackled. "Busted."

"Okay, let's all just sit down and talk this through. Please?" He turned to the woman. "Rock, this is my wife, Sasha McCandless-Connelly. Sasha this is, um, Rock."

Sasha twisted her lips into a skeptical bow but transferred her coffee from her right hand to her left and offered a handshake. "Hi, Rock."

The woman slid her eyes over Connelly and then settled her gaze on Sasha's face. She seemed to make up her mind about something. She gave Sasha a genuine smile and took her outstretched hand. "It's Petra, actually."

"Oh, so she gets to know your name?" Connelly pouted.

"She's not a dirty pig. Are you?" Petra directed the question to Sasha.

"If by dirty pig, you mean federal law enforcement officer, no. I'm not. I'm an extremely tired civil litigation attorney, mother of eight-year-old twins, and, um, wife of a dirty pig. But, I'm not kidding about being exhausted. I've been traveling all night, and I'm dead on my feet. Can we please sit down?"

She stared pitifully at Petra, who must have realized how close she was to falling over. She led them back to the two-top where she and Connelly had been sitting when Sasha spotted them.

Connelly grabbed a third chair. "Thanks," Sasha said as she dropped into the seat.

"So ... what *are* you doing here?" Connelly probed.

"We found Cinco last night."

"Where was he?"

"Hiding in his closet."

"Didn't see that coming," Connelly admitted.

Petra arched an eyebrow, listening intently.

Sasha took a long gulp of coffee. "That makes two of us. Long story short, Cinco got a visit from Bella Steptoe—you remember, the real estate agent who tried to kill Maisy?"

Petra's expression was one of sheer fascination. "What kind of life do you two lead?"

"A complicated one," Sasha told her.

"Okay, yeah, I remember Bella. What does she have to do with Cinco?"

"Leith Delone sent her to threaten Cinco to keep his mouth shut. Connelly, Delone's behind Landon's death. Landon sold his stupid AI thing to Delone, who wants to turn it into … something even worse." She reached into her bag and pulled out Cinco's sketches.

She smoothed them out on the table and gestured toward the one with the hammer. "This one, *'Unintended Consequences'?* It's a warning about what might happen if they successfully turn Cesare into Thor's Hammer."

What little color Connelly's fatigued face contained suddenly drained away. "Mjölnir."

"That's the word Maisy used last night on the phone. She said you have something to tell me. So, tell me."

Petra leaned forward eager to hear what came next. Sasha took close note of Connelly's uncomfortable, defensive body language. He crossed his arms over his chest and averted his gaze.

"I know I should have told you this sooner. Believe me, I *know*. I should've told you right away because the more time that passed, the more I rationalized not telling you."

"Not telling me *what?*" Sasha demanded.

"After Landon died, a package was delivered to my office. Hank brought it to the house."

"What was it?"

"It was from Landon. You know that note that everyone thought was a suicide note? It wasn't. It was a draft of a letter to me."

He took out his phone and passed it to Sasha. She studied the picture of the handwritten message from Landon to her husband. Then she read it a second time before handing it off to Petra.

"I still don't know how you figure into all of this, but

since my husband left our twins to come out here and accost you, I assume you have a central role."

Petra said nothing.

Connelly looked queasy. "I can see that you're angry," he said to Sasha in a low voice.

"We'll talk about it later," she gritted out. "I mean, you waited six months, what's another couple hours?"

He blew out a long breath. "So, the other thing in the package was this drive that I was showing Petra when you came in."

Sasha studied it. "Is that thing what you and August had your heads together about?"

"Yeah. Obviously, Landon wanted me to be able to access the program, but I didn't know the PIN."

"August figured it out?"

"No, that was Maisy, actually. It was the date of Josh's murder."

"Of course," Sasha said. That was the least surprising part of all of this.

Petra shook her head. "I'm so lost."

Connelly turned to her, "The important thing to know is a man named Landon Lewis created the AI that Mjölnir is built on and he regretted selling it. He wanted me to destroy it for him, so that's what I'm trying to do."

"And Leith Delone is smack in the middle of it."

"*Leith Delone*? He owns Pinpoint Partners?" Petra gasped.

"Yes," Sasha said.

"Wait, how did *you* find Pinpoint Partners?" Connelly asked.

"Landon's call log. He spoke to someone there a few hours before he died. Apparently, he wanted to talk them out of moving forward and struck out. And after that call, he called a number here in Sun Valley, which Maisy traced to another tech company called—"

"Emerging Tech Solutions or ETS," Petra interjected. "That's where I work."

"So you already knew all this?" Sasha asked Connelly. "That's why you're here?"

"Nope. I'm here because August said he knew a hacker who could help me destroy Mjölnir." He gave Petra a long look. "But I'm finding the notion that the very same red hat hacker who can take Mjölnir down is working on optimizing it a bit more of a coincidence than I'm willing to swallow."

"You have it all wrong. I do work for ETS. And I am a red hat."

"A what now?" Sasha asked.

"A red hat hacker. She's a hacktivist who chooses her hacking targets based on political or ideological reasons. Right?" Connelly sought Petra's confirmation.

"More or less."

"But you work for ETS?" Sasha said. "How do you reconcile those two positions?"

Petra gave her an unamused look. "Well, under late-stage capitalism, a girl's gotta eat. And working for a corporate entity gives me a good cover to do what I do without being suspected."

"So it is a coincidence?"

"Yeah. Well, we're pretty much the best at what we

do. And I didn't work on Mjölnir. My friend, Gar did. And I'm a talented hacker but he's a kick-ass debugger. Like the best. And Pinpoint Partners wanted the best, so they came to Gar." She shrugged like it should all make sense.

Sasha and Connelly exchanged a look.

"You have to admit it's pretty coincidental, though," Sasha told her.

"You mean like it's pretty coincidental that two parents abandoned their children and flew separately across the country overnight without telling each other only to end up at the same coffee shop at the same time?"

Petra had a point.

"That's fair."

"Did Gar ever mention a Landon Lewis? He called your office about the program. Would he have spoken to Gar?"

"No. If he called the main number and asked about Mjölnir, he probably would've been transferred to Antonia, our supervisor. And she wouldn't have told some random guy on the phone anything. She's a stickler for proper procedure." She rolled her eyes.

Connelly was focused on something else. "You said Gar worked on Mjölnir, past tense. The project's over?"

She nodded. "He uploaded it to the FTP yesterday."

"What's an FTP?" Connelly wanted to know.

Sasha was eager to answer. "Oh, I know this one. It's a file transfer protocol server you can use to securely upload files to a network. We use them sometimes to exchange files with a client when there's a big document review or production in discovery."

"That's right. Gar uploaded the debugged program to the FTP yesterday morning. Then he left his ID on his desk and took off."

"He quit?"

"Not formally. He just ... left."

"Without saying anything to anyone?" Sasha pressed her. "Not even you."

Petra's expression turned stony. She didn't answer.

"Petra?" Connelly prompted.

"He left a gag gift on my desk. Along with a cipher."

"A cipher?" he repeated.

"A note written in code."

"Did you decipher it?"

"What kind of question is that? Of course, I did." She pulled a folded-up sheet of paper out of her shirt pocket.

A string of gibberish was written on the top half of the page:

nGmni akr bogpitr Fmeorcbi usxfyyr uiw!

Beneath it, in different handwriting, it read:

I'm a coward but you're not. I left a back door propped open for you.

"It's a polyalphabetic encryption algorithm called a Vigenère cipher," Petra explained.

"Did you and Gar invent it?"

She laughed at Sasha's question. "No, it's been around since the fifteen hundreds if you can believe it."

"What did he mean that he left a back door open?" Connelly wanted to know.

Sasha and Connelly finished their coffees while Petra considered her answer. Finally, she sighed. "I assume he means he left a way for someone to get back into Pinpoint Partners' FTP server if that someone wanted to send them a message."

"He knows you're a hacker," Sasha said.

Petra nodded. "He's one of maybe three people who know I'm Rock."

"If we uploaded the worm to the FTP thing, would it work? Would it destroy every copy of Mjölnir in existence?" Connelly asked.

Petra stared down into her mug as if the remnants of her tea bag held the answer.

Connelly reached under the table and squeezed Sasha's hand. She considered pulling away, but the truth was she understood the impulses that had led him to hide this from her. She didn't agree with them, but she understood them. And she wasn't entirely sure she wouldn't have done the same thing if their roles had been reversed. So instead of yanking her hand free, she interlaced her fingers between his.

They waited in silence for Petra to come to her decision.

When she lifted her eyes, they blazed with determination. "Yeah, it would. I can't access the back door remotely, so we'll have to go into the office to do it. We should wait until tonight when nobody's around."

"Oh, good. I could use a nap," Connelly said.

"And I could use a bathtub full of this stuff," Sasha responded, pushing her chair back and standing up. "Anybody else want a refill?"

40

The Offices of ETS, Inc.

A ntonia Glass finished her tour of the utterly uninspired and decidedly mundane office space in the kitchenette, where she offered Stasia a drink.

"Coffee? Tea? Hot chocolate? We have marshmallows and whipped cream."

"No thanks. Do many children work here?" Stasia asked.

Antonia laughed. "No, but sometimes it's hard to tell the difference between children and coders. Several of the people on my team prefer cocoa to 'grown-up' drinks."

"I noticed the toys on the desks."

The manager nodded. "There's actually a business case for those. The rubber ducks, stuffed bears, and troll dolls help when someone's hit a wall in the debugging process. They'll talk it out to the toy, and, more often than not, they'll see their solution."

Stasia was skeptical. "Really?"

"Truly, it works."

"I didn't see any toys on Garwood's desk. You said he was the best debugger you ever hired. Does he not need props?"

Antonia drew her eyebrows together. "That's odd."

"What is?"

"Gar has a rubber ducky. It wears a pirate hat and has an eye patch. It's quite distinctive. He named it Captain Quackers. You're sure it wasn't on his work-station?"

"I'm positive. Did you pack up his things? Maybe Human Resources has it?"

Antonia shook her head so vigorously that her long dangling earrings bobbed. "No. There was nothing to pack up. Just his lanyard. We moved to a hot-desk system a while ago. So nobody really keeps personal items in the office."

Stasia shrugged. "Maybe he took Captain Quackers with him wherever he went."

"Maybe," Antonia said in a doubtful voice.

"And you said Mr. March has direct deposit set up. So, you'll know if he withdraws his final pay once it hits his account."

The manager frowned. "He does have direct deposit, but we don't have visibility into that end of things. That would be an invasion of privacy."

Stasia pushed back. "But if Pinpoint Partners wanted

to know whether he accessed his account, you could find out, couldn't you?"

"I honestly don't know." Antonia straightened her back. "I'm a bit confused about why you're here, Ms. ...." She trailed off when she realized she didn't know Stasia's last name. Stasia let her hang there for an uncomfortable moment.

"We're trying to ascertain that there were no issues with his work. After all, the project Garwood did for us is mission-critical to our business. Surely you can understand why it gives our investor heartburn to know that as soon as he submitted it, he vanished."

"ETS stands behind all our work, but especially behind Gar's," Antonia told her stiffly. "I don't know why he left, but I assure you it had nothing to do with debugging work he performed for your organization. Now, if you don't have any other questions, I think we're done here."

Stasia didn't have any questions. This whole trip was the colossal waste of time and energy she'd expected it to be. And she did have to give the manager credit for her feistiness. Stasia was used to pushing people around. But mousy Ms. Glass wasn't having it.

Good for you, Antonia, she thought as she followed the woman through the maze of desks.

In Stasia's peripheral vision, a bright yellow duck wearing a pirate outfit caught her eye.

"Wait."

Antonia turned on her heel to see why her guest had just shouted. Stasia pointed at the duck.

"Is that Captain Quackers?"

"It is, indeed." She walked over and picked up the rubber ducky, then returned it to its spot on the desk. "How about that? He must've given it to Petra."

"Who's Petra? This is her work space?"

"No, as I explained, the employees don't have assigned desks. But Petra is ... well, she's forceful. So nobody else would dare sit at her preferred spot."

Stasia liked Petra already. "Were she and Garwood particularly close?"

Antonia considered the question before answering. Then she nodded her head. "They were, yes. I always thought Gar had a bit of a crush on her but that he was too intimidated to let her know."

Stasia decided she wanted to meet this fearsome computer nerd. "Where is she? I'd like to speak to her. Maybe she knows where he went."

"I'm sorry. She didn't come in today. She left my assistant a message that said something unavoidable came up and that she'd do some work from home this afternoon. We give our people a lot of latitude to work remotely."

Stasia was growing tired. "Petra what?"

"Excuse me?"

"What is Petra's surname?"

"Oh. I suppose there's no reason not to share it. It's Vuković." She spelled it out.

"Petra Vuković," Stasia repeated, sealing it in her working memory.

"Yes. But, she didn't work on your project at all."

"Understood." She smiled brightly. "Thanks for your time this morning, Ms. Glass."

"Of course." She bit her lower lip. "Do you think your company will be satisfied that everything's fine here?"

Stasia shrugged. "It is, isn't it?"

Antonia's eyes widened. "I think so."

"Then you have nothing to worry about it."

Stasia left the manager to ponder her response and walked out into the hall.

41

Petra pulled into a parking lot on the outskirts of town and killed the engine. "This market is the closest grocery store. The prices are exorbitant because you're in a ski town at the height of the season. And the selection is limited because ... you know, I don't know why. It just is. But it's important for you to understand there's no food at my place."

"Got it," Connelly said.

"I mean it. There's nothing to eat. There's no coffee, no drinks. I have water and spices. Also half a loaf of bread and most of a jar of peanut butter. But I'm not sharing those."

"I have questions," Sasha told her as the trio crossed the parking lot to the store.

"Fire away."

"Do you have a coffee maker?"

"Yes, but no filters."

This answer raised additional questions, but Sasha

decided to stay focused. "Do you have any food allergies or dietary restrictions?"

"No."

"What's your favorite meal that you wish you knew how to cook?"

"I don't know how to cook anything. Hence, the peanut butter sandwiches. Luckily there are a lot of amazing restaurants in this town."

"The question stands."

They walked through the automatic doors into the entryway, where Petra grabbed a handled basket. Connelly shook his head at her and wheeled a full-sized cart out from the line of buggies. She shrugged and returned the basket to the stack.

"Um, I guess roast chicken and vegetables. I know that sounds basic, but I had the most mouth-watering roast chicken at this little country inn in France. Sometimes I dream about it."

Sasha looked at her husband, who nodded. "Piece of cake."

Petra glanced from one to the other. "He's going to make it?"

"Yes, but he's also going to teach you how to make it. Cooking's an important life skill," Sasha told her.

Petra considered this. "Okay. Wait, what are you gonna do while I learn how to roast a chicken?"

"Oh, I don't cook. I'll be taking a nap. Now, if you had to guess, what size coffee filters would you say your machine takes?"

"I literally have no idea. I get my coffee at the office."

"Sacrilege," Sasha retorted. "That's fine. I'll just buy one box of every size."

UNFORTUNATELY, it turned out that Sasha was too wired and too tired to sleep. She tossed and turned on the futon in Petra's mostly empty guest room/office for more than thirty minutes before admitting defeat. She wandered into the living room, where Petra was staring at lines of code displayed on the flatscreen TV hanging on her wall.

Connelly sat beside her on the couch watching her with a bemused expression.

"What's she doing?"

"She ran Landon's virus through a sandbox so she can play with it safely."

"Those are all words." She perched on the arm of the couch.

"It's not a bad worm," Petra said without taking her eyes off the screen. "It'll definitely work. But it's clear he's a developer, not a hacker. I'm going to make a few tweaks." She glanced over. "Unless that's a problem?"

Sasha and Connelly had an entire wordless conversation in one exchange of glances.

Do we trust her?

Don't we have to?

What if she messes it up?

She's one of the most talented hackers in the world.

Yeah, but we only have one shot at this.

She's risking more than we are.

282 | MELISSA F. MILLER

No, you're right.

"No problem," they said in unison.

She shook her head and tried to hide her smile.

"Didn't you sleep?" Connelly asked Sasha, rubbing her arm.

"I'm too keyed up. Between the time changes, being up all night, and then all the coffee this morning, I couldn't. I'm exhausted, and that's dangerous, but I can't sleep."

"Why is it dangerous?"

"It would be good to be firing on all cylinders tonight when we break into an office building to sabotage a maniacal billionaire's dystopian weapon, don't you think?"

He scrunched up his face. "You make it sound so dramatic. Really, we're just strolling into Petra's office, where she has every right to be, while she pops a USB into a drive for, what, ten minutes?"

"Tops," Petra told them. "And that includes getting in the back door, loading the worm to the FTP server to infect it, and getting the replications started."

"See? Easy-peasy," Connelly said.

Sasha shook her head. Maybe she was just out of sorts, but it didn't feel easy-peasy. It felt heavy and hard. "I guess. I'm gonna take a walk and check in with Ellie. I could use some fresh air. When I get back do you want to call the kids and do a video chat?"

"Sure thing. Enjoy your walk."

She leaned over and brushed a kiss across his lips. "I will."

~

WHEN SASHA RUSHED BACK into Petra's apartment twenty-five minutes later, Leo could tell something was wrong. Her mouth was set in a thin line and her shoulders were stiff.

"Is everything okay with Ellie and Cinco?"

Sasha glanced over at Petra.

The hacktivist was still staring at the television, playing with Landon's virus. Unlike August, her fingers didn't fly over the keys. She worked surprisingly slowly for a hacker. Not that he had a lot of experience watching hackers at work. But she was methodical and precise. Every keystroke seemed to be measured and considered. She was also lost in her own world. She hadn't responded to anything Leo had said beyond the occasional grunt.

"She's in a trance," he told his wife. "We're not going to bother her by talking."

All the same, Sasha pulled him into the hallway.

"What's up?"

"There's someone watching the house."

"Are you sure?"

She gave him an unamused look. "Go see for yourself."

Petra lived on the first floor of an old Victorian that had been turned into three separate apartments, one on each level. She used the room in the front of the house as her living room. It had a bump out with a big bay window complete with a built-in window seat. Leo returned to the living room, crossed behind Petra on the couch, and pushed the curtain to one side. He eased himself down onto the seat.

Sasha was right. A statuesque woman with long, shiny blonde hair was leaning casually against a wrought-iron fence across the street, pretending to scroll on her phone. But her attention was locked on Petra's front door.

"Crap."

Sasha appeared at his side. "Told ya."

"Is she alone?"

"Yeah. I'm pretty sure. I circled the block twice and didn't see anyone else. But, if she's working for Delone, we have to assume she has backup."

"How would Delone know we're here? There's no way we're on his radar. I mean, right?"

"I would think not. But nothing else makes sense." Sasha groaned. "I could make up an excuse to call Delone's lawyer. Just to see how she reacts to hearing from me. I'll make sure to mention the weather in Pittsburgh or something stupid."

It was weak sauce, but it was better than his idea, which was nothing. "Yeah, there's no harm in it."

She snorted. "Easy for you to say. You're not the one who has to talk to ATJ."

She pulled out her phone and pressed the contact card for Amanda Teale-James. Leo kept his attention on the striking blonde. She wouldn't have been his first choice to do field surveillance. She didn't exactly blend.

"It's ringing," Sasha told him.

Across the street, the blonde looked away from her phone and reached into the pocket of her scarlet winter coat—another interesting choice—and removed a second cell phone. She looked down at the screen, and he saw her forehead crease. She seemed to be trying to decide something.

"Still ringing," Sasha volunteered.

The woman outside gave a small shrug, thumbed the phone, and raised it to her ear.

"Hello."

Leo watched the woman's mouth form the greeting and, an instant later, heard the word through Sasha's handset. He reached over and jabbed the button to end the call.

"Hey," Sasha protested.

He pointed through the glass to their watcher, who was ending the call on her end. She dropped the phone back into her pocket and resumed her fake scrolling.

"She has Amanda's phone?"

"It looks that way," he said.

Sasha released a string of profanity that broke through Petra's concentration and drew her attention away from the worm.

"What's up?"

"We have a complication," Leo told the hacker.

STASIA WAS GETTING COLD. She would've considered that a weakness, but she was in Idaho, in the dead of winter, and she'd been standing outside for four hours. She flexed her fingers in her gloves and stomped her boots against the pavement to get her circulation going.

Her phone rang. *Bruce.*

"Did you find her?"

"Yeah, I sent you a bunch of pictures, her firm bio, and a couple newspaper articles. Who is she?"

"She's the lawyer who ATJ met with in Pittsburgh."

"Hey, where'd ATJ go, anyway? I thought she'd be on the Airbus yesterday. Did she fly commercial back to SFO or something?"

"Or something." Her tone didn't invite further questions from the pilot.

"Okay. So I got you the stuff you wanted on the McCandless-Connelly woman? Do you need anything else?"

"No. But there's been a change of plans. We might not be leaving here until later tonight. So you have time for a couple more runs down the mountain."

"Cool."

"Bruce?"

"Yeah."

"No booze."

"Jeez, okay."

She ended the call. He could be as salty as he wanted. She was a passable pilot, but she wasn't interested in trying to take off from a mountain. He needed to be able to fly.

She pulled up the text he'd sent and nearly dropped her phone in a snowbank when she saw the first picture. Sasha McCandless-Connelly, the lawyer who'd called ATJ's number not fifteen minutes ago, smiled at her from her firm's website. She was the same woman who'd come out of Petra Vuković's apartment, taken two turns around the block, then gone back inside.

Why would the Pittsburgh lawyer be visiting a programmer who just happened to work for the company that had debugged Mjölnir? It couldn't just be a coincidence. Could it?

She thumbed through the rest of the pictures. There was one grainy photo of Sasha with her husband. It had obviously been taken with a long-range telephoto lens, as if it had been shot by a paparazzo. Or an agent on a stakeout. She searched for Leo Connelly online and got a suspiciously small digital footprint. Not a total blank, which would have been an obvious red flag, but an unusually thin background. As if it had been scrubbed. Leo Connelly was a cipher. He could be working for foreign interests. Or one of Leith's competitors. Or the feds. Or he could just be a dude who didn't like social media. She had no way of knowing.

When Petra had returned home from the grocery store with the couple, Stasia had thought nothing of it. She assumed they were friends visiting from out of town, maybe for a ski weekend. So the coder had called off work to entertain them. Harmless. So harmless, that Stasia had almost left then. But her field training and curiosity had won out, so she'd decided to stay a while longer.

Shit. Shit. Shit.

This was a complication. And if there was anything Stasia hated, it was complications.

42

Petra finished editing the Mjölnir Killer worm, and the three of them moved into the kitchen by unspoken agreement. Connelly started banging around in Petra's cabinets, taking out mixing bowls and measuring cups. He found a cutting board and a knife and arranged them on the counter at precise right angles to the edge. Then he added Petra's meager spice collection to the lineup.

"What's he doing?" Petra asked out of the side of her mouth.

"It's called *mise en place*," Sasha explained. "It's something they do in French restaurants—or, I don't know, all restaurants? You gather all the equipment and ingredients and get them organized before you start cooking."

"We could just order a pizza," Petra suggested.

"Absolutely not," Connelly said with his head in her vegetable bin. He emerged holding several carrots, a giant onion, and some celery stalks. "Everyone should know how to prepare their favorite dish. Besides, we have several hours to kill, and there's no better use of an afternoon than to devote it to roasting a chicken."

Petra dug in her heels. "Does she know how to make her favorite dish?" She pointed at Sasha.

"Her favorite dish is dark chocolate and red wine, so yeah, she's got it down."

Sasha shrugged. "He's not wrong."

They fell into an easy rhythm. Connelly was a good teacher, and Petra was a quick study. While they assembled the *mirepoix,* Sasha spent the time video chatting with Finn and Fiona, responding to emails, and getting an update from Ellie. Cinco was resting comfortably—that is, when he wasn't fretting about spending the rest of his life incarcerated or hiding from Leith Delone. She told Ellie to tell her dad to hang in there for another day, then she turned her attention back to the cooking lesson.

She waited until Connelly and Petra had salted and peppered the chicken and stuffed the fragrant sautéed vegetables and aromatic herbs into the cavity, followed by thin slices of fresh lemon. After they'd buttered the bird, trussed it, and slid it into the oven to roast, she finally addressed the six-foot-tall platinum-blonde elephant in the room.

"Look, that woman outside is either here for me or Petra."

"How do you figure?" Petra asked, genuinely confused.

"Simple. She works for Leith Delone. Delone knows I knew Landon and that I represent someone whose interests are adverse to his. So he could have sent her to follow me, but I don't think he did. I'd have noticed someone tailing me across the country. Pretty sure you would have, too, right?"

She directed this last part to Connelly, who looked up from the sink where he was washing dishes and nodded. "Definitely. She wasn't on any of my flights. And they don't know about the package Landon sent me. She's not here for me."

"So, the fact that she has ATJ's phone confirms that she's tied up with Delone, but not that she's interested in me. That leaves you, Petra. It is *your* apartment she's staking out."

"But, why? You don't think they know I'm Rock?" Her face went pale.

"Doubtful. I don't have any reason to believe they know about the worm that Landon created. But they do know your company did the debugging work for Pinpoint Partners. They may be worried that Gar said something to you."

"They'd be right. But, like, how worried do I have to be?"

Sasha and Connelly exchanged a look.

Petra shook her head. "No, uh-uh. Don't do that married couple telepathic communication bullcrap. Talk to me."

"That's fair," Sasha acknowledged. "You're probably in a moderate amount of danger if you go through with the plan to help us."

"A moderate amount?"

"If we don't all leave together, we might be able to

outsmart her. Or at least delay her. If she's sitting on you, Connelly and I could leave separately, sneaking you out through the back door or something. She'd either have to pick one of us to follow or sit here, watching an empty house. Eventually, she'll realize what happened, but it'll give us a head start if nothing else."

Connelly grinned. "That could actually work."

"Thanks, honey."

"Can we get back to the moderate amount of danger?" Petra asked.

"There is a risk. We'd be lying if we said otherwise. But, Connelly *is* a highly trained federal law enforcement agent."

"And what about you?" Petra demanded.

"She's the five-foot-nothing badass who broke my nose and my trigger finger the first time we met. And she's the smartest person I've ever met," Connelly said gravely.

Petra was momentarily distracted from the danger outside her door. "Is that true?"

Sasha shrugged.

"She also took down some machete-wielding mercenaries who crashed our wedding," he added.

Petra was stuck on their meet-not-so-cute. "She broke your nose and your finger, and you married her?"

It was Connelly's turn to shrug. "What can I say? I like my women small and violent."

When Petra stopped laughing and caught her breath, she threw her hands up in a gesture of submission. "I'm in. Let's kill Thor's hammer."

43

The sun set, and still Stasia stood across the street from the house, her head bent over her phone but her attention on the movement inside the first-floor apartment. At last, her patience was rewarded.

The husband and wife walked out the front door. They stopped on the porch and turned back to the inside of the house as if saying their goodbyes to their host. They descended the steps to the sidewalk side by side, and then they embraced briefly. She set off down the street, and he unlocked Petra's car and got behind the wheel. Stasia had expected them to stay together.

Now what? The wife was walking at a steady, but not rapid, clip toward the town center. The husband started the vehicle and sat, either allowing the engine to warm up or waiting for Petra to exit the house, or both. There was no sign of motion from within the home.

Her priority on this mission had been to find out if Garwood March had told Petra about the project. But priorities shift, and this one had. The presence of Leo Connelly and Sasha McCandless-Connelly had changed things. Now, she had to decide: Follow her, or wait and see what he did.

Her gut told her to go after the woman. She'd be easy to overtake and, not for nothing, she appeared to be a soft target, regardless of what her glowing press accounts might want Stasia to think. She sat with the decision for a heartbeat, then nodded. It felt right. She pushed off the fence and jogged away from the house.

She kept her attention locked on her target's back. She didn't turn around. If she had, she would have seen Leo push open the passenger door while Petra Vuković raced down her steps and hurtled herself inside the car.

SASHA SMILED to herself when she heard the faint slap of shoes against the sidewalk. She didn't turn around, but she knew if she did, she'd see a blonde woman jogging down the other side of the street. She'd taken the bait.

Her plan had survived the first inflection point. If Delone's woman had stuck around to follow Connelly and Petra, they would have had a problem. But now, Sasha just needed to lead the blonde on a merry chase through the center of town. Petra had sketched out the route for her—a meandering two-mile journey that would end at ETS's office after giving Petra and Connelly ample time to upload the worm to the FTP server and destroy Landon's racist, authoritarian fever dream once and for all.

Sasha didn't love using the office as the rendezvous point, but as Connelly had pointed out, with one car, they had limited options, and the less time they spent split up, the better. Luring the watcher to the office after it was too late for her to stop Petra and Connelly would tip the balance in their favor to two trained, experienced people (plus one hacker) versus one ... whatever the woman was. If they could detain her, they had a chance to tie Delone to everything he'd done, which would go a long way toward helping Cinco out of any legal jeopardy he might be facing. It was a convoluted, complicated plan, made more so by her sleep-deprived state. But it was the only plan they had.

She let her eyelids flutter closed while she visualized the map Petra had drawn. Turn left at the corner. She opened her eyes and made the turn, catching a glimpse of platinum hair in her peripheral vision. There, two storefronts in from the corner, was the bakery with the big windows that Petra had mentioned.

Sasha slowed her pace and then came to a stop in front of the display window. She pretended to study the whimsical cupcakes and the six-tier tower of colorful macarons as she clocked her follower's location. The woman had stopped and stooped to untie and retie her shoelace. Sasha waited until the woman had untied the lace again and then started walking. She knew it would cause the woman only the smallest, pettiest of delays, but it made her happy anyway.

She resumed her stroll, stopping in front of shops to window shop at seemingly random intervals. After twenty-four minutes, she crossed the street and wound her way through a public green space in the center of the business district. The trail was only lightly used. She saw two dog walkers, bundled up and pleading with their pups to do their business already. The woman wisely fell back so Sasha wouldn't spot her. But her bright red coat flashed through the trees. She was still there.

Sasha emerged from the trail and exited the park. She wove a path through a residential neighborhood and past an urgent care center. She crossed the street and stood in front of the entrance to a business park. ETS's offices were on the other side of the small campus. All she had left to do was to wind her way along the walking path that ran through the office park and reach the ETS building in twelve minutes. If all went according to plan, when she arrived Connelly and Petra would have deployed the virus and would be waiting for her in the car, doors unlocked and engine running.

She loved it when a plan came together.

She entered the business park and walked to the first white gazebo that marked the beginning of the insurance company-funded healthy habits trail. That's when she realized: she'd lost her tail.

She waited a solid minute, her heart thumping in her chest, but there was no sign of a tall platinum blonde wearing an eye-catching red winter coat.

Sasha started to run.

44

L eo wheeled over the desk chair from the closet desk to Petra's workstation and sat behind her and slightly to her right. He'd been pleased to see that she sat with her back to the wall, facing the door. He felt a pang of sympathy for the coders, developers, and programmers who had to sit on the opposite side of the big room. He would never be able to accomplish work sitting with his back to the door. Not to mention with his monitor exposed to anyone who walked into the room. The so-called bullpen was, he decided, a terrible office design.

He'd done one full circuit of the floor when they'd arrived and had confirmed that the office was empty, just as Petra had promised it would be. Now he scanned the hallway for shadows while she booted up her desktop machine and popped a pair of sound-canceling headphones onto her head.

He lifted one pad from her ear and said, "Really? This is poor situational awareness."

"I need them to focus. This won't take long. You be aware of the situation while I work." She moved the pad back into place. Then she flipped over a cube timer on her desk. It flashed green, and the illuminated display began counting down from ten.

Eleven minutes to get from the house to the office. Four minutes to search the floor. Ten minutes to log onto the server and upload the virus. Five minutes to leave the office and get back into the car, engine running to wait for Sasha for approximately six minutes. The schedule was tight, but not impossibly so. They could fudge a minute here and there. And Petra said she could probably beat the ten-minute timer.

Still, his pulse raced. This was it. In ten—he glanced at the timer—no, in nine-and-a-half minutes, events that had been set into motion on October 13, 2007, when a man named Calvin Tennyson murdered Josh Lewis in an alley, would come to an end. The world's eight billion souls would never have to know just how close they'd come to being controlled, monitored, and spied on by a billionaire who wanted to probe their every thought, fear, and secret to predict when they'd run out of milk, ovulate, or cheat on their taxes and then sell those predictions to the highest bidder— corporations, governments, cult leaders, strongmen, terrorists, anyone who was willing to pay to get inside all those heads.

He shuddered. Lewis' impulse was understandable, but anyone who'd ever watched a science fiction movie could have told him it was a dangerous, indefensible idea. He flicked his eyes to the countdown timer. Seven minutes left. Sasha would have just entered the business park and would meander her way across the campus for the next twelve minutes. Everything was ticking along according to plan. He just needed to keep his tightly coiled energy in check.

He tapped Petra's shoulder. She twisted her head to frown at him.

"I'm going to do another lap around the floor."

She nodded and turned back to the screen.

He walked out of the room and entered a long hallway lined with four managers' offices down the right side and two restrooms, a storage room, and a server closet down the left. The hallway came to an end at a large kitchenette located beside a set of fire stairs. The elevators were on the other side of the building.

He strode down the hall, pushing open the unlocked office doors and giving each dark, quiet room a cursory scan. He zigzagged the hall, checking both empty bathrooms and testing the knobs on the locked supply room and server closet. Nothing had changed. Nobody was in the building except for him and Petra.

He paced down to the kitchen and flipped on the overhead lights. The old bulbs buzzed to life. He eyed the ancient industrial coffee machine. They were only here for another six minutes or so. Not enough time to make a pot of coffee, no matter how much his tired brain might want a cup. He opened the cabinets in search of a jar of instant but only found hot chocolate packets and tea bags. He considered both options for a moment, then shook his head. He didn't want cocoa. Or tea. He wanted coffee.

On a whim, he picked up the stainless steel carafe and shook it. Liquid sloshed inside. There was no telling how old the leftover coffee might be. He shrugged. Sasha would've been appalled, but in his view, old coffee was better than no coffee. He could microwave a mugful and throw a pinch of salt into the reheated stuff to cut the bitterness. Then he noticed the 'reheat' button on the machine. Even better. He returned the carafe to its spot on the warming plate and clicked it on.

Then he heard a clatter on the stairs. He froze and listened hard. Nothing. But the fine hairs standing up on his arms told him not to write it off as his imagination. He abandoned his dream of subpar coffee, hit the switch to turn out the lights, and crept out of the kitchen. He paused at the top of the stairwell and looked down the stairs. Nothing. He stood there for a long moment, waiting and listening, before he hurried back down the hallway to check on Petra.

She looked up as he entered the room and flashed him a grin.

"I'm in."

He walked around to stand behind her, then leaned forward and studied the screen as if the information on the screen could possibly mean something to him.

"The back door worked?"

"It did. Took longer than I would've liked." She glanced at the timer, and his gaze followed. Just over three minutes to go.

"Can you still get it done in ten?"

"I think so. If you stop talking to me."

He clamped his mouth shut and calculated. They still had eight minutes until they were supposed to be in the car and six more after that until Sasha would arrive. They were fine. But the finger of unease tickling the base of his neck said otherwise. He should check the elevators. No. He should stay right here and guard Petra for three more minutes.

45

Once Stasia realized where Sasha was leading her, she knew she'd been duped. If Sasha was slowly wending her way to Petra's office building, that meant her husband and the coder were probably already there doing something they shouldn't be. She wasted a few minutes berating herself for allowing a pair of civilians to make her and outsmart her.

Then she regrouped. Having taken her morning run through the parklet, she knew that the woods backed up to the business park's campus. She sprinted through the trees and bushes on a diagonal while Sasha strolled along the path. She estimated that at Sasha's current snail-like pace, she'd beat her to the ETS office building by ten minutes, at a minimum.

When she reached the front door, she bypassed the card reader with ease using a credit card from her wallet. She laughed to herself as she eased the door open and went inside. If businesses knew how easily their state-of-the-art card readers could be circumvented, they'd think twice about installing them.

She paused just inside the door to arm herself. She didn't like guns—too loud, too messy. But she never left home without her tactical knife. She unsheathed it from the ankle sheath strapped to her right leg and hit the button to extend the spring-loaded blade.

Holding her knife with a relaxed grip, she fixed the layout of the floor in her mind. The kitchen was at the top of the stairs to the right. The long hallway led to the bullpen where Petra worked, with the door to that space to the right. Petra's workstation faced the door.

Once she could see her route forward in her mind's eye, she began her silent trek up the stairs. Her foot slipped on the fourth step and she careened to the side. The knife struck the metal railing with a clang that echoed off the walls.

Stasia pressed against the stairwell wall and froze, her eyes glued to the opening at the top of the stairs. After a moment, Leo Connelly's face appeared. She flattened herself even more, as he swept his gaze across the stairwell.

She stayed in that position for a full minute after he disappeared from view. She listened to his footsteps overhead as he walked down the hallway, presumably headed for the bullpen. When her heart rate slowed, she resumed her silent trek up the stairs.

She had just reached the top of the stairwell when she heard the entrance door down below click shut. She slipped into the kitchen and flipped her knife closed.

SASHA RAN through the office park, sucking air into her burning lungs. Between the cold, the elevation, and her lack of sleep, she knew she was running too slowly. She tried to pour on the speed, but her legs wouldn't cooperate.

Come on, she urged herself.

But it was no use. She felt like she was running through syrup. She stumbled to a stop and pulled out her phone. Panting, she pulled up an old text thread with Connelly and typed out a hurried message:

> She stopped following me. I don't know where she is.

Then she stowed the phone and resumed her labored running.

When she reached the building, she drew up short in front of the card reader at the door and checked the time. Eight minutes until Petra and Connelly should be in the car waiting, and fourteen minutes until they would expect to see her leading the blonde their way.

They needed to come up with a new plan that accounted for the fact that the woman working for Delone had vanished. She was pulling her phone out to call Connelly when she noticed that the door wasn't actually fully closed.

She frowned. *Sloppy.* He should have made sure the door had locked behind him and Petra. But she decided not to be too cranky about it, as it inured to her benefit.

She eased the door open and stepped into the dark, silent lobby.

"Hello?" she called. Her voice echoed and called back to her.

She spotted an emergency staircase and remembered that Petra had said she worked on the third floor. Sasha entered the stairwell and began to climb the steps. When she reached the third floor, she exited into a hallway and stopped to get her bearings.

As she stood there, the smell of coffee—stale, overheated coffee, but unmistakably coffee—wafted through the air. She turned to her right and spotted the entrance to a kitchen or break room. A cup of bad coffee would make everything better. She walked inside and hit the wall switch to turn on the overhead lights.

WHILE THE FLUORESCENT bulbs overhead were still coming to life, she crossed the kitchen. A large industrial coffeemaker sat on the counter next to the sink, its 'Rewarm' button flashing red.

Sasha turned to her left to open the cabinet where she imagined the mugs were kept and came face to chest with the tall blonde woman.

Play dumb.

"Oh, you scared me," she said truthfully. Then she flashed a smile. "Are you working late, too? I'm just grabbing a cup of coffee. Want one?"

She watched the blonde watching her, saw her calculating her next move.

After a moment, the woman returned Sasha's smile. "Sure, why not?"

Sasha gestured for her to move to the side, then opened the cabinet, and pulled down two mugs. Her heart raced, and her mind raced faster yet. Petra was almost finished deploying the worm. She could only need another minute, maybe two. All Sasha had to do was stall. She could do that.

She filled both mugs with the muddy-looking coffee and handed one to the blonde. "Careful, it's hot."

The blonde took it and placed it on the counter behind her.

Sasha gave her a questioning look, then raised her mug to her lips and took a cautious sip. She grimaced. It was as bad as she'd expected and even hotter than she'd imagined. The ideal drinking temperature for coffee was, in her personal judgment, one hundred and fifty-five degrees Fahrenheit. She estimated that this swill was hovering somewhere around two hundred degrees. Maybe the blonde had the right idea to let it cool down first.

Sasha turned and rested her mug on the counter, and a glint of metal flashed on the periphery of her vision. She turned back and found herself staring at the blade of a wicked-looking knife.

Her stomach sank. She hated knives. Knife fights were tricky under the best of circumstances. And she was decidedly not in top form at the moment.

"So, we're doing this?" she asked, trying to keep her voice even.

"Looks like. But you can decide if we do it the easy

way or the hard way. Where are your husband and Petra Vuković, and what are they doing?"

"They're at Petra's desk uploading a virus to Pinpoint Partners' server to destroy Mjölnir."

The blonde's eyes narrowed and her nostrils flared. "I don't believe you."

Sasha shrugged and kept talking. "Suit yourself. But if I'm telling the truth—and spoiler alert, I am—your boss isn't going to be happy with you. Because from what I've seen Leith Delone doesn't like loose ends or messes."

The countdown clock in Sasha's head hit zero. Petra had either uploaded the Mjölnir Killer worm by now, or she'd failed and been locked out of the server. Either way, time was up.

The blonde grabbed Sasha's right arm and yanked it up behind her back, then she jabbed the knife into the side of Sasha's neck. "Let's go find your husband. I hope for your sake that we're not too late to stop him."

She's not going to kill you. She wants to use you as a bargaining chip, and she can't do that if you're dead.

As Sasha was being marched forward, she tracked the women's abandoned coffee mug from the corner of her eye and willed herself to be patient.

Not yet.

Not yet.

Now!

Sasha stretched out her left hand, grabbed the blonde's abandoned coffee mug, and swung it up and back over her shoulder in a high arc in one swift motion. The hot liquid splashed over the woman's face, and she howled.

Sasha twisted out of the woman's grip and wrapped her hand over the knife. She slammed the woman's wrist down into the edge of the counter to dislodge the knife from her grip. It clattered to the floor, and Sasha kicked it under the refrigerator.

Now it wasn't a knife fight, it was just a fight.

The blonde whipped her elbow up and smashed it into Sasha's cheekbone. The sting of contact sent Sasha stumbling back a step. She raised her fists in a defensive gesture.

The woman laughed. "I read about your Krav Maga training. It's cute. I guess you're not bad … for a civilian."

Sasha aimed a kick at the woman's knee.

She blocked it easily, as if she'd anticipated the maneuver, and Sasha realized she had training of her own.

"Israeli Special Forces?"

The blonde spat on the floor. "Mossad."

That was arguably worse. There was no move Sasha could make that this woman wouldn't see coming.

Then flip the script. If she knows what you're going to do, do something else.

Sasha's stomach lurched at the thought of ignoring her training, but in this instance, following her training guaranteed defeat. Her instructor Daniel always said the most dangerous part of a street fight against an untrained opponent was the unpredictability. There was no telling what they'd do. She just had to act the part.

Sasha grabbed the woman's hand. She couldn't believe what she was about to do. She shoved the hand into her mouth, biting down on the webbing that connected her thumb and index finger until she tasted coppery blood.

The woman's blue eyes widened in surprise and pain. She hissed and pulled back her free hand, then drove it forward, executing a powerful palm strike that connected squarely with Sasha's breastbone.

Sasha released her bite and gasped for breath.

The woman shook her hand, spraying droplets of blood across the floor.

They circled one another like cage fighters. The woman moved first. She clenched her arms around Sasha's neck, raised her right knee, and started to force Sasha's head down while pulling her knee up.

Sasha threw out both forearms and jammed them into the woman's hip to block the knee strike, then she wrapped her elbow around the woman's knee while she pushed her head up against the woman's neck with as much force as she could muster and drove the woman backward.

Connelly ran into the room with his gun drawn just as Sasha head-butted the woman's forehead. The blonde stumbled, and Sasha kicked her left leg out from under her. Her opponent crumpled to the floor.

"Took you long enough," Sasha panted, still winded from the palm strike.

"You were supposed to meet us in the car," he reminded her.

She choked out a laugh and looked past him into the hallway. "Where's Petra? Did she do it?"

"With fourteen seconds to spare. She added a little flourish, too. Every time the worm replicates, a crudely drawn middle finger flashes on the screen along with the words 'F U Delone' written in Comic Sans. She's sitting there watching it, giggling like a twelve-year-old boy."

The blonde rolled over onto her side.

"Uh-uh," Connelly warned her, pushing her back down with his foot.

"My left shoe," she said.

"What about it?"

"Cut the heel open. There's a micro-SD card inside."

Sasha and Connelly exchanged a look.

The woman continued, "I've recorded every conversation I've ever had with Leith Delone. I transfer the recordings to a new micro-SD once a month. Call it an insurance policy. This one has over four thousand hours of audio on it, going back at least five years. There's more where that came from."

"You want a cooperation deal?" Connelly asked.

"New name, new identity, full immunity, and I'll give you everything I have."

He turned. "I need to call Hank. You got this?"

She nodded.

He extended the gun, and she took it warily. He went out into the hall and ducked into an empty office, already pulling up Hank's number on his phone.

Petra appeared in the doorway, wiping tears of laughter from her eyes. She looked down at the blonde and then at Sasha.

"You have a bruise on your cheek. Do you want some ice?"

"No. But will you grab her left shoe for me, please?"

The hacker raised an eyebrow but yanked the sneaker off the woman's foot and handed it to Sasha.

"There's a knife under the refrigerator. Could you get it?"

Petra fished the knife out from under the fridge and held it with two fingers. "This is a serious-looking knife."

Sasha used it to slice through the hard rubber heel. The heel fell away to reveal a tiny memory card wrapped in a scrap of bubble wrap and taped to the shoe. She removed the card, slipped it into her pocket, and let the rest of the shoe fall to the floor.

"You know, I thought you and your husband were a total mismatch. But, I think you might be the complementary flavors of weird."

Sasha laughed. "I guess we are. Word of unsolicited advice?"

Petra shrugged, "Sure."

"When you meet someone who's the right flavor of weird, don't overthink it."

46

Two weeks later
The offices of McCandless, Volmer & Andrews

Sasha looked around the long conference room table at the assembled team. "Who's missing?"

"Ellie's on her way," Will told her. "She was helping her parents pack up their van."

"I take it the U.S. Attorney signed off on Cinco's cooperation agreement?"

Will had volunteered to represent his old partner in negotiations with the Department of Justice over his involvement in the events that led to Landon Lewis' death.

"Yes, to be honest, Cinco is such a small fish in light of everything Anastasia Cohen gave them on Delone, he's not even on their radar. He's—I don't know, what's smaller than a minnow?"

"A guppy," Sasha suggested.

"A mosquito fish," Naya declared with authority.

"He's a very small fish."

"So, they approved the Prescotts' move to New York State?"

"Signed, sealed, and delivered," Will confirmed.

"Thanks for taking that on," Naya said.

"I *am* the criminal defense attorney here. Some people seem to forget that." He gave Sasha a reproachful look.

"Sorry, Will, next time I'm in a knife fight with a former Mossad agent, I'll totally tag you in."

Naya choked on her donut hole.

"When are they going to indict Delone?"

"Within the next day or two. Thanks to the tip from Hank, the feds got to Brian Rosen at Pinpoint Partners before Delone did. And Stasia's pilot is also cooperating. His goose is cooked."

"Music to my ears," Sasha told him.

"Oh, and, you may be pleased to know that based on Cinco's sworn statement, the district attorney revoked Bella Steptoe's home confinement agreement and she'll be awaiting trial in her case in county jail. So, I wouldn't be surprised if a few nights sleeping on thin, scratchy, low-thread-count sheets and the loss of her personal Pilates privileges convince her to cooperate, too."

Sasha grinned at the image.

The door opened a crack, and Ellie slipped into the room, mouthing 'sorry' as she took the seat closest to the door.

"Thanks for coming in early, everyone. We have just

a quick administrative update, and then it's all donuts and coffee and chitchat," Sasha promised. "Naya, it's your show."

"Okay, people. Listen up. As the partner saddled with facilities issues, I've been tasked with negotiating with Jake for additional space so we can build out and expand the office. I *thought* we had a deal, but our beloved landlord/coffee shop owner has backed out and given the space to someone else."

A chorus of groans and grumbles went up.

"Now, hold on. I found out who is taking over the rest of the floor, and if we have to share, I guess it's a pretty good neighbor to have."

Naya nodded at Caroline, who had obviously been waiting for the signal. Caroline pulled open the door.

Maisy sashayed into the room followed by Jordana. "Well, hello, neighbors! I'm just stopping in to let you know that the Farley Files can't wait to engage in all sorts of office buddy events with all y'all. We're talking Margarita Mondays, Taco Tuesdays, Watermelon Wednesdays—"

"Watermelon Wednesdays?" Sasha interrupted. "In February?"

"I got on an alliterative roll and got carried away. The point is, Jordana and I are gonna be very good neighbors, and we can't wait to move in."

"On that note, Maisy said anyone who stays after work to help us carry in all our stuff is welcome to join us for our first, um, Fiesta Friday this evening." Jordana delivered the bribe with a pained expression.

"What just happened here?" Sasha asked Naya.

"I got outplayed by a bubbly blonde, and now we're going to have endless parties," Naya groused good-naturedly.

47

Ensenada
Baja California, Mexico

Gar grabbed a cerveza from the fridge, slid open the door, and stepped out onto his balcony. He was leaning against the railing and staring down into the sparkling turquoise waters of the Sea of Cortez when his off-brand phone buzzed in his pocket.

He took a pull on the icy beer and then thumbed the display open. He had a notification from Nomad-Coders, the job board that was keeping his alter ego of Rodrigo Pablo Roberto in beer and fish tacos. He frowned when he saw that it was a private message and not one of the jobs he'd bid on.

His frown bloomed into a smile when he read the sender's handle: Captain Quackers.

There was only one person that could be. He pulled up the message:

> ASSUME BY NOW YOU'VE SEEN THE
> NEWS. ROCK HACKED LEITH DELONE'S
> DYSTOPIAN HELL APP. THINKING ABOUT
> MOVING ON FROM HERE. UP FOR A VISIT?

He messaged back:

> I'LL PICK YOU UP IN SY. LET ME KNOW
> TIME AND DATE.

The response came back as a Vigenère cipher. It took him two more beers to decode it, and when he did, he still wasn't sure what it meant. The details about time and date made sense, but at the end, Petra had tacked on one more sentence: You're my favorite flavor of weird.

He shrugged and returned the phone to his pocket. He'd find out in person the day after tomorrow. But right now, he had a sunset to watch.

48

Sasha raced into the house and pulled the door shut in a hurry. "Brr!"

Finn and Fiona ran over to greet her. "Mommy's home!"

"Did you bring the pizza?"

She gestured toward the large white box with red lettering that she'd just placed on the coffee table and gave them a sidelong look. "Nope. Totally forgot to pick up the pizza."

Giggling, they raced off to let their dad know she was home. She kicked off her boots and was hanging up her coat when Connelly walked into the room holding a glass of chianti in each hand.

"Happy Friday." He handed her one of the goblets and gave her a warm kiss.

"Happy Friday yourself." Before he could grab her boots and line them up like little soldiers, she kicked them into the closet and pulled the door shut.

"So, you know how we agreed not to withhold information anymore?"

"If that's not an ominous opening, I don't know what is. I *think* we agreed not to withhold information unless it was classified as top-secret national security secrets, lawyer-client privileged, or anything we pinky-swore with the kids not to share."

"I stand corrected, counselor."

"But yes, I remember." She studied his face. "I've forgiven you for the Landon thing, but I don't think I want to know if you've had another 'please save the world' package delivered. It's the end of a long week, Maisy stole my floor space, and I'm tired, Connelly."

"Maisy stole your floor space?"

"More accurately, Jake *gave* it to her because his crush is out of control. I'll tell you later. What's your news?"

"Well, it's *not* that we need to stop artificial intelligence from taking over the world."

"I'll drink to that. What is it?"

"I can't keep this from you any longer. I donated the Monopoly board to the game library."

"You did what?"

"I couldn't face another Friday night playing socialist Monopoly. I reached a breaking point."

She sipped her wine and tried not to laugh. "I hear you."

"But I bought a new game to replace it, and I think you and Finn are gonna love it."

"Oh?"

"Yep. It's a cooperative board game where you go

foraging for nuts and berries and work together to survive in the wilderness."

"All important life skills," she said.

"At least as applicable as learning to build hotels to maximize the value of your real estate holdings."

"I can't wait until Fiona turns this game on its head and starts selling the herb poultices to the highest bidder."

"Mommy, Daddy, the pizza's getting cold!"

"We're coming," he called back.

He looped his arm around her waist and pulled her close. "Oh, also, Hank and I have new jobs in a new agency that I can't tell you anything about."

She took a deep breath and counted to four before exhaling. "Just for that, you're on Finn's team."

THANK YOU!

Thanks for reading *Insidious Threats*. This artificial intelligence arc has turned out to be an adventure that's spanned four books (*Inevitable Discovery, Independent Sources, Steeltown Magnolia,* and now this one), kicked off a new series (*Steeltown Magnolia*), and, at the time of publication, is as "ripped from the headlines" as any topic I've ever touched on!

It's been satisfying for me to dig so deeply into one theme, and I hope it's been enjoyable for you to read. I am definitely ready to move on to new ground now!

To get updates about release dates and other book news, sign up for my newsletter on my website where you can always find an up-to-date list of the titles in this series, as well as my other books on my website, www.melissafmiller.com.

In addition to new release alerts, newsletter subscribers receive notices of sales and other book news, goodies, and exclusive subscriber bonuses.

Share it. This paperback book is definitely lending-enabled; so please lend your copy to a friend.

Review it. Please consider posting a short review to help other readers decide whether they might enjoy it.

Connect with me. Stop by my Facebook page for book updates, cover reveals, pithy quotes about coffee, and general time-wasting.

Keep reading. Check out the first book in one (or all) of my other bestselling series:

Critical Vulnerability (Aroostine Higgins Thriller No. 1):

Aroostine relies on her Native American traditions and her legal training to right wrongs and dispense justice. She's charmingly relentless, always dots her *i*'s and crosses her *t*'s, and is an expert tracker.

Dark Path (Bodhi King Forensic Thriller No. 1):

Bodhi is a forensic pathologist and a practicing Buddhist who's called upon to solve medical mysteries and unexplained deaths while adhering to his belief system. He's thoughtful, unflinching, and always calm in an emergency.

Rosemary's Gravy (We Sisters Three Humorous Romantic Mystery No. 1):

Rosemary, Sage, and Thyme are three twenty-something sisters searching for career success and love. Somehow, though, they keep finding murder and mayhem ... and love.

ABOUT THE AUTHOR

USA Today bestselling author Melissa F. Miller was born in Pittsburgh, Pennsylvania. Although life and love led her to Philadelphia, Baltimore, Washington, D.C., and, ultimately, South Central Pennsylvania, she secretly still considers Pittsburgh home.

In college, she majored in English literature with concentrations in creative writing poetry and medieval literature and was stunned, upon graduation, to learn that there's not exactly a job market for such a degree. After working as an editor for several years, she returned to school to earn a law degree. She was that annoying girl who loved class and always raised her hand. She practiced law for fifteen years, including a stint as a clerk for a federal judge, nearly a decade as an attorney at major international law firms, and several years running a two-person law firm with her lawyer husband.

Now, powered by coffee, she writes legal thrillers and homeschools her three children. When she's not writing, and sometimes when she is, Melissa travels around the country in an RV with her husband, her kids, and her dog and cat.

Connect with me:
www.melissafmiller.com

Made in United States
North Haven, CT
29 September 2023

42139484R00200